THE HIDDEN CONGREGATION

THE HIDDEN CONGREGATION

A REVEREND CHRISTIE MYSTERY

WILLIAM T. DELAMAR

INTEGRATED MEDIA
NEW YORK

All rights reserved, including without limitation the right to reproduce this book or any portion thereof in any form or by any means, whether electronic or mechanical, now known or hereinafter invented, without the express written permission of the publisher.

This is a work of fiction. Names, characters, places, events, and incidents either are the product of the author's imagination or are used fictitiously. Any resemblance to actual persons, living or dead, businesses, companies, events, or locales is entirely coincidental.

Copyright © 2015 by William T. Delamar

ISBN: 978-1-5040-8257-0

This edition published in 2023 by Open Road Integrated Media, Inc.
180 Maiden Lane
New York, NY 10038
www.openroadmedia.com

My wife, Gloria Delamar, my inspiration.

THE HIDDEN CONGREGATION

CHAPTER ONE

"Bishop, I know you have doubts, but he's young, dedicated, and trusting . . . really trusting." Reverend Darner leaned forward, his withered hands pushing a set of sheets across the desk. "These are his divinity school records. His professors all recommended him for his current pulpit. I'm sure they would again, if we contacted them. We need someone young, someone with strength enough to carry the cross, so to speak." Reverend Darner nodded his bald head knowingly.

Bishop Markham pushed his fat frame up in his chair and adjusted his glasses to study the resume placed in front of him. He examined the material then leaned back in his chair. "And what a cross. Strong and trusting. I think you're right. He'll accept. By now, he's looking for the next post. He'll jump at the chance." He shook his head. "I feel rotten about what's happened there. Maybe that's what turned my hair so white. I used to be young. Now I'm like a pink overweight rabbit."

"I'm sure of it," said Reverend Darner. "No, not that you are a pink overweight rabbit. I'm sure he's dedicated to the church."

"I almost feel guilty. He'll have no idea what's ahead of him. Young, dedicated, and innocent."

"We can't waste time. I am certain the police will never stop looking." Bishop Markham nodded his head. "Better to bury the past."

"So to speak," said Reverend Darner.

CHAPTER TWO

Ox woke up at 5:30 a.m., now his usual time, but stayed in bed. He was tired. He had been pushing himself for a year and wanted to rest more, but he knew he had to get moving. Yesterday, he had scraped and painted the little church and strained muscles he hadn't used for years. This was his first pulpit and his church was finally growing. One of these days he would be able to afford a sextant or bring in a carpenter to help with repairs. He stretched and forced himself to sit up on the edge of the bed, taking care not to wake Barbara.

He had dreamed of her in the early hours . . . not the kind of dream he could mention in a sermon. Morning light was creeping in under the shade. He put on his bathrobe and tiptoed out of the room. He rubbed his sore muscles.

The day was starting like all the hot summer days in St. Louis. He ran his fingers through his hair before stepping out on the porch to pick up the paper. *Wouldn't want the neighbors to see a minister disheveled.* He wondered if the apostles or saints ever combed their hair.

He paused on the small plank porch and inspected the clear sky. A buzzard glided on an updraft. "One of the advantages of being on the outskirts of the city," he thought out loud. "The people inside St. Louis don't have this. No sirree."

The little house was shielded by cedar trees bent and grown to the structure over the years. But they didn't screen the flies off the porch. He swatted one buzzing around his ear, stooped and picked up the folded newspaper near the steps.

He opened the paper and turned to the religion page. There was the ad he had run.

"Come to a small family church where you can grow. Look for the good in life. You may have it and not know it. It's there."

He moved into the house and the screen door slapped behind him. The kitchen was dark. He flipped the light switch and stood looking at the small, cramped room with its tiny windows, not enough cabinet space, barely room for one person. He heated water, got out the instant coffee, and selected a mug to start the day with—bright orange with a unicorn on it, a symbol of healing in mythology. Just what he needed. He was tired and his muscles ached in rebellion to every step.

He had left the paper open on the counter and a headline caught his eye.

"Seven Churches Burn to the Ground."

He picked up the paper and stood under the single light bulb.

"Philadelphia. Over the past two months, seven churches in this city have been destroyed by fire. Fire Chief Russo says they are suspicious and he suspects arson . . ."

He had heard about it on the news. He scanned the rest of the article. Investigation under way. No suspects. Different denominations. He put down the paper to mix his coffee. He set the mug on the counter and stared at the paper. He let his hands run down his chest and aching legs. *Churches engulfed in the flames of hell. Wonder how many bars have burned. It doesn't say.*

Barbara rushed into the room, still gathering her robe about her. "Why are you rubbing your body? Do you need some help?" She put her arms around his neck and kissed him. "Good morning, cornstalk. You didn't answer my question."

"Why 'cornstalk?'" he asked.

"Because your hair's all tousled like yellow corn silk. Why are you rubbing your body?"

"Sore muscles from all the physical activity yesterday. I've either got to do that more often or stop altogether."

"You tossed and turned all night. Have a bad dream?"

"I don't remember."

"Oh? Did you have a sex dream? How do you want your eggs?"

"I don't have sex dreams. I'm a minister. I just dream of my congregation. I'll have a pair, sunny side up."

"Oh, we were dreaming of one of the women in the congregation, were we? Did she look like me? You better say yes. Do you want your eggs on your head? Oh, wear your hair like that all the time. You look so rustic."

She cracked the eggs into the pan, turned, put her arms around him and kissed him again.

He rubbed her back. "Come to think of it, she looked like you. I better rub around in case you have some sore muscles." He let his hands drop lower.

She rubbed against him and breathed, "Is that appropriate behavior for a minister? I wonder what your congregation would say if they knew you started the day off rubbing your wife's behind?"

"Just because I'm a minister doesn't mean I'm abnormal. Maybe there'd be less bickering in the church if they all rubbed each other's buns."

"I should say so. And I can just imagine the Sunday service you could conduct. You could sell it to Hollywood." The eggs were already sizzling as she laid out the plates. "You think we're going to be in this dinky place for the rest of our lives?"

"We've only been here a year. I've got to prove myself before I get a call for something bigger. They don't give plums to just anybody."

"Prove yourself?" She flipped the eggs. "You've already doubled the size of the congregation and lowered the average age from sixty-eight to fifty-two. Can't just anybody do that. Now sit and get ready for your eggs. Tell me about this bimbo you were with last night."

She plopped the eggs in front of him. He began to eat without looking. The toaster sprung the bread just in time.

"There were some churches burned in Philadelphia. Who would burn churches?"

"And that upsets you?" She sat and started eating, too. "Tell me about it."

"Your counseling training is showing."

"Am I right? Are you upset?"

"Of course not. Everybody ought to burn churches."

"When you dreamed of the church bimbo, did you get stimulated?"

"Helluva question. Ministers don't get stimulated."

"It's not a helluva question and you're evading it. Did you get stimulated?"

"You don't ask ministers questions like that."

"I'm asking this minister." She poked his chest with her finger. "Answer the helluva question."

"No, of course not."

"That's a helluva an answer."

"I'm a minister."

"Well!" she said. She finished her eggs.

"Okay, psych major. What would it mean if a minister had a sex dream?"

"Beats the hell out of me." She jumped up, grabbed the dishes and put them in the sink.

THE HIDDEN CONGREGATION

"Beats the hell out of me," he mimicked. "What kind of a counselor are you? Beats the hell out of you. My muscles ache and this afternoon, I'm supposed to counsel one of my parishioners and I can't even half walk." He leaned forward to sip his coffee.

"I'll be glad to come in and help."

"Some help. You'll tell him it beats the hell out of you."

"Which one of your dirty old men are you counseling?"

"That'd be breaking a confidence. I can't tell you that."

"Hey. We just talked about sex dreams. You can tell me. So tell me."

He laid his head on the table and laughed. "You're a piece of work."

She put her hand on his neck and massaged it. "You'll be okay, Babe. By two o'clock, you'll have at least one sore foot on the ground. The problem is, you believe you can help everybody."

He pushed up from the table. "Got to get dressed. Have to get to the church."

"What's the rush?" she asked, letting her robe slide off to the floor and untying the bow at the top of her gown.

His feet stuck to the floor. "Have to be there to answer the phone. We can't afford a secretary, you know, and I have no volunteers for today."

"Why does the phone have to be answered? Anyhow, does a phone in the forest ring if there's nobody there to hear it?" She let the gown slide off her shoulders and onto the floor.

"I suppose I could be a little late."

"Mommy, I woke up," came a small voice from the doorway. It was their three-year-old, Billy.

"That happens at least once a day," she said scooping him in her arms and kissing him. She deposited him on a stool by the table. She put a bowl and spoon in front of him. "Give me a minute and I'll put something in that for you."

Oxford Christie leaned against the kitchen doorjamb and smiled at his son and naked wife. Her auburn hair needed brushing. It was curly and full of energy, like her. She caught his look and gazed at him with those gray-blue eyes, and the rest of his world dissolved.

"I love your body and soul," he moaned. "But we've got a situation. Don't you think you ought to put on some clothes?"

She walked over to him. "I want to check the muscles on your chest." She opened his robe and quickly unbuttoned the pajama top. She rubbed her hands on his chest. "This part of you looks okay. Let's see your back. Off with the robe."

Ox allowed her to yank off the robe and pajama top. She made a sudden swooping motion downward, pulling his pajama bottoms to the floor and kneeling on them.

"This part's okay. Everything is just the way it ought to be. Not a hair out of place."

"Barbara. Our son is watching."

"Well, great, Ox." She stood and pressed herself next to him. "See, Billy. Your father and mother have bodies, and we're different like you and Martha." All the while, she was standing on the pajama bottoms and wrestling with Ox to prevent him from pulling them up.

"Barbara, what if Martha were to come in. She's five."

"I hadn't thought of that. Here. This will only take a second." She jerked the pajama bottom and pushed him. "I want Billy to see you as naked as me. Let go." She got it and scooped it with the rest. "Okay. Billy, you take off your clothes." She stuck her head out of the kitchen door and called, "Martha, are you awake?"

"Yes, Mommy."

"My God," said Ox.

"Come on down here. Quick."

THE HIDDEN CONGREGATION

Ox grabbed for his pajamas, but Barbara ran out to the entry hall as Martha came down the steps. He ran to the kitchen as Barbara threw the garments up the steps.

"Take off your clothes. I want you to be naked like me." Barbara held her arms out to Martha.

"Okay." She dropped her nightgown on the steps.

Barbara took her hand and led her out to the kitchen. By this time, Billy was naked and held his pajamas out to her. Martha stopped and stared at her father.

"Okay, Children. To your places. Billy, get your little bare bottom on the stool. And Daddy, we know you have to go to work." She was blocking the doorway. "So, you sit for just a moment," she pointed, "at the head of the table."

Ox jumped onto the chair and scrunched to the table as far as he could.

"And I'll sit where Mommy sits." She sat, hands at back of her neck, and stretched. "Now we all know what Mommy and Daddy and the little girl and little boy look like. We're a family and we're naked."

Martha gazed at her mother's breasts and at her own chest. "When I grow up, will I get big like you?"

"Yes. Maybe bigger, maybe smaller. Everybody has their own size."

"I want to be big like Daddy," said Billy.

"And so you will be," said Barbara. "And now, I'm going to go upstairs with Daddy to help him get ready for work."

She grabbed Ox's hand as he rushed to leave, and blocked his way so the two of them were facing the children. "Martha, you get some milk out and pour it very carefully for each of you. Then you sit and think very carefully about what you want for breakfast. Then . . ." Ox was trying to push her toward the door, "very slowly, you get out all the things we'll need to make breakfast, and line them across the table so you can surprise me when I come back. Then, you sit and teach Billy what they all are."

Ox and Barbara stumbled up the stairs.

Martha called after them. "Mommy, can we do this every morning?"

"Yes, darling, for as long as you like," Barbara said, then to Ox, "That's how you handle that kind of situation."

"Dear Lord, I hope what she meant was fixing breakfast."

CHAPTER THREE

Ox loved his family. He had known Barbara all his life. They had grown up together in Davenport, Iowa. Their children were just a natural result of deep love. He wanted a dozen of them. They both did.

Driving to his church in his twenty-year-old Chevy, he felt good. The car overheated if he went over thirty-five, and the body was rusting, but it got him there. And his life got him there, too. It was satisfactory. Everything was good.

He thought of the burning churches and the old wooden structure of his church—a tinderbox. There were some crazy people in the world. Thank goodness, he didn't have to deal with them.

His brakes squealed as he parked in front of the Church of the Crossroads, a crazy name, but apt. Nothing there but a crossroads. The other three corners were fields. He got out and slammed the door.

Well, he thought, *what will be, will be.* "Listen to me," he said out loud. "I sound like a fortune teller."

The warped side door led into a committee room that connected to a workroom and the minister's study, all of which had been living quarters for the previous minister who had been unmarried and didn't need much space. *I've got to do some work on this place.*

The phone was ringing and he rushed into the study. "Church of the Crossroads, may I help you?"

"Dr. Christie?"

"Yes, this is Oxford Christie."

"Oxford, this is Bishop Markham in the Eastern Diocese. Have I caught you at a bad moment?"

"No, Your Excellency. There's nobody here but me and the crossroads."

"Well, Oxford, we've been watching you and the Crossroads. You've been there for almost a year and your progress has been notable. Most notable. Some might even consider you a miracle worker."

"Thank you, Bishop Markham. That's nice to hear, but I've been fortunate. There's a new settlement of young professionals a few miles away . . ."

"Oxford, it was fortunate they were there, but you attracted them. You brought in the sheaves, so to speak. I'm going to get right to the point."

He paused and Ox felt like saying, "What?"

"We would like to call you to the Church of the One Soul in Philadelphia. What would you say to that?"

"Bishop, I'd go wherever you decided is best. This is certainly a surprise." Ox couldn't help but smile.

"It will be a challenge of a different sort, Oxford."

Ox began to mimic a rain dance.

"The congregation is smaller than the Crossroad's. The church is much larger," the bishop said.

Ox climbed on the desk and pretended to be shouting for joy.

THE HIDDEN CONGREGATION

"The building is in constant need of upkeep and capital expenditures."

Ox shook his head at the dilapidated quarters surrounding him and laughed silently.

"It's in a declining section of Philadelphia, but the worst part is that the congregation, such as it is, loved your predecessor and will be slow accepting you."

"What happened to my predecessor?" The words "*my predecessor*" carried a feeling of excitement.

"Dr. Petersen got called away to the Greater Pastures."

Ox was about to ask where the Church of the Greater Pastures was located, when he realized what the bishop meant. "Oh, I'm sorry."

"I'm sure he's got his own golden cloud. Well, what do you think?"

Ox climbed off his own double pedestal cloud. "Bishop Markham, isn't this a decision the congregation usually makes?"

"To tell the truth, they've been too stunned to give it much thought. It might be more accurate to say they don't want to think about it. They asked me to make the selection, and I have. What do you think?"

"Bishop Markham, I accept, but what about my replacement here? These people have invested their time and money here, and . . ."

"Don't worry. We've got it worked out. We have a young fellow your age. Single. Good carpenter. He'll live there and continue what you started, and he'll repair the building in his spare time and get some of those young professionals to help. It'll work. Don't worry. They'll like him. We'll expect you in Philadelphia in one month. You'll need to find a house. You'll be able to afford a bigger one on your new salary, and I'll get an official letter in the mail to you."

The bishop gave him details regarding the congregation (average age sixty-eight), the church building (sprawling stone cathedral over two hundred years old), housing in Philadelphia (Mount Airy/Germantown area), concerns the bishop had about reviving the church, the church budget supported by generous giving from old members, some of whom were no longer able to get out, and the salary (nearly double his present one).

When the conversation was over, Ox let it sink in. He was to rejuvenate what had been one of the flagships of the denomination. An important assignment. The Church of the One Soul was a symbol of the entire movement, like going to the source. Just this morning, Barbara had asked how long they were going to be in this dinky place, and even then the decision had been made. He grabbed the phone and dialed.

"I was wondering when you were going to call," she said. "I just got a call from the Eastern Diocese saying they were going to send me material on housing and schools in some crazy section of Philadelphia. Is there something I should know?"

"You bet. I've been asked to go to Philadelphia to a large church at double the salary."

"Well, it's none too soon. Martha went next door and told Susie what's-her-name, you know the blond bombshell with eyes for you that you were built just like Billy. Susie was concerned, wondered if you were stunted. I told her it was a real problem."

"We must be careful that Martha never talks to the bishop."

"I can't tell you how happy I am about this. I mean, besides you getting the recognition you should be getting, we need the money for another baby. If my calculations are correct, this morning should've been a direct hit."

"You had it all planned, didn't you?"

"You know me, Babe. Leave nothing to chance."

THE HIDDEN CONGREGATION

"And we'd have taken the shot even if the kids had stood there and watched. Right?"

"Good thing Martha's interested in planning breakfast."

"I hope her interests don't change for a long time."

CHAPTER FOUR

Sergeant Oster was rooting though cold case files in the third level down in the police round house. He was surrounded by a semicircle of detectives and junior officers.

"Here's that crazy Church of the One Soul. Who wants it?" Oster's beefy face carried a slight sneer. "It might mean going to church."

"I'll take it," said Emmett Roberts. "I hate hypocrites—holier-than-thou do-gooders."

"Fine. Jessie May Fremont, you go with him. He needs someone to rein him in."

"I don't need no babysitter."

"Can we have the box of files?" asked Jessie May.

"I expect you to memorize them."

"Shit," said Emmett.

"No. No shit."

"Yes, shit. I want to hit somebody."

CHAPTER FIVE

Ammahn Nical Laval, Ph.D., lay flat on the moss-covered mat in the greenhouse that formed the northeastern corner of his study, high on the top of the old stone house. A black silk turtleneck concealed his massive chest, blending body and darkness. Ammahn stretched his long arms by his sides. He concentrated on his impatience, reducing it to occasional spasms in his heavy hands.

He focused on a goatskin, head and hooves intact, suspended from the top of the greenhouse. The moonlight filtered through the glass, casting a dim halo around the goat. It still possessed a face that seemed to be laughing at its own fate.

"It is your destiny to wear the face of your skull. It's mine to have a brain cursed with perceptions of human insignificance."

He closed his eyes and slipped into the energy of the night, the movement of shadows and gnarled cedar trees towering outside—three thousand years old—messengers of the earth. Deep underground, rocks shifted, grinding their story.

"You, goat, have made your contribution. I have collected you. Some day, I will be collected. Only Death has a permanent collection."

He smelled the moisture in the earth and, farther away, the heat of the desert, and the dung heaps of man and beast. He could hear the clattering voices of hate and anger like anxious birds of prey—cries from the evil side of the mind's duplex. And from the good side, wails of despair and shattered hope. He could taste the decay of death and feel the persistence of rebirth.

A vibration in his throat like the growl of an animal came and went with his breathing. His muscles tingled.

His brain searched for visions of the past and flew into a single thought, and roosted there. The gift of our third layer of brain, the gift that lifts humans above the snake and the rat, is a mind that excuses error. The most humble human is self-righteous compared to any other creature; sanctimonious clingers to the earth.

He remembered Philadelphia, the Church of the One Soul.

The room was still, unlike the shadows outside. He opened his eyes. There was something he had to do. It was time—past time by some clocks. His mind moved to the letter still lying on the desk—Department of Archaeology, University of Pennsylvania. An invitation to return to present a guest lecture series.

Ammahn jerked to his feet with one easy motion, arms still straight by his body, his short legs and long torso creating power in motion for a tall frame—power needed in crawling through crevices, underground tunnels, tombs, and ancient cities; the deserts of the past—chronicles of the future.

He had arranged for an early flight: 8:15 a.m. Philadelphia, there was unfinished business; something unanswered—Nehmi and Petersen. How many years had it been? It didn't matter. By the clock of the earth, the great timekeeper, it was seconds ago.

He watched the shadows dancing outside. The shadows in Philadelphia called—bone and rock and sand. Why not just forget them? Time would bury them and preserve them

THE HIDDEN CONGREGATION

for future digging. The past, the good, the evil—what did it matter?

But still, they called. He would have more time this trip, more time to dig. His bags were already packed.

The powerful jet whistled and left the ground, circled toward the east, climbed and gathered speed, a six-hour flight. The clouds shut out the ground. Eastward, toward the source, but the source was everywhere.

The seats were wide and the one next to him was empty. He adjusted his chair to lay flat and allowed himself to relax, thrusting feet first through space, toward the rising sun.

Sand, ancient rock, and a wailing wind escaped from a corner of his mind, something about ancient stones that dwarf all human importance; the ice age lying in shale, waiting for a trigger. Destination: Cold Point, Pennsylvania; a prophetic name. It was a cold prophesy of the past—the shallows of a great Pliocene lake, gone but still emerging, like light years; a wink in the eye of infinity. There were creatures not mentioned in Holy Writ lurking at the edges of the unknown.

"Sir, would you like a cup of coffee or tea or juice?" asked the stewardess.

"No. Thank you. You're very nice, but I'll just lie here and restore my energy."

She smiled and moved on. He could hear her recite her liturgy. "Would you like a cup of coffee or tea or juice?"

He let his body sleep as the earth and its creatures swept beneath him on a moving tapestry. Through the windows of his mind, he could see the stars, whistling cold through space and burning hot to the touch. The plane, too, was a star, while the spinning earth below brought the burning sun from the other side of the world slowly overhead.

They crossed mountains and rivers. Far below and to his right, lay the grasslands of Kansas. He could feel its rich heat in the thin light over Missouri. Evolution was taking place as time's invisible presence processed earth and air. Flesh cracked open and bone turned white. He could feel the blood in his veins, flowing at a steady pace, like the continuing kaleidoscope below him.

Time sang, bathing space—the origin of all music—centuries of music in a calling note; cries of ecstasy and terror. His blood sang and the world sang with it, from air to grass, from fire to rock, to silent chalk. All the life that had surged and died, fluid eyes long closed, reduced to powder, a sweet dust with pungent mystery, unknown but to a few of his colleagues in archaeology.

Mid-afternoon: the cries of life beyond the chalk blended with the whisper of the jet as it began its descent into the thicker air.

"Sir, you need to bring your seat to an upright position and fasten your seatbelt."

We're all fallen angels. The House of Sleep was rising toward him—the archive—the bone land. He would haunt the past.

The old business in Philadelphia had only aged a few grains of sand. There would be time. There would always be time. The figures in the Museum of Man were silent witness to that. The findings, whatever they might be, would hardly change the balance of good and evil.

Insignificant, except to certain people.

CHAPTER SIX

Cynthia Neal was trying to recover from a bad night. She'd had a cup of tea and two aspirins, and her head still pounded. All night, she kept waking to the same nightmare. Two animals fighting, or maybe they were dancing, or maybe they were mimicking sex. A crazy ballet. Two strange animals with large liquid eyes. Half human, half something else. And throughout the charade, they would pause, the music would stop, and they would turn their heads and leer. Then, exaggerated gyrations again and growling organ music.

She couldn't get it out of her mind—the images—the music. During the last two weeks, every night of her concert series, she would come home exhausted, go to bed and dream. Was she one of the animals? Was she both? Was it something she ate? Was it her music they danced to? Had cells in her brain run wild? Was there something inside her brain that wanted out?

She fingered yesterday's mail, still unopened beside the phone: one from Philadelphia, the String Instrument Society.

Light filtered through the glass door from outside. "Six-thirty. Too late to go back to bed," she said.

She slid the door open and stepped out on the balcony. She breathed the fresh air deeply. Maybe it would clear her head.

There, twelve floors below her was the Cuyahoga River. To her left, far upstream, was Cleveland, but across the river were the woods, nothing but woods. Here the country could be a hundred years ago—two hundred. She wasn't on a balcony. She was on a mountain, looking across a river at the woods, listening to the birds, smelling the earth and underbrush in the heat of summer, and feeling the morning sun as it climbed in the sky and dried the air.

In her mind, she wasn't in Cleveland. She was in Richmond, looking across the James, smelling the boxwood, feeling the soft world and holding it close. The wind sifted through the trees and carried messages. The leaves sang.

She glanced to her left, and there was Cleveland, still shimmering in the distance, concrete and smoke. No singing leaves, only progress: dirt, noise, and progress. Things must have been better a hundred years ago, simpler.

Her head began to clear, the pounding more like an itch on her temples. She leaned against the door and thought of Richmond. She had just come home from Julliard, and there was the remarkable letter from the Cleveland Symphony. First violinist. She had arrived. At Julliard, they had told her she was a genius.

The air was sweet, there in the house on the James River, in the house that stood like a monument to spite the floods; in the house with her father, beginning to turn old, who had always understood her need to be one-with-music. He could hear the leaves, too, and the flowers, and the grass drying in the fall with singing colors. And her mother who loved her, and loved her, and loved her. Her mother, who had turned old, but didn't mind.

Cynthia gazed across the river. The air was getting warmer. She looked at her watch. It was time to practice.

In her living room, she fingered her violin. Since she was

THE HIDDEN CONGREGATION

seven, she had been playing. The strings stretched and vibrated tones of her father and mother, and their fathers and mothers, and their fathers and mothers. Her music came from the dust of her beginnings.

In her apartment, sound barely carried from one room to another. Closing doors made a room soundproof. The playing wouldn't bother the neighbors. She caressed the violin. She felt the cool wood against her cheek, inhaled its odor, aged, peaceful. She could almost hear music drifting from the sound hole.

She played a few arpeggios she had composed herself. They reminded her of the wind at night, a few drops of rain, leaves rustling down a pathway, a moon trying to break through the clouds, and herself not being lonely or strange.

When younger, she had cried when she played. The music was so beautiful. But skill brought self-control. She channeled her emotion into the music. The violin did her crying and singing. She was the instrument, the wood, the strings, the fingerboard, and the soundboard.

The program that night was all Schubert. She thought about the music, ran it through her mind, allowed it to surround her.

That evening, she placed her violin on the passenger side of her Datsun and maneuvered onto the throughway into town. She walked into the concert hall with time to spare.

Olivia Brown was there already. She liked to practice and tune up before the rest came in. "Hi, Cynthia. All ready for Schubert?" She concentrated on the strings and began to play her bass.

"Not as ready as you, but I'll get into it."

Olivia stopped. "You were born in it. I have to work into it." She tilted her head and asked, "Do you ever get out of it?" There might have been a trace of irritation.

Cynthia went to the curtains and peeked through. People were already coming in. She gazed at the audience as the house began to fill. They made their own music. She took her place and tuned her violin—the opening ritual.

When the house lights dimmed and the maestro made his entrance, the applause set the tone of excitement, an integral part of the concert for her. Now she could play. Her music would blend with the others.

Passage after passage, wind and rain. The notes were things, as real as flowers or stars or clouds. They were falling leaves or graceful birds.

Intermission.

It always came quickly. The visions stopped almost as soon as they began. She became aware of her chair and surroundings.

When the concert ended, a void hovered for a moment; it was over. The mood was broken. She closed her violin case and left the hall.

In her car, she sat for a while, then started the motor and crept southward, once pulling to the side of the road where cedar trees framed an open field. She sat in the small car for what must have been an hour, absorbing the moonlight, shadows, smells of summer, and the music of the stars.

It was long past midnight when she opened the door of her apartment and saw her reflection in the glass balcony door across the living room. *Hello again. Are you me or am I you?* She studied herself. The image disappeared as she slid the door open.

On her balcony, Cynthia watched the sky and the eastern horizon turn light, heard the birds wake, one note after another, and finally felt the sun's warmth. She didn't feel tired, but closed her eyes when she felt the urge and listened to the music of the world. She lay back in her chair, felt the sun and turned off her mind. She might have slept for a while.

THE HIDDEN CONGREGATION

She walked into the living room just as the phone rang.

She glanced at her watch. Almost ten-thirty. She let it ring two more times and picked it up.

"Miss Neal?

"Yes?"

"This is George Watts of the Philadelphia String Institute. I had hoped to catch you after the concert last night, but somehow, I missed you. I assume you got my letter."

"Oh, yes. But it just came and I haven't even opened my mail."

"I'll get right to the point. Our Board has asked me to talk to you about a position as professor of violin, first violinist and solo artist. It will involve some teaching, but not a lot. The letter goes into more detail."

She tilted her head back and felt a rush.

"If you are interested, perhaps we could have lunch and go over particulars."

The silence on the line told her he was waiting for a response. "I'm sorry. What did you say?"

"My apologies. I've called at a bad time. I said if you are interested, perhaps we could have lunch and I could go over particulars with you."

"Uh, I would be delighted."

"Fine. Wonderful. If we met at noon, I could make the three o'clock flight. Would that be too early?"

"No. No. Fine. What time? Uh, I mean, what restaurant? Any place is all right."

"I'm staying at the Top of the Square. I understand they have a fine restaurant here. Would that do?"

"Yes. I'll see you at the Top of the Square at noon." She had regained her control. "Oh, this is exciting."

"Wonderful. I'm excited, too. I'll see you there."

She placed the phone in the cradle and held her hand on it while the impact moved through her.

Quickly, she reached for the letter and tore it open. Yes, it was all there.

She picked up her violin and played the arpeggios. Eyes closed, she could hear the soft wind of night and drops of rain on dried leaves on a pathway, while a moon tried to break through. What music would Philadelphia bring? She opened her eyes and stared at her reflection in the balcony door. "Music, music, is music all I am?"

CHAPTER SEVEN

Emil Nehmi raked the flagstone walk running alongside the church from front to back. It was covered with twigs and leaves from several years of neglect. A tangle of weeds grew up between the stones. He knelt with his clippers to cut through the mess. He had to make things look good. There was a new minister coming. Things would change . . . someone to take orders from. He would no longer be his own boss.

He laid down the clippers, grabbed a trowel and scraped off some mold from a stone. He glanced at the grass badly in need of cutting. He would have to get that done, too. The minister would wonder what he did round here. Oxford Christie. He wondered how much of a stickler he was. He might be walking into something over his head. Young, married, time would tell how strong he was.

He glanced again at the grass—it needed the weed whacker. It was too long for the lawnmower. He left his tools on the walkway and opened the basement door. He scurried down the steps.

Things would have to look right. He wondered how perceptive this new minister was. The One Soul, no longer abandoned.

Time would tell.

CHAPTER EIGHT

Ox babied his old Chevy up the few blocks to the church. The car had behaved itself for most of the trip from St. Louis, and the family was now at the new house—a real home for a change. He chugged through the weary neighborhood slightly blighted by neglect, and pulled to the curb by the Church of the One Soul, a castle-like building surrounded by decay.

A broken flagstone walkway stretched the length of the building on the right side. He decided to look around. Ten feet beyond a back entrance the property came to an abrupt end with a cyclone fence protecting the unwary from dropping off the high cliff. Far below, the Schuylkill River and the parkway traced side by side into the mist.

A children's swing set, a seesaw, and a jungle gym nestled into a forest of weeds, cans, bottles, and papers. Off to the other corner of the church, the grass was knee-deep. He wandered over to look.

On the opposite side in the back, he was surprised to see a stone archway forming an entrance into a lot buried in grass. Over the arch were wrought-iron letters.

"My Soul Is Set Free From This Tired Body"

A cemetery. He could see a few headstones visible above the

THE HIDDEN CONGREGATION

grass, but the plot was mostly inundated with ragged bushes, an aspen tree, and miscellaneous saplings. A cicada droned a song of heat. Grasshoppers flitted from one wave of grass to another. Bird nests clung throughout the bushes—trash catchers dried out by the years. A wall on that side blocked him from the front of the church.

He retraced his steps past the swing set into the broken flagstone walk. The woodwork around the stained-glass windows needed painting. The windows were dark. The church secretary, Mrs. Rush, knew he was coming at 9:30. Maybe her day didn't start until 10:00.

A faint breeze disturbed the heat. The ground released damp odors: a stew of grass, leafing trees and blossoms. He could taste the healing elixir.

The neighborhood was quiet. Nothing moved except a little dust.

He walked to the front with a sense of wonder at the size of the place. On the other side, the building formed a U-shape into a courtyard set back about fifty feet from the street. He made his way up the cobblestone drive.

To the left, nosed in close to the building, was a small black car, its paint oxidized—an old Studebaker, one made in the U.S. before the company moved to Canada—older than any car he had seen in years. He spotted a lighted upstairs window and tried one of the doors. Locked. But a high-pitched voice cried out through a small speaker above the door.

"Who is it?"

"Oxford Christie."

There was a loud buzz and he grabbed the brass knob and opened the door into a small, musty passageway. To the right, there was a set of double doors, probably to the sanctuary. To the left, a stairway led to the upper floor. He paused to look at a bulletin board. There was one notice, a yellowed three-by-five-inch card.

"Women's Auxiliary Discussion Group," it read. "Every second Monday afternoon at 2 p.m."

Ox wondered how long it had been there and whether anyone met on those Mondays. A voice pierced down the stairs.

"Dr. Christie?"

"Mrs. Rush?"

He took the steps two at a time and, making the first turn, and came face to face with a small, gray woman—large blue eyes etched in sorrow. She might've been pretty at one time—a faded photograph—straw flowers in winter.

"How nice to meet you," she said. "It gets lonely in here when you're all alone."

"Not much traffic through here during the day, I guess." Lonely when she's all alone. Well, why not? He shook her small hand warmly and detected the faint smell of lavender.

"Let me show you your office, and I'll give you a tour of the building." She sounded almost apologetic as she walked back up the stairs.

She pointed to a dark walnut door just to the right of the stairs, and taking out a key, unlocked it—a corner room. He walked across the worn carpet and looked out on the children's play sets, the cyclone fence, and the valley beyond. He turned and touched the desk. Two stuffed chairs and some old wooden ones, painted black, stood stiffly in a semicircle in front of it. To the left of the door were built-in bookcases climbing halfway up the wall, almost empty.

"There's a small powder room here." Mrs. Rush pointed to a door next to the entrance, as though seeking approval.

Ox nodded. His eye had caught a bright blue book on one of the shelves. He walked over and picked it up.

The Conquest of Illusion, he read. *By J. J. Van Der Leeuw.*

Mrs. Rush handed him a set of old jury-box keys, the kind found in some hardware stores. There were evidently no tumbler locks here.

"This one is to your study. This one is to the church office, and this one is to all of the outside doors." She led him through the count. "And this last one is to the key case on the wall in the church office. That's where all the rest of the keys are kept, including a skeleton key that fits most of them." She paused as though uncertain about what to do next.

"Thank you," said Ox. "Let's go see the rest of the building. How about the sanctuary?"

"Right this way." Mrs. Rush was out of the door and down the steps. "I've got the answering machine on in case anyone calls."

Ox bounded after her, surprised by her agility. They passed the bulletin board and the courtyard entrance. At the double doors leading into the sanctuary, Mrs. Rush paused to flip a series of light switches. She opened the doors and smiled—a pretty smile in a sad way.

He walked in and stopped. The sanctuary was huge. He stared at the frescoes and paintings on the high ceiling. The worldly eyes of cherubim, angels, and bearded old men stared from a torment of clouds.

He caught himself staring back. "Whoever did those must have been inspired. The rich colors. If people get tired of my sermons, they can stare at the ceiling. I might do it myself."

"Dr. Christie, I'm certain no one will be staring at the ceiling when you are in the pulpit."

"Oh, by the way. My name is Ox. I prefer to be informal."

Mrs. Rush looked surprised and uncomfortable. "Well, mine is Angel." She managed a smile and paused. "A whim of my parents. Actually, it's Angelica."

Something made him assume she lived alone. A solitary figure, she moved along the rail of the chancel toward the center aisle, her hand caressing the wood.

The stained-glass windows hadn't been so colorful from the outside. In the center aisle, he turned slowly, taking them all in. In the back of the chancel, in vivid reds and blues, were Jesus and the lamb. The sanctuary was cross-shaped, and at the far side of the transept were windows with a profusion of stained-glass flowers honoring Faith, Hope, and Charity. He glanced at the balcony and the clerestory. Other smaller windows were glowing there.

"This room is incredible. The wood paneling looks like it's been waxed from floor to ceiling. The pews shine. Is it all oak?"

"Yes, the pews are. I'm told the paneling is walnut and chestnut. It was built over two hundred years ago."

She glanced round the room, one hand nervously playing at her mouth. She kept taking steps forward as though to keep moving.

"Who takes care of it?"

"Mainly it's Mr. Nehmi. He's been here a long time. He takes care of the place as if it were his own."

Ox walked down the aisle, feeling the pews, looking at the ceiling and the walls. The chandeliers were all different, hanging on long, delicate chains until about twelve feet above the pews.

"My Lord. Twenty-four, a sanctuary like the huge European cathedrals."

Mrs. Rush was fidgeting.

Ox felt uncomfortable for her. "I hope you'll forgive me. I'm overwhelmed. Let's go on. I can come here later and marvel."

She pointed to the front of the building. "I ought to show you the tracker organ." He followed her through double doors into

THE HIDDEN CONGREGATION

a large narthex, the main entrance to the church. They crossed it to go up narrow stairs curving a hundred and eighty degrees. He ducked his head as they came into the choir loft. From there the sanctuary looked even larger, but distant. In the center of the loft squatted the huge tracker organ.

"Wait until you hear it. Mr. Pregle practices on Thursday night, maybe tomorrow night at the reception. Everyone is just so anxious to meet you." She almost sounded excited, but her voice trailed off.

"I can't tell you how anxious I am to meet them." But he felt a twinge in his chest. A spasm or a premonition. He spotted another door. "Where does that go?"

"The steeple." She opened the door revealing old-style steps with high risers covered by stacks of sheet music and hymnals. The air was musty.

"This is Mr. Pregle's storage room." She laughed nervously.

Ox supposed it was natural for her to be nervous, meeting the new minister. They returned to the narthex.

"Maybe I should show you the lower level in the front."

Through a small door and down narrow steps, they came out into a duplicate of the narthex above. Angel switched on a floor lamp at the bottom of the steps. It did the job, but the corners were dark and the air stale. There was a door at the end.

"I noticed a cellar door by the walkway outside."

"Mr. Nehmi uses it when he's working in the yard."

She moved down the long hall and opened a door on the left, and Ox was looking into a nursery.

"We keep this, but it hasn't been used for a while."

"Angel, how many young families are there in the church?"

"Well, actually, not many."

Ox interpreted that to mean none.

There was another door on the opposite side of the nursery. He crossed over and tried the knob. "What's in here?"

"That leads into the unfinished space under the sanctuary. We keep it locked. I don't have the key with me." She turned toward the stairs. Ox worked the knob one more time. He turned to follow her, but his eyes locked upon a large oil painting he had missed just inside the nursery door.

"Angel, who is this a portrait of?"

"Oh, that's Dr. Petersen."

Ox stared at the dignified face. The gray eyes stared back. "Why is his portrait hanging here?" Ox moved to his right without breaking his gaze. The gray eyes stared straight across the room.

"Oh, I guess there just wasn't space upstairs." Angel headed for the steps. Ox glanced again at the face of Dr. Petersen and hurried after her.

Upstairs, they moved past the bulletin board and into a large kitchen. In the middle was a huge table.

"Good place for cooks to collaborate," said Ox. "Have many potlucks here?"

"Not lately. A few of us used to have lunch in here. Maybe you can get something started." She pointed off to the side of the kitchen at another door. "We can go into the dining room this way." She opened it. "We have coffee after service here."

Ox surveyed the huge room, easily forty- by sixty-feet. The floor shone like a ballroom. "Does it get used any other time?"

"Not lately."

Mrs. Rush continued into the dining room, but Ox stopped. There were stairs to the left, curving up through a maze of paneling.

"Is there another large room above us?"

"Yes. The meeting room. We'll come back through there. I want to show you the small chapel."

THE HIDDEN CONGREGATION

"Let's wait. I want to assimilate all I've seen before taking in the rest of it. This place is enormous."

"There's so much to see here. It's been a special place." She sounded like she was trying to reassure herself.

Ox wondered why she used the past tense. "Yes. It certainly is a special place."

He followed her back through the kitchen and up to the church office. Her window overlooked the courtyard. Everything was clean and neat. Nothing out of the ordinary. No family pictures on the desk, no cartoons tacked on a bulletin board; no signs of individuality.

"You've been here a long time?"

"Yes. I grew up in this church. I've seen a lot of things change around here."

"How long was Dr. Petersen here?"

"Oh," she said, only it was more like a moan. "He was here for forty-six years." She took out a wadded tissue and held it to her nose.

"I guess you miss him very much."

She sat on a side chair next to her desk. "Yes, but we're all hoping you can fill the void."

"I don't know about filling the void, Angel, but time can place a soothing veil over memories."

She nodded. "There are constant reminders, you know."

"Is that why his portrait's in the basement?"

Mrs. Rush jerked slightly. "No. No. We'll probably move it again some time." She twisted the tissue in her fingers.

"How old was he when he died?"

"He was seventy-six, and brilliant to the last moment. Everyone loved him. They really did."

Was she trying to convince herself? "I've a tough act to follow. I'm going to need your help."

"I'll try."

"The community around here has changed, hasn't it?

"Yes. There are no young people anymore. They all moved away or got older."

"Has that happened to the congregation, too?"

"Yes, and the giving's not what it was. When someone dies, they leave something to the church. We've cut the budget. There aren't enough of us to do much with bake sales."

Ox was assured by her concern. "When I get settled in, we'll go over the finances. But the primary issue is new members." Her shoulders slumped. "How many have joined in the past year?"

"Well, actually, none. There's just nobody around anymore. If we could just move the church somewhere else or bring in a new neighborhood. But all we've got is us."

Ox let Angel get back to her work and retreated to his desk. He wanted to work on his sermon, but something wasn't quite right. He hadn't connected with Angel. She had barely gone through the motions. He looked at the phone. Barbara. Time to call to see if the phone was installed. He hadn't liked leaving her with all the mess the movers had left.

He dialed and felt encouraged when the phone rang.

"We're sorry. The number you have dialed . . ."

"Rats." He hung up the phone. Almost noon. He walked back to Angel's office.

"Angel, I'm going to go and get Barbara and the kids and take them out for hamburgers—get them out of the house of boxes, but I'll be back."

Although only a few blocks away, the house the bishop's office had found for them was in a less eroded neighborhood. Two little boys about Billy's age sat on the front steps. "We're waiting for Billy to come out," one of them volunteered. "He had to go to the bathroom."

The house, itself was another of the big old stone places, typical of the area—about a hundred years old, but cared for.

Barbara opened the door. "Welcome to the Christie warehouse. Whatever you're looking for, I can't find it, unless it's me you're after." She wrapped her arms round his neck and kissed him. "How does the church look?"

"It looks great. The phone's not been disconnected because of non-payment. The entire Church of the Crossroads could fit into half of the sanctuary. After I've learned the place, I'll give you a guided tour. It'll knock your socks off. But I've a hunch the congregation gets swallowed by all those pews. Let's go get hamburgers."

"You're on. The kids are upstairs fixing up Martha's room."

"I thought Billy was going to the bathroom. Bulletin from the kids on the front steps."

"That's what he came in for, but she said she needed him. He was trapped the minute he came out of the bathroom."

"Call them down and we'll free him from her clutches. I had a bigger sister, too."

They spent the next hour relaxing in a McDonald's.

"I've got my quota of cholesterol for this week." Ox stretched his arms and shoulders. He glanced at his watch. "It's time for me to scoot."

Ox pressed his brakes to turn in to the courtyard. The cellar door was open. He heard a lawnmower and guessed Nehmi was cutting the grass.

He decided to look over the sermon he had written and touch it up, add a few allusions to the church building. He wanted the first sermon to be one to remember. Ox walked over to the study window. The river and the parkway moved side by side as a reminder of the constant marriage of civilization and nature.

Movement near the swings caught his eye. There was a man holding a rake. It had to be Nehmi. Straight as a post. Something about the way he stood defied any weight that could be placed upon him. He was looking at the grass around one of the end poles of the swing set. He bent down and scooped something out of the grass. He held it in his hand for a moment and laid it on a flagstone; a small animal skull, bleached white. Maybe a large cat or small dog.

Nehmi got something from his wheelbarrow and went back to the skull with a hammer and a chisel. He split the skull in half and carefully placed it where it had been.

Nehmi turned and met Ox's gaze. He waved, a thin smile slowly growing. Ox raised his hand, noticing how clear the face was of wrinkles, lines, or expression. But the eyes—they were different. All expression centered there. Clear, penetrating, and unblinking. The eyes of a watcher. What are the eyes of a watcher? He wasn't sure where the thought had come from, but Nehmi was watching. He slid the window open.

"Mr. Nehmi, don't leave without our having a chance to talk."

Nehmi nodded and bent for a discarded bottle beside the seesaw. Ox returned to the desk, his sermon in front of him. He'd need the computer to make changes. It didn't make sense to do it by hand and type it again.

He glanced at the wall over the bookcase. At one time there had been a picture hanging there. There was a smudged outline of a frame. He stared at the empty space.

Finally, his eye rested on the dark blue book on the shelf below, *The Conquest of Illusion*. He rolled his chair over. Title page, 1928, J. J. Van Der Leeuw, LL.D. author of *The Fire of Creation*, and *Gods in Exile*. Must've had something to say. Was it new then? Would it be new again? He flipped a few pages. *Our very consciousness is terra incognita; we know not the working of our own mind.* An interesting thought, but not new.

Who left this here? Petersen? What about any other books? Only three in all. He examined each of them. *Nature and the Supernatural: As Together Constituting the One System of God* by Horace Bushnell, 1858. He stared at the thick, brown cover. Future reading if for no other reason than curiosity. *Modern Religious Cults and Society* by Louis Richard Binder, 1933. Modern as spats and straw hats. But do cults ever change? Maybe as modern as needed.

There was a tap on the open door. It was Nehmi. "Welcome aboard." He stepped in and extended his hand, at the same time glancing at the book Ox was holding.

"I'm amazed at the condition of the sanctuary. I had to meet the man who could keep it looking the way it does."

Nehmi showed only a whisper of a smile. "It represents the heart of the church, the beginning and the ending."

"One gets the sense things are just beginning. It looks so new."

"Yes."

"The wood, the windows, the chandeliers. And the ceiling, those frescoes, who in the world did them?" Ox realized he was babbling.

"Yes, the ceiling." For just a moment, Nehmi gazed as though he could see the frescoes. "The ceiling. It was that way in the beginning. Very special." Then he spoke apologetically. "It's time for me to finish the outside. I've let it get ahead of me. The inside will just about take care of itself. We'll have more time to talk at the reception." Nehmi's face hardly changed as he talked. Almost like a mask. "I have to leave earlier than usual. Tomorrow, I'll make up for it. I want to get the place looking good for the reception. I'd better get all the tools inside."

"I'll see you tomorrow. Maybe you can fill me in on what some of our larger maintenance problems are."

Ox heard him retreating down the steps then nothing. He looked out the window. The weeds were all gone from around the children's play sets. The skull reflected like a bleached marker. Why hadn't he just thrown it away?

CHAPTER NINE

Ox continued to gaze out the window. The traffic on the Schuylkill River was fascinating, all that life flowing like ants. Then he remembered. Time to try Barbara again.

"Hello."

"I see the phone has finally been installed."

"He left ten minutes ago."

"I guess this is the first phone call you've received."

"Second."

"Second? Who beat me to it?"

"Insurance agent. But he won't call again."

"Why? What'd you tell him?"

"I told him your occupation was bridge worker and you were seventy-six years old and had the trembles, and we desperately wanted insurance. He said he'd call another time."

"I hope he doesn't have a brother who sells cemetery plots."

"I should've had the man give us an unlisted number."

"Welcome to the big city. Come to think of it, I'll have to ask Angel how she discourages nuisance calls. I haven't heard the phone ring all day."

"Who's Angel? A saintly haunt?"

"The church secretary."

"A church secretary named Angel? A bit much. Is her hair golden, and does she run around in a flimsy little white robe and a white halo?"

"No. It's more on the order of silver, maybe pewter."

"Slightly tarnished?"

"She hasn't shared her considerable past."

"I'll have Martha come in and talk to her. What time will you be coming home for dinner?"

"We had a late lunch. It's going on four-thirty. Can the kids hold out 'til seven?"

"Sure. Martha's got the little boys in the backyard playing school."

"What's she teaching them?"

"The last time I checked, she was teaching them how to be excused."

"Wait a minute."

"Don't worry, she was just showing them how to raise their hands."

"Whew," said Ox. "I'll see you later."

He looked out the study window. Late summer, it wouldn't get dark until seven-thirty.

Mrs. Rush tapped on his door.

"Will I see you tomorrow morning?" she asked.

"Yes. I'm a morning person, so I may be in early."

"Have a nice evening." She waved and trotted down the steps.

The courtyard door slammed behind her. Her car started. It sputtered and clunked with a nervousness to match her own. The building was quiet.

His eye rested again on the blank spot on the wall. In the quiet of his mind, he could imagine a voice. "Take care of my congregation."

He walked down the steps, past the bulletin board, and into the sanctuary.

No lights; he wanted to see it through the filtered light of the stained-glass windows. The ceiling was immersed in its own night, an empty void with chains suspending clusters of pearls. The wooden paneling was dark and ageless, harboring its secrets.

He sat in the last pew and focused on the chancel at the far end of the long sanctuary, narrowed in the dim light, walls leaning secretly inward. He could sense echoes rising in the silence, echoes from two hundred years of sermons, christenings, weddings, and funerals. Moments calling to be remembered. He envisioned himself standing in the pulpit. Then he envisioned Dr. Petersen standing there.

Take care of my congregation.

He peered toward the ceiling for ancient eyes penetrating the gloom.

Dark. Nothing.

Nothing at all, and yet . . . something. The air was as old as the wood, as old as the dark.

The oak pews felt cool. Near the chancel, subdued light crept in through the large stained-glass windows. How many people had breathed this air in and out, over and over, sharing it and their secrets? Living, sharing, dying; their history hiding in the walls.

We all have secrets. Maybe they are splintered parts of a bigger secret, history in the walls, waiting to be read; past congregations hiding in the walls.

The hidden congregation.

He had a new sermon for Sunday.

CHAPTER TEN

Cynthia drove past the Church of the One Soul and pressed the brake pedal. She backed over to the curb. A few days ago the place was scraggly, a monument of a church blighted by weeds and debris. She had felt an attraction and repulsion, and had kept driving toward her apartment, but now there had been a transformation. The grounds were clean and trim. It made the whole building worthy of a sonata.

She got out of the car and stood on the sidewalk. Joining the sound of her mental violin were heavy chords of a massive organ. She could hear mystery, and beauty, and something else. Death? Danger? And there were other strains, the barest thought of song. Was it *Der Zarovitch*?

Cynthia walked up the flagstone walkway that curved next to the old stone building and discovered the children's swings and seesaws. They looked as though they were waiting for someone. She squeezed into a swing and sat facing the large cyclone fence overlooking the valley.

Then she stood at the fence and gazed across the river and parkway at the communities buried in the trees. It was like Richmond and Cleveland, but it was neither. The music was different. It was faster, more exciting.

THE HIDDEN CONGREGATION

She studied the building with a quiet exhilaration and maybe a little fear. The setting sun and the glare in her eyes made the windows seem dark, and through the quiet, she could hear the lonely strains of an oboe, restrained excitement. Was there movement in one of the windows at the far end?

She glanced toward the swing set, and there on the grass laid two white objects. She stooped closer: halves of a small skull. The music stopped. Silence, then a different music merged: soft kettle-drums, a bow seesawing crazy chords. She knelt and touched the bleached bones, one after the other. Her stomach lifted and she jerked away. They were so out of place. She didn't want to look at them, but felt drawn. She retreated to the flagstone walk.

She stopped in front of the stained-glass windows. With no light coming through them, they were black, dull. Her music began to change again. What was inside this building? She walked back to her car. The grass was so neatly cut. Why was the skull there? What had brought her here in the first place? George Watts of the Institute had suggested the area and the ad in the Sunday *Inquirer* had sounded promising. But the skull. She couldn't erase the feeling when she had touched it. Something crawled inside her.

Cynthia's apartment was the third floor of an ornate stone house that had to be over a hundred years old. It was just four blocks beyond the Church of the One Soul. She closed her door softly. The front windows faced east over the valley with the river and the parkway curling along together. The wind scurried through the foliage of the split-leaf maples that concealed the yard below and most of the street. A thin strip of land bordered the other side of the street before the ground dropped into a valley. Mimosa trees, still in bloom, shed pink fairy blossoms. And her music was unrestrained. She forgot about the skull.

The telephone had been installed, right where she had asked it to be placed. There was a note taped to it. It was barely legible.

"Miss Neal, I let the phone man in this afternoon and showed him where you wanted it. I hope I got it right." It was signed Hilda Danziger.

Cynthia thought of Miss Danziger, hunched over and crippled with arthritis. She lived on the first floor because it was difficult for her to climb the stairs. She must have labored up the steps to show in the phone man. A sweet lady, old and somehow sad. Miss Danziger had pronounced the "miss" as though making a statement about the term *Ms.* She wanted there to be no mistake. The poor soul was alone, had no family to share the huge house with. Cynthia guessed she had grown up here.

There were still boxes to unpack. They were all stacked in the central sitting/dining room.

On the north side of the apartment was the bedroom. On the south side was a kitchen that probably had been a bedroom at one time, since it was the same size. All three rooms had stained-glass windows in the back, like Tiffany's. She could hear the music of crystal as the late afternoon sun reflected rainbows of color through them—rainbows of hope. She felt a sense of magic as she looked round at the colors on top of this old mansion, empty except for Miss Danziger and herself—an exquisite loft on top of a private mountain—her own hideaway.

She picked up her violin and fingered the strings. There was beauty and hope and despair, and also fear of the unknown, and maybe the thrill of mystery. She let the bow slide across the strings.

Cynthia never kept a journal. Her music was her journal. She would play her feelings, and after she had replayed and edited, she would write it. The title was usually the date and place. Her feelings now were so mixed: hope, fear, anxiety, the new, the old,

THE HIDDEN CONGREGATION

and the unknown. She thought of the church building and all her feelings surged out in heavy notes and chords that changed quickly to light cries, questions, and answers. She felt the beauty and the unknown together—hope.

It was after eight o'clock before she realized it was time to fix something to eat. It was still light outside, but the rainbows were gone. She turned on the light in the kitchen then heard a tapping at her door. It was Miss Danziger. She carried a tray.

"I brought you a cup of tea and some German cookies, springerle and pfeffernusse. I made them this morning. I just loved your music, but I couldn't place it. Who were you playing?"

"It was my own." Cynthia inspected the cookies and decided she didn't need a balanced diet.

"Oh, my. It was beautiful. What is it called?"

"*Hope in Philadelphia.*"

"Did you compose it since you came to Philadelphia?"

"Just now."

Miss Danziger looked so surprised and pleased, Cynthia had to laugh.

"Music is my life." As an afterthought, she added, "I guess it's everything. Please, sit."

She moved a box from a chair.

"Oh, I don't want to impose."

Cynthia laughed again. Miss Danziger had brought two cups of tea. "You're not imposing. I had just finished and the next task was unpacking. I'll gladly put that off."

Miss Danziger put the tray on top of a box and sat.

"There," she said. "The springerle are hard as plaster. You nibble off a corner and then blow in them. They'll get softer."

Cynthia followed the instructions. "They're delicious."

Then on a sudden impulse, "Miss Danziger, do you know anything about the Church of the One Soul?"

In spite of the fact that Miss Danziger held her cup in both hands, it shook enough to spill.

"Oh, dear." She put the cup down slowly and brushed off the front of her apron with her handkerchief. "Well, it's a wonderful old church. It's been there forever."

Cynthia waited while Miss Danziger brushed her apron some more.

"Dr. Petersen was there for more years than I can remember." She glanced at her apron and brushed it again. "I was still a young woman when he came, and my family were all alive." She looked in the direction of the church as though she could see it. Her eyes watered. "Papa and Mama, all of us." Her voice dropped almost to a whisper. "The congregation would have followed Dr. Petersen anywhere. I guess we did." Memory filled her voice. "Once, we were a large congregation, but not in the past few years. Well, it doesn't matter, anyhow. We didn't need anybody else." She said it as though that settled an argument. "We came to depend on each other." She seemed to forget her train of thought, then continued. "He died. He was seventy-six. His time had come." Her voice got louder. "We have a new minister coming. He starts this Sunday." She started to pick up her teacup, but didn't. "Maybe things will be all right."

Cynthia felt a hurting sadness in Miss Danziger, almost like a violin crying.

"It's so good to talk to someone who's a member. What do you know about the new minister?"

Miss Danziger was still studying her apron. "Well, he's thirty-eight. He comes from St. Louis. He's married and has two children. We were told he could do magic things with a church, and we need that. The congregation's getting old, like me. We need a new start, some young blood." She looked up at Cynthia. "Why don't you come?"

THE HIDDEN CONGREGATION

"I . . . I thought I might drop in."

"Oh, please. Go with me. Let me introduce you. It would make me so happy." Miss Danziger's eyes watered again as she reached out and touched Cynthia's arm.

"Yes. Yes, I'd like that. Thank you."

Miss Danziger looked worried. "I hope you won't be put off by so many gray heads." Cynthia gazed at Miss Danziger. She sensed something was troubling her. "Gray heads don't put me off. Thank you for coming all the way up here to let the phone man do the installation. I know it isn't easy for you to climb those steps."

"Oh, I so rarely come up here. Someone might as well be using this space. And I do like having someone else in the house. It's such a big place. My sister used to fill the house with her music. She played the piano, but it's been fifteen years. I still hear her echoes. Now maybe it won't sound so empty." She smiled and her face shined. "I could hardly hear your music coming from way up here, but it was so special. Please don't ever think it's a bother to me. And at night, when I go to sleep, I always close my bedroom door. It won't bother me if you play."

Cynthia soaked a cookie in her tea. "These taste like licorice."

"Anise," said Miss Danziger. "It's an old recipe of my mother's. She used to make them every Christmas. But Christmas isn't so special anymore, and besides, I like them all year round. Try the pfeffernusse." Miss Danziger looked round the room. "You've got work to do. I'm going to slip downstairs and get out of your way. I just wanted to let you know again how welcome you are here. This is your home. If you need anything, just let me know."

She put her hands on her knees, pushed herself up and made her way across the room.

"Thank you for making me feel so welcome in your wonderful home. It means a lot. It's so beautiful here. And that wonderful old staircase, so wide with those ornate banisters."

Miss Danziger turned and stared at her for just the slightest moment. "You are welcome, you know. You are so welcome. There's another staircase in the back up to the second floor. But it's narrow with high steps. It was put in for servants, but we never had any." She opened the door. "Would you mind dropping the tray off downstairs in the morning when you pass through? There's no hurry."

And she was gone. Cynthia cracked her door open and listened to the old lady descending the creaky stairs. It took her a long time to plod down the two flights. The door downstairs closed and latched. It was quiet.

On Sunday, she would go to church with Miss Danziger, the Church of the Gray Hair. But now, there were boxes to unpack.

Clothing first, then dinner. The soft, sweet music of Miss Danziger carried something of the mystery of the church.

A new minister, unknown to everybody. He would know her as well as he would know anybody else. She wouldn't be the stranger in his eyes. The Church of the One Soul. What would it be like, and the people, and the music? An unusual name. What hung like a shadow in her mind about the place? She carried a box of clothing into the bedroom.

CHAPTER ELEVEN

Ammahn carried his bags through the crowded terminal. There were no windows—like being in a concrete tunnel, a bunker to keep out the world. But he knew the world was out there, waiting to come in, waiting as though it knew the people were only temporary.

People scurried, creating a murmur of seconds on the clock of the universe. The earth surrounds, and people, like moles, blind to rock and wind, burrow through existence. Roots of trees burrow ever inward, searching for entrance into humanity's monuments. The mouse and the cockroach had found the way; he could see the traces at the base of the walls. The great clock moves and concrete crumbles. Only cries from the swamp are permanent.

Outside, he breathed the unfiltered air and found the limousine from the university, the driver standing beside it, waiting.

"Dr. Laval?"

"Yes."

"Let me take your bags."

"No, no. I'll not transfer my burden to you. Show me where to put them."

The heavy car sealed off the outside sound, but he could feel the wheels on the road as the driver inched across early evening traffic, heading north.

The driver tilted his head and leaned back. "We left a car for you at your place. Housekeeping went in and cleaned everything. Looked like nobody's been there for a long time."

"Fifteen years. You've gone to a lot of trouble for me."

"Dietary stocked your kitchen. That's quite a place out there. I don't think I've ever seen anything like it. Just kind of hidden away there."

"Yes, hidden is the word."

"Ten minutes from the Blue Route and the concrete, and you're in the country. Real country. A different world."

Ammahn felt his body moving with the powerful car, a collaboration of motion. It moved as he willed. He moved as it willed. His body blended with the black velvet cushions.

"It must get lonely living in a place like that," the driver was making conversation.

"Lonely, yes. That's what archaeology is. Doing lonely things. Lots of lonely places."

Moving north on the Blue route, he remembered the turn-off and the small country road that led away from civilization and through Cold Point to the farm and the silent house. Ammahn stood on the solid plank flooring of the porch. It blended with the dusk, like the rest of the exterior, mellowed by age.

He closed his eyes and breathed the elixir of grass and leaves and earth. The smell would be different inside. He read the familiar words on the heavy brass plaque bolted into the hardwood by the front door.

Good and Evil co-exist,
The flip sides of the soul.
Good grows through Evil's action,
But Evil through Good's lack thereof.

THE HIDDEN CONGREGATION

He rubbed his fingers across the words. So some think . . . so some think. Softly, he pushed open the heavy oak door. He paused outside, peering into the small front room before entering. The air inside was so earthy, he could feel it on his tongue, in his nose, on his fingers. It was always thus. He had instructed the department to tell Housekeeping to use no cleansers.

From below the floor came the odor that set the place apart. It drifted up and opened doors to his memory. On the far wall hung the skin of a calf, its head hanging down as though licking the floor. To the right on a small round table sat the skull of some ancient creature dug up at the edge of the marsh near the bottom line of his property.

He stood in the center of the room and removed his shoes and socks. He reached down, swept aside a throw-rug and pulled a trap door open. He gazed down, trying to see beyond the darkness, listening for any silent sounds from the underground cavern that began at the back wall of the cellar. Cool air crept across his feet.

Cautious, he placed one foot on the top step. Solid. He descended into the cellar-cave below, his private cavern. Dust plumed up as his foot touched the dirt floor. He closed his eyes to smell its dryness, its history. Creatures unknown to man had moved through this sightless space. Secrets from beyond the first ice age.

He felt the earth with his feet. Slowly, he knelt in the center of the floor, letting his hands caress the loose dirt. He let the soft silt of the past sift across his hands. The dust of ages engulfed the room. The diary of the dirt intrigued him, what it had been, what it had seen. It settled on him, covering him as it had covered all that came before him. He walked across the carved-out room to a small cabinet mounted on the stone wall. Inside were white candles. He lit one.

"I will leave my light here, to let them know I have come."

He knelt again and forced the candle upright in the dirt.

Ammahn held his hand just above the flame. He moved his fingers and watched the shadows dance on the plank ceiling and rafters above him. The flame moved with some unknown current, its wax aroma overpowering the dust. Beyond the wooden stairs the entrance to the cave beckoned: dark, forbidding, and irresistible. He had crawled there before. He would crawl there again; hidden rooms and pools below the earth's crust.

Ammahn climbed back up the steps, leaving the candle burning.

Before mounting the narrow staircase to the second floor, he inspected the kitchen in the back of the house. Herbs hung from the ceiling above a long cutting table in the center of the room. The kitchen sink with its brass fixtures had been added a hundred years ago. There was a wood-burning stove beside it and a box filled with kindling. On its other side was a large oak icebox. He checked. Filled. Cold. Looked like they'd done everything he had asked them to do.

The walls of the second floor slanted in to a point with four gabled windows, one on each side of the large, square room. The room was the way he wanted it, a mat on the floor, a desk-table facing the southeast gable. He stood by the table. Over there through miles of distant haze, beyond the foliage and civilization, the Church of the One Soul was waiting. His feet felt the worn wooden floor beneath him—centuries of wear. He sat at the table, his gaze to the southeast broken, but his mind still there. His hands lay palms down. He closed his eyes and remained motionless, feeling again this place.

They are there. Doing what they have been doing. Hiding behind themselves.

He opened his eyes. The evening sun colored the dust

THE HIDDEN CONGREGATION

particles red as they danced before the southwestern window. Chromosomes of time.

Tomorrow, the university. Sunday, the Church of the One Soul. The great clock had brought them together. It was never too late to search out the past, because the past was always there.

CHAPTER TWELVE

Ox and Barbara drove to the church instead of walking because rain was the forecast. They had been lucky enough to find a teenage girl a few blocks away to baby-sit. Already, the early evening sky was dark. Black clouds lay like fingers of scud reaching from the west, blotting out the sunset. Stepping out of the car in the courtyard, Ox felt the cool breeze carrying the scent of rain. He could hear the distant rumble of thunder.

"We're going to get a good one." He glanced up as they hurried inside.

Angel met them at the door. "Oh, it does look like we're going to get rained on." Raincoats were lying across a table just inside.

At the reception for Ox there were only fifteen people and they looked as though they were in mourning, black being the predominant color. He envisioned them in a funeral parlor.

He was trying to recall what it was they reminded him of when Barbara, standing beside him, whispered, "Poor baby."

Angel began the introductions and the six men and nine women shuffled into a makeshift reception line.

"Miss Danziger, Hilda, this is Oxford Christie. He prefers to be called Ox, and this is Mrs. Christie."

"Barbara. Please call me Barbara."

THE HIDDEN CONGREGATION

Nehmi stood off to one side in the chilled community room. In his dark suit, he was an apparition of a banker or a floorwalker watching the store. He certainly didn't look like a caretaker.

Ox thought of what the six men reminded him of. The men in El Greco paintings: tall, thin, dark, shadowy figures. There was a sameness about them, almost a mystique. Their faces were translucent and their eyes carried the anguish of unrelenting life. *The Opening of the Seventh Seal.* That was the painting. He remembered the eyes.

"This is Elmer Weiss," said Angel, and she continued the litany.

Elmer's gray hair was all but gone. That gave Ox something to tell him apart from the others. He shook his hand and discovered he had a grip like a rock.

"I hope you aren't discouraged by the poor turnout this evening," said Elmer. "A few of the congregation don't go out at night. Those that do live close by. We could probably use a few more members." It was hard to tell if Elmer's eyes were gray or blue. They seemed filtered as though by something he didn't want known. His Ben Franklin reading glasses were perched halfway down his nose.

"We're going to have to work on that," said Ox. "But it's the quality that counts. Angel, how many people are you expecting to come?"

Angel winced. "Some of them don't like to come out when it looks like rain." It sounded like an apology. "There'll be more on Sunday."

Ox glanced at Barbara, who whispered out of the corner of her mouth, "Standing room only."

"I did hope more would come, but after you get settled in, they'll all be around," said Angel.

"If they live that long," mumbled Barbara.

"It's just as well," said Ox. "Fewer names to remember."

"This is Hosannah Lewis. Dr. Christie likes to be called Ox. And this is Barbara Christie."

"So good of you to come, Dr. Christie, Mrs. Christie."

Ox refrained from saying it was an opportunity, like he was benefiting from Dr. Petersen's death. "It's my pleasure. Thank you. I'm looking forward to being with you."

Hosannah managed a thin smile, but tears seemed to be a permanent condition of her tired old eyes. And it occurred to Ox that the women, all dressed in black, could've stepped out of an El Greco, too. The entire group seemed to be immersed in their own collective shadow.

Barbara mumbled, "An Angel and a Hosannah. How can you go wrong?"

Nehmi came over and Ox commented, "I imagine you get pleasure out of seeing the beauty of this building."

"The building is like the congregation in many respects," said Nehmi. "It's old and requires a lot of maintenance. Some of the parts are just as they should be, some need work." His voice was calm, assured, sounding a sharp contrast to the tone of the meeting and, again, not like a caretaker. He wrapped an arm around Ox's shoulder. "I'm very pleased with it. So this is Mrs. Christie." He took her hand in his. "I'm pleased to meet you. Your husband has quite a challenge here. Wouldn't you say so, Joe?" He pulled the next man in line over. "Joe Clyde, the Christies, Ox and Barbara. And we're all going to work together to revitalize, aren't we?"

Joe became animated.

"Yes, we've all got to pull together." His smile revealed yellowed teeth as he pressed his waxy hand into Ox's. But his eyes wavered and looked away, his narrow shoulders sagging just a bit.

THE HIDDEN CONGREGATION

Ox tried to note something about each member to help him remember the face with the name.

"And Mary Jane Clark has volunteered for just about every job in the church in the past." Nehmi pulled her over to Ox. "You'll pitch in, won't you Mary Jane?"

"Well, I'm sure we'll all pitch in." She glanced toward the others and a few heads made slight nodding motions.

Mary Jane would be easy to remember. She was built like a fireplug and there were still traces of red in her hair. Ox guessed she had been an assertive worker, but the fire had gone out.

"This is Elizabeth Smith. She's one of *the* Smiths." Nehmi smiled at his own brand of humor. Elizabeth had a pasty face and a trembling lower lip. "And here is Carolyn Carver, and Marjorie Bannister, and Fred McCreedy." He pulled them all past the receiving hands.

Ox was trying to keep up with the names and any distinguishing features. Carolyn Carver—bushy eyebrows, Marjorie Bannister—downcast eyes and hair in face, Fred McCreedy—trembling hands.

Nehmi continued, "Rebecca Crum, Harold Warren, Patricia Stallings, and Sam Cheek. This is the nucleus of the church."

Ox shook hands hoping he would be able to put the names to the faces later. He liked the change of pace Nehmi had brought, but was surprised by the man's assertiveness. He almost seemed to play the role of leader.

Ox thanked everyone for coming out on such a bad night. "I'd like to think of this not so much as a reception, but as a prelude to a series of planning sessions."

"I don't know what any of us could contribute to plans for the future, but I guess I'd be willing to try," said Joe.

"Me, too," said Mary Jane, glancing round at the others. Some of the heads nodded again, but without enthusiasm, and a cloud seemed to be settling over the group.

"Some of us can't stay up as late as others," said Hilda. "If you schedule it for six-thirty, a few more people might come."

Then it was as though everyone had run out of anything to talk about. They stood around as though they were each alone, not in clusters, but by themselves. The sound of heavy rain outside began to permeate the room.

Ox noticed Nehmi's eyes were intent in their watching. Unblinking. "Mr. Nehmi, what would you think of hanging Dr. Petersen's portrait over on that wall instead of in the basement? I think he ought to be visible when we start our planning."

"I'd be glad to move it up here. It used to hang in your study."

"Oh," said Angel. Her hands fluttered to her face. "It . . . it's so much better where he is. I . . . he . . . it's quieter there. It's private. Ethan . . . Dr. Petersen would prefer . . ." Her eyes pleaded with the group. She bowed her head and ran into the kitchen.

Ox could think of nothing to say or do. Hilda trotted after her and Ox started to move also, but Elmer put his hand on his shoulder.

"Angel had become very close to him."

"I guess I touched a nerve. Is that why the portrait is hanging in the basement?"

Elmer thought a moment before answering. "That . . . could have a bearing."

They were all looking toward the kitchen door when the sound of the rain got louder as someone opened the outside door. Ox turned to greet whoever it was.

"Hi, I'm Lawrence Pregle." The wet figure stripped off his raincoat.

Ox walked over to shake hands. "I'm glad to meet you. I'm looking forward to hearing you play the organ."

Lawrence was by far the oldest person in the room. He

held a frail hand out to Ox who grasped it carefully in fear of crushing it.

"And I'm looking forward to hearing you. I play. You pray."

In spite of the timing, Ox was pleased to hear any form of humor, and noticed Pregle was pleased with it himself. Even so, he appeared as one of the group, the same dark, slender figure, a silhouette of a man.

"Call me Larry." Then he seemed to notice they were all watching the kitchen. "Is something wrong?"

Nehmi explained. "Angel is feeling depressed."

"Oh," was all Larry said.

"I think I may have caused it. Maybe it's not a good idea to bring up the portrait." Ox started toward the kitchen again, but this time, Nehmi put his hand on his arm.

"She has to work it out for herself. Hilda is with her."

The kitchen door opened and Hilda beckoned to Elmer. She shrugged an apology to Ox. "Excuse me." Elmer, head down, walked into the kitchen, closing the door behind him. Ox was torn over whether or not to follow him. But he realized he should wait. He had been restrained twice.

Barbara pivoted her foot to touch his.

Nehmi draped his arms across their shoulders. "It's something that has to run its course."

They could hear the rumbling of the thunder. "Just like the weather," he added. In a few moments, Elmer emerged from the kitchen, Angel behind him, followed by Hilda.

"We've talked it over and decided it would be a good idea to hang the portrait here," he said.

"Yes," said Angel. "It's time. We should bring the portrait up here—where we can all see it—and remember."

"Oh, I'm not so sure," said Hosannah. "Maybe we ought to think about it."

The increasing sound of the rain almost drowned out the voices.

"No." Hilda stepped forward so she could be heard. "We've talked it over. It's best to remember what can't be forgotten anyhow. Like Angel said, it's time."

"Yes," said Elmer. "It's time." He turned to face the small group. "Things can't get any worse, and now that Ox is here, they may get better. Joe, let's go get the portrait." He turned to Ox. "I know you don't know why this is so difficult, but in time, you may."

Elmer and Joe skittered through the door and were gone. Nehmi went into the kitchen and returned with a hammer and a large picture hook. They all watched as he placed it and drove in the nail. Hilda clutched her arms across her chest for protection against the chill.

Barbara stood beside Ox and commented quietly, "There are no Mr. and Mrs. here. They are all either single or widowed."

Nehmi stood in the center of the group. "Sooner or later, you're going to have to take Ox into your confidence."

"I confess," said Ox, "I feel there's something strange going on." He walked over to the wall where Nehmi had placed the hook. "From what I've been told, I would think you would all want that portrait hanging from the highest place of honor." He pointed to the wall. "Will someone fill me in?"

No one talked. For several slow minutes, they listened to the storm sounds invading the building. The thunder was vibrating through the structure. Finally, Mary Jane spoke, but it was barely audible. "We can't."

Ox tried to make eye contact with each of them, but they all avoided his gaze, staring at feet, hands, or corners of the room.

"Will you tell me you'll consider it?" He knew something was deadly wrong.

THE HIDDEN CONGREGATION

"We can't," Mary Jane repeated, her eyes almost pleading.

"Are you saying you won't or you can't?"

"I'm saying we can't." This time she said it clearly.

"All right. I'll take that to mean that if you could, you would, and you will therefore consider it." He scanned their faces—no affirmation, no spark, no life.

The two men came in carrying the portrait as though they were pallbearers. Ox moved aside for them and Nehmi helped them position it. And there were the grave eyes staring through the dimness of the room.

Ox shivered from the damp air. He gazed at the portrait and an echo from his mind said, "*Take care of my congregation.*"

The small congregation hovered, silent, facing the picture. Almost in a single motion, they turned away. Hilda and Angel said goodnight and left together. The others all bunched around the raincoats and left as though by the same signal.

Ox stood in the doorway and watched the dark figures fading into the rain and darkness.

Barbara touched his elbow. "I tell you what, Babe. You've got yourself a tiger by the tail."

Nehmi stood behind them. "You don't know it, but you've already begun to make a difference."

CHAPTER THIRTEEN

Ox looked at his congregation. So this was it, twenty-one, counting Barbara. They were outnumbered by the chandeliers. They were all huddled toward the front. They could rent space for a bingo game in the back of the church and nobody would know they were there.

Hilda had brought a guest. Ox knew she was new because Hilda had introduced her to others nearby. Also, she was a young woman. And she didn't look sad. Maybe he could encourage everybody to bring a guest. They could swell the congregation to a whopping forty.

He would call a planning session next week. The rebuilding couldn't begin too early and he would have to seed the discussion with some of his own ideas. So far, there hadn't been any suggestions penetrating the cloud of woe hanging over his waning congregation.

Larry Pregle was creating a tornado on the tracker organ with *Bernstein's Mass*. The floor vibrated. Even the air vibrated.

A man came in and slipped into the back pew as the last chord echoed into silence. Tall, but not thin or frail like the rest. He draped a long arm along the pew on his right and scanned the meager congregation, then focused on Ox. Ox glanced away and back. The man seemed to be sizing him up, examining him, maybe challenging him. *Oh, good. Another fan of Dr. Petersen.*

Ox began his sermon.

"One can stand on this spot and almost hear the echoes in this long, precious repository, echoes from two hundred years of sermons, christenings, weddings, and funerals. Moments crying to be heard, events to be remembered."

The man in the back stared at the gray heads. He gazed around the sanctuary.

Ox continued, "We have a history that forms the basis for our church community, our culture, our personality, our collective being."

The man seemed to be searching for something or somebody. Ox scanned the faces in front of him. "How often was there music vibrating through these walls as there was this morning?" Hilda's guest had her eyes shut. "How often has the truth spoken here shocked?"

The man focused on the ceiling, then on Ox.

"How will that influence the ideas spoken and thought here in the future? Dr. Petersen was a man of vision."

The man in the back studied the stained-glass windows.

"What events happened here in all that time that changed the course of lives? How many lives were changed, never to be the same again? Listen quietly. These walls have secrets to tell us. All of the congregations of the past are in their hidden seats, waiting to exchange thoughts with us. They are our history. They are us. They, with us, are the future."

Ox was shocked by an audible gasp from the front of the congregation. He lost his train of thought for a moment. He couldn't tell where the sound had come from. They all looked shocked.

Angel's face seemed frozen into a mask concealing any emotion. Hilda's forehead was creased with concern. They sat frozen in a moment of terror. Hosannah's mouth was suspended as though in the middle of a scream. Mary Jane's eyes seemed glazed by shock. Even Elmer seemed stunned. Joe shook his head to shake off what he had just heard. He swiveled around to the others for support against some threat, but they all stared straight ahead. All but Nehmi. He was calm and intent.

The man in the back had focused on Nehmi.

Barbara looked puzzled. She'd evidently heard the gasp. She smiled reassuringly and mouthed the words, "Okay, Babe."

"In checking through old records and archives, I find that next year this church will mark its two hundredth year. Dr. Petersen led this congregation for almost one-half of one of those centuries. There can be no doubt he led you and some who are no longer here, through both difficult and good times."

This time they whispered as though they were a swarm of agitated bees.

"Mr. Nehmi made a comment to me the other night. He compared the building and these walls to the congregation. Some parts are excellent, some need work. It's always been that way. It was that way with those past congregations whose souls inhabit the walls. They understand the human condition. They know a community has to help itself. We use the past to build the future."

When the service was over, Ox asked the congregation to join him for coffee in the community room. Nehmi was the first to shake his hand.

"You touched more than a few chords."

Mary Jane started to shake his hand and darted past him instead. Hilda brought her guest over.

"Dr. Christie, this is Miss Cynthia Neal." Hilda stumbled for words. "Miss Neal is new here."

THE HIDDEN CONGREGATION

"Please join us for coffee," said Ox.

"I loved the way you pulled the past into the present and the future," said Cynthia. "It's so true."

But she had a puzzled look. Had she felt their reaction?

"Yes. Yes," said Hilda. "That was nice." But it was as though she hadn't been listening. Her thoughts were elsewhere.

Barbara had decided to shake his hand, too. She leaned forward and spoke low. "I don't know what happened, but you knocked their socks off—mine, too, and I'm wearing pantyhose. Let's go home soon, okay?"

He was still smiling when Hosannah gripped his hand. She chewed her words before she spoke them. "I don't know what you found in those old archives, but don't believe everything you read."

She was gone before he could ask her what she meant. When Angel came by, she kept her eyes down and thanked him.

He had thought the sermon uplifting, but he seemed to have stumbled into a secret vault of their past. He felt as though he was standing on an elevator that dropped a few floors and stopped, and dropped again and stopped and dropped again. When would he hit bottom?

Elmer had waited as the others filed past. He came over and gave him a limp hand and a strange smile. "I don't think there can be any doubt you are the right minister for this pulpit." He paused and it was obvious there was to be a "but" as he struggled for the right words. "But you need to know this congregation has experienced something of an extreme shock in the past."

"I know losing someone who was as important as Dr. Petersen can take time to get over." But Ox knew that wasn't what was bothering them.

"No, no, it's not that. It's . . . it's . . . difficult to describe." Elmer turned and walked away. "Maybe you don't need to know." The latter comment was apologetic and more to himself than to Ox.

The man from the back pew strolled into the dining room and stopped in front of Dr. Petersen's picture. Angel, Hosannah, and Joe were in a quiet and serious conversation on the other side of the room. In fact, everyone was quiet.

Ox decided before he would start hanging crepe, he would join the three of them to find out what was going on. Before he could, however, Cynthia Neal came over to him.

"How does one go about joining the church?"

Ox forced his thoughts away from the others. "It's simple. If you feel you're ready, all you do is sign the membership book."

"I'm ready."

"Wonderful." He felt relieved to think of something more positive. "You're my first new member. That makes this special. The book's in my office." He motioned for her to follow him. "Don't be shocked to learn yours will be the first signature in over fifteen years."

"I've a feeling there'll be more."

The old book lay open on a stand next to the bookcase.

"I calculated the average age of the congregation, Cynthia. It's seventy-one. I hope all the gray hair won't put you off. I'm going to try to attract as many younger people as possible. I want the average age to be around fifty."

Cynthia laughed. "Miss Danziger made the same comment. She was worried all the gray heads would turn me away. They don't. I already feel this to be my church. I liked your comments about building the future. And I love this building."

She studied the book, the signature prior to her own. "Sam Cheek. Eighteen years ago. It's strange no one joined the church in all those years. You have to wonder why."

"I do. There's bound to be a reason, but I haven't found it. It's incredible. But at least your signature represents a turning point."

THE HIDDEN CONGREGATION

When they went downstairs the only people left were Nehmi and Barbara.

"Where is everybody?"

"Mr. Nehmi and I were just talking about that. They all just left. Maybe Dr. Petersen scared them away." She glanced at the portrait.

"Mr. Nehmi?" asked Ox. "Was he or wasn't he a revered figure?"

"He was, but there are circumstances that hang on. I'm sorry I have to leave. I liked your sermon." He stopped and turned back. "It carried a special message." Then he left.

Driving home, Ox mentioned Cynthia's joining the church. "In one week, I've attracted more new members than Dr. Petersen did in the last eighteen years. What a record."

"Yeah, and it doesn't hurt that she's beautiful, does it?"

"If she's attractive, she might encourage new members of the opposite sex."

"You know," said Barbara, returning to what had happened in church. "Something intimidated them today. It wasn't the portrait."

"You're right, but maybe I'll put it in my study. It belongs there. He can watch me and keep me on the straight and narrow. But it wasn't the portrait. My sermon spooked them." A black sedan with an emblem on the door pulled past them— University of Pennsylvania. Ox couldn't be sure, but the driver might have been the man from the back pew. Where had he been? He thought he and Barbara had been the last to leave.

CHAPTER FOURTEEN

Ox sat by Angel's desk. He had decided to take a direct approach. He had to. He looked directly into her eyes without blinking. "Angel, what happened to this congregation?"

Angel concentrated on the computer keyboard. "It just sort of dwindled." She hit the wrong key and backspaced.

"I know. What caused it to dwindle?" He leaned forward.

"Why, uh, people got older."

"Angel, I need to know. Where did they go?" Then another thought poured out. "And why are there no couples in this church? And why have there been no new members for eighteen years?"

"Oh," she cried. She jumped up and grabbed a tissue and ran past him toward the door.

He could hear her thumping down the steps. He listened for the outside door, but she evidently retreated into the bathroom. He could wait for her in her office, but felt it more prudent to go to his study until she returned. There was no turning back, but the tension had to be resolved.

Angel in the toilet. That would make an interesting sermon title.

He stood, looking out the window and making a mental list

THE HIDDEN CONGREGATION

of people to talk to today: Nehmi, Elmer, Hosannah, and Hilda. Nehmi had a detachment suggesting objectivity, and Elmer appeared as someone the rest trusted and followed even though he was obviously as troubled as any of them. He had to get to the bottom of it, at least identify the problem.

But first, Angel. He couldn't just ignore her reaction to his questions.

After a while, she came quietly up the steps and into her office. Ox waited. When her chair squeaked, he strolled into her office. She huddled in her chair, covering her mouth and nose with both hands.

"Oh," she said and started to her feet.

Ox grabbed her firmly by each arm and gently sat her down. Her whole body shook as she stared at him, eyes wide.

"Angel, I apologize. I didn't mean to put so much pressure on you. I know you've got something burning inside of you, and I know you need to get it out. But you take your own good time telling me. Your own time. That could be today or a year from today. Okay? I'm sorry."

"Oh," she cried again, then jumped up and wrapped her arms around his neck. "Thank you." She turned away and dabbed at her eyes. "I don't think I can talk about it." She fell into her chair and stared at her computer screen. She dabbed some more. "I can't talk about it. I can't even think about it."

He couldn't pressure her any more than he had. He would have to dig the information from the others. "It's locked inside you and you need to get it out."

She cringed and turned her head.

"I'll be here for you. You set your own time. But it'll help you to talk about it."

Ox returned to his study. There wasn't any sign of Nehmi, so he called Elmer. "This is Ox Christie. I wonder if I could

73

drop over and spend a little time getting acquainted?" Elmer was a block away on a side street. The two-story stone house was modest compared to the others in the neighborhood, but it was still large, maintained, and freshly painted. The others were huge and run-down.

"I just put on some coffee," said Elmer. "Come on back to the breakfast nook." He seemed to have recovered from the Sunday sermon. Elmer was tall, thin, and agile, moving without effort. He wore a dress shirt, but no tie.

"You by yourself in this big place?"

"I am now." Elmer reached up to a line of cups hanging in the window and grabbed two. "How about some pastries? I bring them all the way from a place in Mount Airy called The Working Man's Gourmet." He put the box on the table.

"You found my weakness." Ox waited for Elmer to sit before taking a chair. "Not that I don't have other weaknesses."

"If that's your worst one, you'll live a long life." Elmer poured the coffee and placed a carton of milk and a bowl of sugar on the table. Then he sat.

"Gotten all settled in, have you?"

"Slow by slow," said Ox. "It's a big house and there's a room filled with unopened boxes. Between the kids and the unpacking, Barbara's managing to keep busy."

"You and Barbara . . ." Elmer was searching for words. "You have a good life together?"

"Yes, very good. I've known her all my life."

Elmer gazed past Ox. He seemed to have drifted someplace else. He jerked himself out of whatever it was. "Yes. Moving is an unpleasant business." Elmer added milk to his coffee. "I've considered selling this place and moving to something smaller, but I put off thinking about it."

"You have children?" asked Ox.

"Two. But they are out on their own, leading their own lives."

"Is it just the three of you?"

"My wife died fifteen years ago." He said it matter-of-factly.

"I can see why you might think of getting something smaller." Ox assumed a nonchalant air. "It came to me as a bit of a surprise when I noticed there are no couples in the church."

"Yes, we're all widows and widowers, except for Hilda. She never got around to marrying."

"What about Angel? Has she ever been married?"

"Yes, her husband died . . . quite a while ago."

"It's not a large congregation. Are you all close?"

"Close? You don't mean geographically. You mean drawn together, right?"

"Yes, close-knit."

Elmer pondered the question. Ox began to wonder if he was going to answer it.

"Yes. Yes, we're a close-knit group."

"In most congregations there are segments, cliques. Is it because the congregation's small that you're all so close?"

Elmer's eyes seemed to fasten on Ox and at the same time look right past him. "I guess it would be more accurate to say we are drawn together by circumstance."

"I know I sound like I'm digging, but I felt a strange reaction to my sermon yesterday, a kind of group alarm. Something happened to the congregation while Dr. Petersen was here, didn't it? You alluded to it after the sermon."

Again, Elmer took a long time to think, hunched over his cup. It was obvious he was going to answer, but he appeared to be searching for the right words.

"Yes, something did happen. Something . . . traumatic, but it's over now, except for those of us who remain. But it's over for the church." Elmer gazed without blinking at Ox. He talked very deliberately. "What it means is that you have to start from scratch. You've got to build a new congregation."

"Elmer, what happened?"

Elmer gave an impatient gesture. "Ox, I want to help you rebuild, but what happened is dead and will be buried when we all die. Many have already. We were a large congregation. Best to let it go to the grave. That way, nobody's memory is tainted."

"I might be able to help."

"Maybe," said Elmer. "But I think it's best this way."

Ox realized he wasn't going to shake Elmer's resolve, but the congregation had suffered through something they didn't want to talk about. He tried a different tack.

"It was unusual for the bishop to make the decision for me to come here instead of a search committee from the church. Was it because of a lack of enthusiasm?" He emptied his cup and waited. He smiled as if to say, "I'm digging."

Elmer smiled as though to say, "I know." He poured them each another cup. "Eat another pastry."

Ox ate and waited.

"I think none of us thought we knew what was best for the church anymore."

When Ox left Elmer's house, he knew more than he had, but only a little. And Elmer wasn't going to tell him any more. He found Nehmi trimming grass by the sidewalk in front of the church.

"You realized I stumbled into a sensitive area on Sunday, didn't you?"

"Maybe it was by design." He eyed Ox for a moment and continued to trim. "You had to sooner or later. The sooner the better."

"The question I've not had answered is, what happened?"

THE HIDDEN CONGREGATION

"The real question is, can you turn the tables?"

"I need to know what happened first. It involved the entire congregation."

"They all got trapped in it," said Nehmi. "I was busy working on the church."

"You mean the church building."

Nehmi continued to trim. He paused and turned his eyes on Ox. "Yes, the church building, more or less."

Ox persisted. "When did it happen?"

"It started right after Dr. Petersen came here."

Ox felt a dropping sensation in his stomach. "That long ago?"

"It started slow and built. It culminated about fifteen years ago."

Ox stared. "Fifteen—does the fact there are no couples in the church have any bearing on it?"

"I expect it does." Nehmi examined the grass by the sidewalk and began to gather clippings.

"What exactly happened?"

"You would best find out from those who played a role."

"But you know."

"Their viewpoint is what you need." He turned toward the flagstone walk and the cellar door. "You have to know what they feel. It may take a while. On the other hand, maybe not." He piled the clippings by the cellar door and started down the steps. Stopping, he added, "When you find out something, I'll be glad to verify it, if I can." Then he was gone.

In his study, Ox began work on next Sunday's sermon, "Trust, Love, and Perseverance: Conquering Adversity." He was frustrated knowing something had happened and everybody— even Nehmi—knew what, but him. He was frustrated Nehmi hadn't volunteered more information. Nehmi, surprisingly, had the answers.

He would call on Hosannah and Hilda in the afternoon. He was damned if he was going to wait until they all died. He wasn't going to turn his back on them.

His eye rested on a piece of paper sticking out of the purple book, *The Conquest of Illusion.* He pulled it from the shelf and opened it. It was a note. Faded type on yellowed paper. Old. Brittle. It marked the place at chapter seven, The Phantom of Evil.

He could barely make it out.

"Fools that step into my circle will lose theirs. Welcome to your new congregation." Was it an old message to Dr. Petersen? He had leafed through the book days before, but hadn't seen it then. He stared at the note. Was it for him?

CHAPTER FIFTEEN

Ox was surprised to see Hosannah's house so filled with the trappings of wealth: Oriental carpets, tapestries, and teakwood furniture. He followed her down a long corridor of original oil paintings into a library filled with leather-bound sets of books that would make a collector salivate.

Every step seemed an effort for her. Her eyes were flat, dull as empty space. But she had a pit bull jaw. She motioned him to a large leather chair angled to a fireplace. She sat in its mate. Between them, on a small walnut table, sat a silver tea service that might be matched in the Vanderbilt mansion. The tea was already poured in delicate china. He felt as though he was watching this scene in a movie.

"Hosannah, you made the comment I shouldn't believe everything I read in the archives. Was there something in my sermon yesterday that bothered you?"

"Elmer called me just a while ago to tell me you were going to ask about that." Her voice was hard, with sharp corners, but still there was a hint of kindness. "There's not much I can add to what he told you." She took a sip of tea and placed the cup carefully on the saucer. She studied him with a sad kind of smile. "We've had a difficult time, but we think you can rebuild the church. I'm sorry if I sounded curt. All of us will help you any way we can, but we don't want to dwell on the past."

It was a rehearsed response.

"Hosannah, it would be helpful if I had a better idea of what happened."

"We think all you need to know is that something happened."

She was drawing strength from the *we*. Ox knelt in front of her chair and held her small hands in his. He spoke gently, "I want to help. I won't turn my back on you. I won't press you. It was something terrible, wasn't it?"

She said nothing, but leaned forward and placed her head on his shoulder. She cried softly. "I can't tell you."

Surprised, Ox put his arms around her. She felt fragile.

"I'll always be here for you, Hosannah."

"I can't tell you. It was dreadful. I don't know what came over us." She searched for a handkerchief and settled for a napkin. "Dr. Petersen finally saved us. It was so bad when his wife died. He was so filled with remorse."

She pulled away to dab her eyes. Her chin quivered. "Well . . ." She took a deep breath and picked up her cup of tea. "Have you gotten unpacked, yet?"

Ox suppressed a laugh. He was certain the question hadn't been rehearsed, but it sure changed the subject. He guessed it would be asked again with each visit.

"It'll be a long process," he said. "But we're making headway. Moving is a task. I hope to be in this area for a long time. How long have you been here?"

"I was born in this house."

"You were born in this house, not in a hospital?"

"Oh, yes, right here. Upstairs in my mother's bedroom. In those days, hospitals weren't the place to get born."

THE HIDDEN CONGREGATION

"How old are you, Hosannah?" He knew he could ask that question of someone as old as she.

"Ninety-two. Ninety-three in September."

"You're in good health."

"Yes, I was the lucky one." Her eyes grew moist again. "Stuart was in poor health. Oh, I wasn't going to talk about that. That was then."

"Fifteen years ago?" asked Ox.

Her hand jerked and she spilled some of her tea. "Yes, fifteen years."

"How long were you and Stuart married?"

She put her cup on the tray. "We were married fifty-seven years when he died. We were married when I was twenty. He was twenty-two." She began to dab her eyes again and her chin quivered. "He's been gone a long time and I'm sorry for everything." She stared at the mantel, through and beyond the silent porcelain figures counting time there. A solitary tear crawled down one cheek. "I guess he knows that now. I hope."

But there wasn't any hope in her voice or anywhere in her eyes.

Her sadness, her despair, reached into him and held him. "When you want to share with me, Hosannah, I'll be here for you."

"Elmer says we should let it die with us."

Ox walked to the church slowly. He was cataloging the facts he had gathered. He knew it was going to take time for him to get the whole story. He might never. A little later, he would talk to Hilda.

Hilda led him through French doors into a living room from the past century. The drapes were drawn so tight not one beam of sunlight could stray in among the dust particles.

"These are springerle cookies. My mother used to make them." Her eyes were a washed-out blue, but with an occasional flash.

"That's a worthwhile custom to pass down. They're German cookies, aren't they?"

"Yes, they were both German, my parents."

Her hands were cramped by arthritis, but she managed.

"You have a lovely home. Have you been here all your life?"

"All my life. My parents bought this house new in 1890."

"Wow. That's a long time. I wonder how many homes were here when the church was built."

"Not many; in fact, none to speak of. It was all woods, a few frame houses hidden away. Nothing like now."

"It was a church in the woods."

"That was one of its charms. It was a flagship church and people came from miles around. Some of them began to build in the area."

"Your parents included."

"Yes, my father made a lot of money. He owned a machine company that made surveying instruments."

"How long have your parents been gone?"

"Oh, he died in 1917 from that terrible flu epidemic. I was just a young girl. And my mother died in 1927. My sister and I were all alone. But they left us well prepared."

"Where does your sister live?"

"Oh, Anna died a long time ago. I miss her so."

"Fifteen years ago?"

"Oh," she said. "How did you know?"

"Someone must have mentioned it to me. So your family has been part of the church for over a hundred years."

"Yes, our history in the church long preceded Dr. Petersen and . . ." She put her fingers to her mouth as though to say "oops."

THE HIDDEN CONGREGATION

Ox smiled. "Elmer called you didn't he?"

"Well, yes." She sank farther into her chair and smiled in embarrassment. "Yes. We've needed help for so long." She pushed herself up in the chair. "But I agree with Elmer. It's best to let it die with our memories." She reflected for a moment and added. "Mr. Nehmi stopped it."

Ox was about to ask her what Nehmi had done, even though he knew she wouldn't tell him, but he heard the front door open and Hilda called out, "Oh, Cynthia. Come in here a moment."

Cynthia Neal walked in carrying her violin case. "What a surprise," she said.

"Cynthia's living on the top floor. It's so nice to have someone else in the house. You sit, dear. I'm going to get you a cup of tea. Cynthia plays the violin. Maybe she can start a music committee. We don't have one anymore."

Hilda didn't wait for a response, but made her way toward the back of the house.

"A music committee." Cynthia set her violin case beside an overstuffed chair. "I'm not sure what a music committee does, but there is music to that old building. It might be something I could do. Maybe I should come over and talk about it. If you're interested."

"I think it's a great idea," Ox said.

"This Sunday?"

"Fine. I'm sure Larry Pregle would welcome collaborators. Some alternate music on Sundays. Maybe we could even put on some concerts and get people into that building. Maybe we could even get a choir going."

"We had one once," said Hilda, coming back with Cynthia's tea. She paused for a moment before setting down the tea. "But it turned out not to be so good—after a while. There was this man." She shook her head as she sat and picked up her cup. "I wish he had never been there. We were never certain about him. I thought he was there this past Sunday, but my eyes aren't so good anymore, and it's been fifteen years."

"Did you mention it to Mr. Nehmi?"

"No, but if he was there, Mr. Nehmi knew."

Ox commented to Cynthia, "Apparently, Mr. Nehmi has done a great deal more over the years than take care of the physical plant."

"He seems . . . constant. Like the recurring theme in a mass. But secret."

"You think music all the time, don't you?"

"She does. You should hear the music she plays upstairs. It's hers and it's beautiful. This house is blessed by her music."

Ox noticed a faint blush and realized Barbara was right. She was beautiful.

"I don't know about blessed." Cynthia sipped her tea and tilted her head. "I had no idea how captured I was going to be by that church. It just reached into me and held on."

"Yes," said Ox. "There's something there, all right. Something powerful. One of these days, I'll know what it is."

On the way back to the church, Ox's feet were pounds lighter. Cynthia was a bright light in his congregation, maybe the only light.

But all the deaths fifteen years ago puzzled him. He thought of the old graveyard he had seen on his first day. The graveyard, of course. All of their dates would be there. He walked through the building and out the back.

The knee-deep grass and brush concealed most of the stones. The place was unkempt. He'd have to talk to Nehmi. Pushing aside branches, he found a stone for Cyrus Danziger. He brushed dirt off its face. Died November, 1917. And there was the stone

THE HIDDEN CONGREGATION

for Amanda Danziger. Died 1927. No other Danzigers. Where was Hilda's sister?

And there was a new stone for Ethan Petersen, but there was no mate. He lay there alone. Where was his wife buried?

There was plenty of space.

He began to look for any stone with dates of death in recent years.

There were a number of names he hadn't heard, people who had died in the 1800s. Some were obviously the parents of current members: Clydes, McCreedys, Crums, but no Weiss'. Where was Elmer's wife? Where was Hosannah's husband? He searched every plot, every corner. Where were the missing graves?

He walked back into the church. There would have to be old church records for the graveyard. Why weren't those people buried there? He would write himself a note to check with Angel. He would have to start a file of notes.

Then he thought of the note he had found in the book. Brittle, old. He walked into his office and to the bookshelf. He thumbed through the pages.

Empty.

CHAPTER SIXTEEN

Ox and Barbara walked up the hill toward the church. Martha and Billy skipped along in front of them, trying not to step on cracks. It didn't matter if they were a few minutes late to Sunday School. Martha and Billy were the whole class, and Barbara had volunteered to be the teacher.

"You realize this is just until you bring young parents into the church. I don't do Sunday School."

"We'll get them in. The church will grow. But we have two problems. I've got to help the old congregation while building a new one."

"You've got to help the remains."

"An interesting way of putting it."

"Maybe it's their choice to be the walking dead."

"I'm determined not to let any young person that walks in get away."

"If I've got to teach Sunday School, I'd be happy if you even captured some young, nubile women."

"Why? For bait?"

"You got it, Babe."

"I don't see this neighborhood crawling with bait."

"Well, since I'm running the Sunday School, it'll be over in time for Martha and me to be ringers in the audience."

THE HIDDEN CONGREGATION

"Me, too," said Billy, proving again that he had an acute sense of hearing.

"Silly," said Martha. "You don't even know what a ringer is."

Ox watched as the congregation listened to Larry Pregle immerse himself in the tracker organ. Copeland's *Grand Canyon Suite*. Slightly on the secular side, but appropriate for the sanctuary—itself, like a canyon. The whole building vibrated.

The count was up this Sunday: twenty-eight. It was the same cast of characters, all of them sitting in the same seats as before, including the man in the back row, but two young men who had come in together sat about halfway back; and a youngish couple. The man was dressed casual in a sloppy T-shirt, but the woman had on a gabardine pantsuit. They looked mismatched. But they swelled the congregation by another two. He began his sermon.

"In ancient Hebrew, 'ecclesiasts' was the word for 'preacher.' The *Book of Ecclesiastes* was written by a preacher, although scholars know it was in fact, written by more than one person over a period of several hundred years. There are many passages you'll recognize from current usage in songs and sayings, but there's one we hear frequently without knowing of its Biblical origin.

"This particular preacher had been away for a long time. Upon his return, he had these words to say.

"'I returned and saw that the race is not to the swift nor the battle to the strong, neither yet riches to the wise, nor yet food to the industrious, for time and chance happeneth to them all.'

"He had returned and found that over time, things had changed, and those he had expected to be the rulers, leaders, or winners, weren't, and drew the conclusion it was out of their hands. Fate decreed.

"The *Book of Ecclesiastes* is fatalistic. No matter how good you are or how smart or industrious, someone who is your total opposite in all these respects can come out ahead and you can fail. Good people fall by the wayside. And the clear implication is there's nothing you can do about it.

"If that's true, there's no reason why any of us should try. I believe that through honest intention, preparation and perseverance, we can do anything. We can overcome any obstacle; we can right any wrong."

Ox, as usual, scanned the faces in front of him, looking for indications he was getting through. Elmer and Hilda exchanged glances, and Hosannah, eyebrows raised, then looked at her lap.

"How do you succeed? By standing alone against the storms? That's possible. But there's a more effective way. You stand as a group. You bolster each other and by so doing, bolster that thing called community."

Did he see signs of hope in Mary Jane's expression? Or was it anticipation of something else?

"This congregation is a community. You're pulled together by common needs and have a sustained need for each other."

He avoided making his comments any more specific since some might be left out. Was there a glimmer of agreement on the face of the man in the rear? Ox decided to add a few more comments for the benefit of the newcomers.

"Our belief in the Church of the One Soul movement embraces the concept that each of our individual souls connect to the One Soul. Some call it God. Whatever you call it, we are all connected. We share the good and the bad. We collectively work to eliminate all that is negative. We are all in it together. Through love, trust, and perseverance, you can change your world. But it's up to you. You need to make a conscious effort to participate."

THE HIDDEN CONGREGATION

After the closing music, Ox followed the crowd to the community room and found himself walking beside the man from the rear pew.

"I'm Oxford Christie. I'm glad you could join us again this morning."

"I'm Ammahn Laval. Your sermons are thought through very well."

"Thank you. I hope you'll decide to join. We're a small congregation now, but we expect to grow."

"I've been here in the past, Dr. Christie, and I doubt you are destined to remain small."

"I hope you're right."

The way the man walked and carried himself suggested confidence and independence.

But Ox was puzzled. The man seemed independent to the point of being out of place. And he studied everybody, more like examining. Was he the man Hilda remembered?

In the community room, Nehmi shepherded the newcomers. "Ox, I'd like you to meet Tom Fitzgerald and Chris Frankle."

"Tom, Chris, glad to meet you. Let me introduce Ammahn Laval." Nehmi moved off in another direction.

"Are you fellows new around here?" Ox asked.

"Our company just transferred us here," said Chris. "I live just down the street. Tom's found a house in Mount Airy, but we decided to do some advance reconnoitering for a church before our families get here."

"You have children?" Ox felt like he had hit a bonanza. "We each have two," said Chris.

"What kind of work do you do?"

"Computer programming," said Tom. "We specialize in hospital systems."

"This is a beautiful old building," said Chris. "The paintings on the ceiling reflect their colors everywhere."

"Mr. Nehmi keeps the place looking this way," said Ox. "I've come to the conclusion he's responsible for the church being what it is."

Ox wanted to draw Ammahn into the conversation, but noticed his attention was diverted somewhere across the room.

"My wife and I will definitely be back," said Tom.

"We actually got moved in on Friday," said Chris. "But my wife didn't feel like fighting the disarray to get here. We'll be here next week, too."

Ox noticed the mismatched couple standing near the entrance. They seemed to be observing, almost examining the others. Now they were coming over to meet Ox, or it might be more accurate to say, she was pushing him to come over. He was the first to speak. "I'm Emmett Dobson and this is my wife, Jessie May."

"We enjoyed your sermon. The concept makes a lot of sense," said Jessie May.

"Do you have children? We'd love to have them come to our Sunday school."

"No," said Jessie May. "I guess we've just been too busy."

"What do you do?" asked Ox.

"I'm a land surveyor," said Emmett, "and she's a lab technician."

Hosannah, Hilda, and Mary Jane came over. Ox introduced Emmett and Jessie May. "We liked what you said this morning," said Hilda. "And we are all going to pitch in and help you."

"Think about what I said, because it was directed at you and the problem you don't feel you can yet discuss." He paused on the word *yet*.

"We're glad you're here," said Hosannah. "Maybe you really can help."

THE HIDDEN CONGREGATION

Emmett and Jessie May stood quietly, listening.

The congregation lingered a little longer than they had the past week, and there was even a laugh or two.

Ammahn Laval, standing alone, looked at the portrait of Dr. Petersen. It was as though the two were having a staring contest. Nehmi was watching Ammahn—no change of expression. Barbara tugged at Ox's arm. "I'm going to take Martha and Billy home and get lunch started. Don't stay long. By the way, the closest thing to a young nubile woman seems to be waiting for you to stop gabbing. She's standing over there by the brochure rack. In this congregation, she looks like a lonely little petunia in an onion patch."

Ox glanced at Cynthia.

"We won't be long," he said.

"Thanks for another great sermon," said Cynthia on the way to Ox's study. "There was just so much truth in it."

Ox ushered her to a chair. "I think the church's most important mission is to develop community. Every sermon will carry some of that." He sat in the other chair in front of his desk. "Sermons are just talking. It's doing that counts."

"Hilda made the remark this morning that you might save the church, but that she was beyond saving. I didn't get the impression she was joking."

"I'm glad you told me. That was a cry for help."

"She made another funny comment. She said she hoped the same thing didn't happen to you that happened to Dr. Petersen. You mentioned him last Sunday. He was here for half a century?"

"Forty-seven years. It boggles my mind."

"What happened to him? What was she talking about?"

"That's what I'm still trying to find out."

Cynthia reflected. "I sense it's a sinister secret. And the thing is, I feel comfortable here. You hear the voices from the walls. I love that. I hear the music of the place. It's lovely, but sad, and there's an air of mystery, something threatening, almost exciting."

Ox watched the expressions on her face, sensitive, intelligent. Nubile, she wasn't, but still young and attractive, and intelligent.

"Where do you come from?" he asked.

"Cleveland, before here. I was first violinist in the symphony. Julliard before that. I grew up in Richmond, Virginia. I'm first violinist, solo artist, and professor in the Philadelphia String Instrument Institute. I get paid for doing something I would gladly do for nothing." She seemed relaxed. She hesitated. "Tell me about yourself."

"Not an awful lot to tell. I grew up in Davenport, Iowa, not an exotic place like Richmond."

She laughed. "Richmond's not exotic. It's an overgrown small town."

"That might apply to Davenport. I like the place, full of huge oak trees and fat squirrels. From there to Harvard Divinity, then to St. Louis for my first church. And from there to here, a flagship church. Your career is more illustrious. From Julliard to first violinist? That's impressive."

She smiled and slouched in her chair. "What does the music committee do?" she asked. "Besides get people involved."

"It'll help select music and monitor quality and appropriateness. Sometimes we'll want variations, from organ music to a string ensemble, or a flutist, or a famous violinist from the Philadelphia String Instrument Institute."

She nodded.

"And," he continued, "we might want to have special music programs for the congregation and the general public. The sanctuary would be ideal for it."

"I'll do it," she said. "It feels right. Can we go to the sanctuary while we talk about it?"

THE HIDDEN CONGREGATION

"Yes," said Ox, "but I'm going to have to run in a few minutes. You live close by. Would it be convenient to stop by tomorrow afternoon on your way home?"

They walked down the steps and Cynthia replied, "Four p.m. tomorrow would be just fine. And, by the way, I have something of a personal problem which I might need to discuss with you."

"I've done a bit of counseling, if that's the kind of problem you're talking about."

"It could have a bearing on what I do here."

They walked into the sanctuary—empty quiet. Ox wondered what her problem could be.

"If we're going to hear voices or music from the walls, this is the time," he said.

"I hear the music all the time. It's complex."

"I'm not going to turn on the lights. The sun through the stained-glass has a special effect."

In the quiet, the place was like a natural wonder—Natural Bridge without commercialism.

"It makes you feel insignificant and important at the same time," she said.

"Gives you a perspective of yourself. I had the same feeling the first time I saw El Capitan in Yosemite."

She turned around, slowly, taking the room in just as he had done. "Is that a choir loft?"

"Yes. Let's go take a look. Something else we might want to consider is getting a choir going." He added, "Hilda said there was one once, but there was apparently a problem with a member who left."

"Was Ammahn Laval the man Hilda was referring to?"

"She isn't sure. Apparently, it's been fifteen years since he was here. Did you meet him?"

"Yes. Even though he was outgoing, he seemed . . . hidden. I can't quite explain it," said Cynthia. "He spent some time talking to those two newcomers, Tom and Chris."

They walked up the wide steps together, entering the rear of the loft and looking out over the panorama.

"This is a spectacle," she said.

"Exactly. Want to see Larry Pregle's storage closet?" He opened the door to the steeple, revealing books and sheet music stacked on the steps.

"Judging from the sheet music, there definitely was a choir," she said.

They walked back down the steps.

"What's below," she said, looking at the steps curving down.

"I'll show you." Ox switched on the stairway lights.

At the foot of the steps, he turned on the lamp and noticed a wall switch. He flipped it and a series of wall lamps with crystal globes spread muted light every ten feet on both sides of the long, narrow hallway, giving the effect of a subterranean cavern with arched ceilings.

"Wow, I hadn't seen these lights myself."

"This is too pretty to hide away. There could be art shows here, or receptions, or even small weddings."

"Without a doubt."

Why hadn't Angel turned on the lights so he could see the beauty of the place? Maybe she didn't want to linger here because of Petersen's presence. He led the way down the hallway.

"And here's the nursery, although it hasn't been used for a long time." He reached in and flipped on the light.

"Does that lead somewhere?" She pointed toward the door on the far side.

THE HIDDEN CONGREGATION

"No," he said, walking across the nursery. "That's the unfinished area under the sanctuary, but the door's locked. Nehmi calls it the dirt basement." He turned the knob, and to his surprise, it opened. "Oh, I haven't been in here myself."

He swung open the door and stepped into a small area that had been excavated. Around his feet, the dust rose in small clouds from the fine dirt. She stood beside him and they peered into the dark area beyond the spill of light from the door. He became aware of the dust. It had risen to the beams and hovered around them.

"I think this dust likes us," said Ox.

"Actually, I don't find it disturbing. You'd think it would be irritating." She took a deep breath. "It has a nice smell."

Ox allowed a deeper breath. "You're right. It smells sweet. There's something almost special about it."

The small cleared area felt close. The sweet dust seemed to fill it. He stepped forward and stood outside the light from the nursery to acclimate his eyes.

"It's spooky," she said, standing closer beside him.

He stared into the darkness. "Can't see much."

About ten feet from the door, the ground slanted up. Out of the corner of his eye, he spotted an old file cabinet sitting next to the door they had just come through. He stepped over and pulled open the top drawer.

"What a strange place for a file cabinet," she said.

The drawer had several boxes of candles, all black, and there was a box of wooden matches.

"I guess Nehmi must keep these here."

He pulled one out and held it while she struck a match and lit it.

"There's something about this place," she said. "It's like we're on an adventure. Like there's something unknown waiting."

They began to walk up the gradual slope. The ground was uneven and he held her elbow to help keep her balance.

"We're going to be dusty from head to toe." Ox could smell nothing but the sweet dust, the penetrating candle smoke, and Cynthia's perfume. He was surprised by his desire to turn his head and smell her hair.

He peered ahead. No headroom left. They would have to crouch to go any farther. Up ahead, the ground rose to within three feet of the ceiling. It was difficult to tell if it stayed like that all the way beneath the chancel.

"We better turn around."

"Yes," she said.

Neither of them moved for a few minutes. He felt warm and could feel her warmth beside him. The odor of the wax seemed to expand her perfume. He felt drunk—drugged, something running through his veins that wasn't his own blood. They turned to go back, but paused facing each other.

"Time to go back," they said together. But, again, they stood looking at each other, allowing their bodies to stand close, not backing off, making the slightest contact. Ox couldn't think. Her breath was warm. Her eyes were closed. Her face tilted to his. He closed his eyes.

"We have to go back." She had opened her eyes. They were wide like those of a frightened animal.

"Yes. Yes."

They turned back. They stepped into the nursery and Ox realized he was still holding the candle. He blew it out and peered back into the dirt basement at the dust settling. He was covered with it. So was Cynthia.

"Whew. It was close in there. Overpowering."

"Yes," said Cynthia. "Like breathing air spiked with something that wouldn't give up. And incredibly warm."

THE HIDDEN CONGREGATION

He stepped back in, holding his breath. He dropped the candle into the drawer and banged it shut. He closed the door behind him.

"I ought to make sure that door gets locked. I can't think of any reason anyone would want to go in there."

Cynthia moved back to the door and opened it. She stepped in for a moment then came out. "It's quiet in there, and warm, incredibly warm."

She leaned against the wall, closed her eyes, and took several deep breaths. Ox was trying to get his breathing back to normal. "No music?"

"No. Like a lid was clamped on. I could hear the dust settling, but no music." Ox thought of the sound of settling dust. They walked up to the sanctuary.

"I hear music. You hear voices in the walls. I hear dust settling."

"Did you notice anything about the smell in there?"

Her laugh was more like a cough. "Yes. Now that you mention it." She looked away from him. "I'm still trying to get over it. It's still in my nose."

When they had passed through the sanctuary, she asked, "What did it smell like to you?"

"Everything sweet I've ever smelled. Compelling. Powerful."

"Yes. All that," she said. "It was overwhelming for a few minutes there." She blushed and looked at her shoes. "And the dust clings."

The church was quiet. He needed to breathe fresh air. He thought of Barbara and the kids.

Lunch was waiting. "Let's give some thought to some things a music committee can do, and maybe some members for it."

"I've thought of a few things. I'd like to have my students come out and put on a program." She bent down and took off one dusty shoe. She sniffed the dust, shook her head and put the shoe back on.

"Anything?"

"Smells like dust. Guess I better run. I think Hilda wants to give me lunch."

CHAPTER SEVENTEEN

Ox came in early and watched the sunrise from his study. He tried to replay and examine those feelings that had crept into him in the dirt basement. Before, he had found Cynthia pleasing and attractive, but not an object of desire. "Lust" might be a more accurate word.

He knew she was beautiful, but that was a linear fact. He admired her beauty much the same as he admired a beautiful tree, azalea bush, or a stand of sea oats.

There was no easy way to describe his feelings. In the dirt basement, he had wanted to touch her, to smell her. Her scent had become a force. Why? Why did the feeling go away when they came out? And did the feelings really go away?

Barbara was so wonderful and their marriage so perfect. How could he have such thoughts in his head?

And Cynthia. What had it done to her? She had felt it, too. Fought it like he had, but felt it like he had. And today at four o'clock, he had a counseling session with her. What kind of counselor could he be?

And the congregation, some mystic sword hanging over them—he had thought he could help. Little chance if he couldn't control his own urges.

He could still smell that odor, and just the thought of it . . . Ox slammed his hand on the tabletop. He got up. He charged out the door, down the steps, through the sanctuary, and to the basement. He was damned if he was going to lose his grip over this.

He opened the door and stepped inside. The dust plumed up around his feet. He lit a candle and breathed deeply. The odor was faint, but unmistakable. Not as strong as yesterday when she stood close, breath warm and eyes closed. He blew out the candle and tossed it into the drawer.

In the nursery, he faced the spot where Petersen's portrait had hung. The gray eyes, something kindling there. What happened to you? What has happened to me? Am I going to fantasize about her? He leaned against the wall and stared at the dirt basement door, but it was her he saw.

This had to stop—damned for all time. The place was filled with some kind of addictive odor. Or was the desire addictive? From lust thou art. To lust thou shalt return. Was it the dust, the candle, or something else?

He pushed the door open again and stood in the circle of light. He would need a flashlight to see farther under the chancel. A sea of dust engulfed him again, floating in waves. He felt like he was drifting with it, and with Cynthia.

He stepped out and shut the door. Sometime, he would get a flashlight and explore the area, but right now, he had to lock it. Either the problem lurked behind the door or in his mind—some hidden flaw he hadn't identified. Hidden flaws. That was his next sermon. This certainly fit in, flaws and action. He was brushing dust off all the way to the office for the key, and all the way back.

He decided to go home for breakfast even though he had eaten early. He wanted to be with Barbara. He wanted to absolve himself of guilt. He wanted the security of her presence.

THE HIDDEN CONGREGATION

"Hi, Tiger. Conquered the world, yet?" She reached into the refrigerator and laid out the bacon.

"I haven't even conquered myself yet. Trying to resolve problems and write next Sunday's service. In fact, I want to get a few Sundays ahead. Maybe I'll write a couple today."

"You ought to be taking a couple of days off a week, you know. Just like everybody else."

"I will after the initial interviews with the congregation."

"Sit and let me fix you some eggs. You look tired." She ran her fingers through his hair. He pulled her to him and kissed her.

"That does me more good than eggs."

"The kids are still asleep," she said, pulling him toward the living room couch.

"You're insatiable," he said.

"I think of it as voracious. Think of it as a celebration."

"What do you mean?"

"Pregnant, Babe."

"You've seen a doctor?"

"Who needs a doctor? I know my body. You hit the stork's eye in St. Louis."

It was just nine o'clock when Ox got back to the church. He felt exhilarated. Another little one was on the way, another gift from God. Somehow, it gave him added strength to face his own weakness.

He would work on his sermons during the morning and pay a visit to Mary Jane Clark in the afternoon. Even though they weren't telling, each managed to give him another beam of light, and he was getting a vague picture. He believed he could tie his next sermon in with that picture.

But that afternoon, Mary Jane Clark disappointed him, in one respect. She gave him nothing he didn't already have.

"How did Dr. Petersen die?"

"His heart stopped. It was an old heart."

But in another way, she was encouraging.

"We're beginning to think there may be hope, some of us."

"There's always hope, Mary Jane, if we work together."

"We're hoping we won't have to tell you what happened."

That was what was encouraging. *Hoping* they wouldn't have to tell. Before, it was they couldn't or wouldn't.

Then she added, "We saw someone back at church yesterday. At least we think Ammahn Laval was here before, when we had all the difficulty. We don't know what to think. It was a long time ago. Didn't mix much. Sang in the choir when he did come."

"What did he do?"

She seemed to concentrate on the sun streaming through the window to the carpet. "We're not sure."

"You have bad feelings about him?"

"We all do. At least, I think we all do."

When he got back, he darted up the steps and poked his head into Angel's office. "Angel, will you give everybody a reminder call about the planning session?"

"Surely." She seemed relieved to have something to do. "Cynthia is waiting in your office."

He looked at his watch. Ten 'til four. Good. An early start means an early finish. Cynthia was wearing a tan gabardine suit. She could've passed for a bank vice-president.

Ox was prepared to talk about the incident in the dirt basement, but Cynthia seemed to have put it out of her mind.

"I was able to get away early. We only have six students in the Monday group and they're all advanced. It's a delight."

"You really like what you do."

"I love music. I love anything having to do with music. It's everything."

THE HIDDEN CONGREGATION

"You mentioned you hear music from these walls just as I hear voices. First of all, I want you to know I don't hear voices." He wiggled his fingers in the air by his right ear.

Cynthia laughed. "I didn't mean to imply you were wifty. If I thought so, I wouldn't be here today." She leaned back in her chair. "I might be the one that's wifty. I hear music most of the time. I think it's a way of thinking. And the music I hear is my interpretation of the place or the person I see. The music here is harmonious and beautiful." She paused for a moment and added, "Primarily."

Ox waited. Was she going to add something else? "Primarily?"

"The new man at the church yesterday, Ammahn Laval?" She shook her head. "I don't know, but something wasn't right. When he was near Nehmi—a lot of discord—tension. It sounded like the wind blowing garbage cans over."

"I think your music carries intuitive qualities, just like my so-called voices in the wall. You may be picking up on what Hilda said yesterday when she talked about what happened to Dr. Petersen. Or your music may be reaffirming what your intellect sees, but hasn't translated into words."

"I hadn't thought of it that way," she said.

"I'm going to tell you something, and it's not breaking a confidence because you already know almost as much as I do. Hilda knows what the problem is. They all do, but they won't talk about it. They're going to cling together until they die."

"If there's anything I can do to help, I will, but I've got a problem to deal with, too. That's why I asked for your help." She paused and bit her lip.

Ox waited, then asked, "Are you comfortable going into it without talking about what happened yesterday between us?"

"Well . . ." This time, she seemed to juggle her thoughts through a long pause. "I've been confused and thinking about it. It could be related—in a perverse kind of way." She stopped. "This isn't going to be easy. I've never talked about it to anyone, no one. I'm close to my parents and I've never even discussed it with them. I can't."

She was silent for what seemed like a long time. Finally, she just came out with it. "I might be gay. Oh, God. I hope that doesn't make you hate me."

"I couldn't possibly hate you for that. You said '*might be*'. What makes you think you might be gay?"

"Well, when I was in high school and college, I never dated. I never felt an attraction to any male. My friends did, but not me."

"Did you feel attracted to any females?"

"No, I was too busy with my music."

"Maybe if the right guy had come along, you would have."

"Or the right girl, for all I know."

Ox sat silent for a few moments. "Does what happened when we went into the dirt basement cause any questions to pop up?"

"That was confusing. But it seemed so abnormal, so controlled."

"Do you feel an attraction to me?"

They gazed at each other for a long period of silence, both relaxed, both intent on the other and the question. The late afternoon sounds of the Schuylkill Parkway drifted in through the window.

"No," she said. "No, I don't think so. You're intelligent and attractive. Maybe more than attractive. I like you. I respect you. What happened was so unusual. I mean neither of us talked about it. Not until we were out of there."

"True, but I don't think I was in any condition to talk when we were in there. And neither were you."

"I've been thinking about it a lot," she said.

THE HIDDEN CONGREGATION

"As you might guess," said Ox, "I've been through the same self-analysis."

"And?"

"It was so unexpected. I know I have to control my feelings. We both have to control our feelings."

"I'm not sure where that leaves me. Does this mean I'm latently promiscuous? I felt urges for you. If I had ever experienced real love, would that have excluded any unwanted animal urges?"

"Have there been other men who meant something to you, at Julliard, at the Cleveland Symphony, high school teachers?"

"Yes."

"Any animal urges with them?"

"No."

"Do you flirt?"

"No, I don't think so."

"Have you ever done anything outside of our experience that could allow you to think you were promiscuous?"

"I have—never—been with a man."

She blushed with this hesitant announcement, and Ox worried that he might also be blushing. He imagined her going through high school, the most vulnerable years, then college with no sexual relations; an absolutely beautiful girl, attractive and desirable in every way.

"There must've been many overtures, many opportunities."

"Yes, there were. But I wasn't interested. That's what makes me wonder."

The intercom buzzed and Ox picked up the phone.

"Ox," said Angel. "I'll see you in the morning."

"Thanks, Angel."

Cynthia smiled. "A church secretary named Angel?"

"It draws a little attention," said Ox. "Cynthia, I think the best suggestion I could make to you is for you to listen to your instincts. They seem to have been sound all these years." She nodded.

"You are worried over a 'maybe'. You answered it yourself. You had other interests. You've had a singleness of purpose, your music."

She said nothing as she thought about it. "I have worried that if I were gay, I would be excluded from this congregation."

"That wouldn't happen. What kind of church would this be? You are you. What I'd like to suggest is you think about that during the rest of this week and let's discuss it again next Monday."

She nodded. "Okay, I'll think about it."

As they both got up, she added, "Can I talk a minute about yesterday?" She went on without waiting. "That place was strange. It was so still. No music. It was just eerie. I've never been in a place like that before."

"Yes," agreed Ox. "It was strange. I went back in there this morning."

"What happened?"

"Nothing. It was quiet. The dust was everywhere. The sweet odor wasn't as strong as yesterday. I haven't figured out what happened, but I had to see if I could resist whatever it was."

She bowed her head and seemed lost in thought for a moment. "I've got to go in," she said matter-of-factly.

"Why?"

"You went in to prove your strength or goodness, or whatever. I've got to do the same or I'll forever wonder. I want to know. I'm not going to run from it."

Ox wasn't certain.

"Considering my other issue, I've got to work this through. Okay? You needed to prove you could keep your control."

"It's locked. I'll get the key, but I'm not sure I should go in with you."

THE HIDDEN CONGREGATION

"Fine, but I've got to put this behind me."

"I think I know where there's a flashlight you can use. I'll stay in the nursery."

In the fuse box next to the sanctuary light switches, he found the flashlight. They walked through the sanctuary without noticing the surroundings. Ox was thinking about what was under his feet. She led the way as they flipped on lights and passed through the nursery.

Ox unlocked the door.

Then she opened the door.

Ox thought he could smell candle smoke.

CHAPTER EIGHTEEN

Ox watched Cynthia step through the doorway. He could see the dust rise and cling to her. She walked forward to the edge of the level portion and turned back toward him, standing away from the doorway.

"Nothing. Absolutely nothing."

He wasn't sure. There was that faint smell. He stood in the doorway and aimed the flashlight beam through the darkness. She came back toward him.

"Maybe nothing," he agreed. "Even your perfume is faint, not like yesterday."

"But I didn't wear perfume, yesterday, Ox, and I'm not wearing any now."

He shrugged. "Must be your natural odor, but it was irresistible."

"I remember smelling you, too. Heavy odor. Intoxicating."

"I don't use lotion or cologne."

"I guess you've got a natural odor, too." She turned back and took a few steps. "I really think it's okay. I'm not feeling the urges I felt the last time."

Ox was still concerned about the faint candle scent. "I guess there's some candle odor left over from before. It's faint. I don't

THE HIDDEN CONGREGATION

feel like jumping your bones. Maybe it's okay to test it together. In fact, maybe we should, to put it to rest for good." Still, he stayed in the nursery, unsure. Finally, he stepped through the doorway. He remembered the overwhelming feeling he had experienced and didn't want to go through that again.

Cynthia nodded. "I think it's okay. The smell is faint."

He took her by the elbow. "While we're at it, let's see what we can see at the far end." Together, they walked across the flat area and began to walk up the slope. When their heads were against the ceiling, she said, "Hold the light high."

The beam played against the back foundation wall. He let it drop a few feet. It looked as though another space was dug out under the chancel, too far away to be sure.

He began to feel more assured. "The only way to get closer is to duck waddle. You game?"

"We've come this far. Let me take off these shoes." She grabbed his shoulder to keep her balance.

Her sweet smell invaded his mind, but it stopped when she let go.

"Don't let me forget them on the way back."

He hesitated, then led the way until their heads were against the ceiling again. He played the light around some more.

"There's definitely a depression, but we can't go any farther without crawling."

"Good Lord," she said.

"What?"

"I'm covered with this stuff." She brushed her arms and legs.

He shined the light on her. "You're covered from head to toe."

"Shine the light on yourself."

He did.

"I got news. Your hair was yellow when we came in here. Now it, your face, your suit, your tie, are all the same color."

"We're twins." He brushed his jacket and the dust almost blinded him. The dust had a sweet taste. He squinted toward the depression under the chancel. "I want to see what's back there, but I'm not dressed to crawl."

His leg muscles cramped from squatting and he kneeled forward just as she did the same. Her perfume was sweet, overpowering. It was like he was tasting her. She was staring at him.

"Ox, it's happening. We've got to leave."

"Yes."

She fell forward on her hands and lay her forehead on the ground. His head bumped the joist above. He felt closed in. No place to go.

"Cynthia. If we don't leave, it'll be too late." But he didn't care anymore. He didn't move. She lay in the dirt and turned over, gazing up at him. Waves of desire washed through him and he fell on her, pressing into the heat of her body. He kissed her, pushing against her. He let himself sink into a dream of motion. She wrapped her arms around his neck and they rolled over and over. Her body was soft and hot.

He lifted his head. "We have to get out of here."

"Yes, we have to leave." She kissed him. Her breath was hot on his neck.

He pressed his body against hers, his mind in a swirl of vibrations. And through it came Barbara's voice. *You hit the stork's eye in St. Louis.*

He pushed on his elbows. "Let's go." But her body rose against him and he wanted to sink into her.

"I hear music." Her voice was far away. "Like a music box. Same tune over and over. I'm dizzy. Can't move." She wrapped her legs around him.

He let his full weight press on her again. He buried his face in her neck, kissed her and inhaled her. He moved his body

THE HIDDEN CONGREGATION

against her softness. She moved her body against his and pushed her tongue in his ear. *I just got a call from the Eastern Diocese saying they were going to send me material on housing and schools in some crazy section of Philadelphia. Is there something I should know?*

Ox got on his hands and knees, Cynthia still wrapped around him. He crawled toward the door. His movements were automatic. He couldn't think, he just moved. His mind was on hold. He finally crawled through the door and into the nursery. In the middle of the floor, he lay on her again and tried to breathe. His head began to clear. The perfume still swept through him.

"We're doing animal things and I want to do more."

"I won't stop you." She unwrapped her legs from around him and let go of his neck. "Crawling out here was the toughest thing I ever did. I don't want to get off of you." He pushed up on his knees and leaned back on his heels.

"I feel vulnerable with my legs spread out and you staring. And I don't care."

"I shouldn't be staring."

"Guess you better let me out of this ridiculous position."

He wanted to touch, but shook his head and got up.

She reached out her hands and he pulled her up. He let go slowly. Her hands felt like they were melting. She leaned her head against his chest for a few moments and waves surged in his body. He started to pull her to him, but she moved away and leaned against the wall. He reached over and closed the basement door. They were both caked with dust.

She looked down and brushed at her skirt. "It happened again, Ox."

"Something's in there. It's not us." He stared at the door. He should bring Petersen's portrait back. Maybe he was guarding something.

"This is incredible. I'll have to sneak in the front door so Hilda doesn't see me like something from another planet."

"I'll go in for your shoes. You stay here."

"Don't worry. It's difficult enough controlling myself out here."

He found them. The flashlight was nearby, still on. He switched it off and turned toward the door. There was a black candle sitting beside the file cabinet, flickering, trailing a thin string of smoke. He walked over, grabbed it, and carried it to the door.

"This was in here burning the whole time."

Cynthia stared. "How did we miss it?"

"Short wick. Small flame. I don't know how it got there."

"It's got a strong odor. It smells like you. Blow it out." She sank to her knees. "Oh, my God. Blow it out."

Ox stepped into the dirt basement. He blew out the candle and tasted the smoke. He set the candle where it had been, but grabbed it again and carried it into the nursery. "It smelled like you, sweet and warm."

"Are you all right?"

"I'm not going to jump your bones, if that's what you mean."

"That's what I meant."

"Not because I don't want to. How do you feel?" He shook his head to clear it again.

"Wouldn't be wise to tell you." She grabbed hold of a table and pulled herself to her feet.

"Exactly so." He put the candle on the table and brushed at his shirt. "Too much of it. Have to go outside."

"What'll you do with the candle?"

"I don't know, but I think I'll take it to the office and keep it as a reminder of what almost happened."

"It's not what almost happened. It's what did happen. Is there such a thing as an aphrodisiac odor?"

THE HIDDEN CONGREGATION

"I never heard of one. But there's a lot I don't know. What I do know is, we better get out of here. The odor is drifting out here." They stepped outside the nursery, careful not to touch each other.

In his office, she got her purse and stood by the door. "I don't know what to say."

"Neither do I. But we'll have to talk about it. We've got to understand it." He examined the candle, turning it over in his hands. "There's no rational explanation for it. Any of it."

"We both went in rational. We both lost it." Part way out the door, she asked, "Are you over it?"

"In all honesty? Not by a long shot. I still haven't caught my breath. My whole body is exhilarated, tingling. If we were on a date, I would be doing naughty things."

She tilted her head and managed a faint smile. "Just so I'm not alone."

She closed the door behind her.

CHAPTER NINETEEN

Cynthia stood in the courtyard, trying to brush the dust out of her clothes. She looked at the dark windows, black eyes passing judgment on her.

She felt an urge to take off her clothes, all of them, and shake them. She didn't care if anyone saw. She didn't care if all the eyes of the church stared at her nakedness. She could still smell Ox, although faintly, but the memory of it . . . the memory of it. Maybe if she were naked, he would see her.

She knew she was over-stimulated and that her thoughts were dangerous. She brushed off as much of the dust as she could. She was glad she had her car for the short drive. Her hair was full of the stuff. She could feel it on her face. She would take a shower as soon as she got home. She hoped Hilda was in the back of the house somewhere.

Cynthia drove the short distance to the house automatically. Her body and mind were a confusion of disbelief and sensations. But more than anything, she was tired, exhausted. She could hardly lift her arms. Faintly, buried in her mind, a tiny music box sound kept repeating itself.

She parked and sat in her car and closed her eyes, but she could feel his weight on her entire being. She opened her eyes and stared at the overhead upholstery. Nothing seemed real. Had it really happened? Was it a fantasy? She turned off the motor and waited a few minutes, looking at the front door for any signs of Hilda. She closed the car door as quietly as she could.

Crossing the porch, she didn't let her heels touch the wooden floor. She opened and closed the door quickly, and carefully moved up the stairs without pausing.

In her room, she leaned against the door in relief. No explanations were necessary, at least not to Hilda.

She dug a plastic bag out of a kitchen drawer, took off her suit and stuffed it in for the cleaners. In the shower, she watched the streaks of dirt running down her body and across the tub.

"What have I done?"

An endless supply of dirt rinsed from her hair. She had to wash it three times, squirting on shampoo and working her fingers through it. She looked at her hands and was shocked to find them filthy in spite of the soap. She rinsed her hair and shampooed again. The tub was filthy and would have to be scrubbed. She was in the shower for over a half hour. When she stepped out, she wasn't relaxed. She was still keyed up—exhilarated, body tingling.

"I know the term for it. I'm worked up."

She had never felt anything like this before. She stood in the center of the large bathroom, and his smell drifted over her.

Oh, God. It has to be over.

It was like a dream she couldn't get out of her mind. She wanted to think about it. She wanted to think about him. She wanted him. She studied her nakedness in the bathroom mirror. Flushed. Aroused. She imagined him looking at her and became more aroused.

If he were here right now . . .

It was dusk. She turned out the lights and sat by the front window looking at car lights along the Schuylkill. Lights coming and going in waves. People going places. Cars filled with voices. Lights darting and hurrying.

I wish he had done it.

It was quiet. She opened the window to let in the noises of the night. The cars along the Schuylkill had the sound of wind drifting up from the valley. The air was warm against her skin, pungent with summer. She was glad she was naked.

She picked up her violin. Nothing. She couldn't convert the smell and the feelings into music.

She held the violin, felt its cool wood, smelled its special odor, laid her cheek against its back and closed her eyes. She played the music box sound and imagined the sound vibrating all over the world.

Is this my music?

When she finished, she let the violin dangle by her side. She could see Ox staring down at her. She wanted his hands on her. She lay the violin down and moved about the apartment randomly, not knowing what to do. She paused in front of the refrigerator. She poured a cup of cold milk and drank it.

Naked, she crawled into bed.

CHAPTER TWENTY

Ox called Barbara. "I'm sorry, I'm running late and didn't call. I'm going to be a while more."

"You got something going with Angel?"

"Nothing that tame," he said. He put the phone in the cradle. "Nothing that tame."

Ox looked down at himself, dirt and dust, just like Cynthia. No, not just like Cynthia. He tried not to think of her body. *I won't stop you.*

"My God, what have I done? What happened?"

The sweet odor, the warmth, the softness, all of it was her. The swirling darkness in his mind.

Cynthia, how close we came ...

"My God, how can I face her? How can I face Barbara? How can I face myself? What's down there?"

He ran through the sanctuary, into the basement, through the nursery, and grabbed the knob.

What?

He turned and twisted the knob. He pushed the door.

Locked. It can't be.

He held the knob. Shook it. Tried it again. Maybe it was just stuck. He pulled it with all his strength. He yanked and jerked, but it was definitely locked.

"What the hell?"

He put his ear against the door—no sound. He walked to the center of the nursery and stared in all the corners: no one here but him. He peered through the door to the vestibule. The cellar door was closed. The long room was empty, silent.

He tiptoed up the stairs, feeling watched, exposed. He ran through the sanctuary and up to the office. He grabbed the master key and ran back. He paused on the first step to the basement, catching his breath. He walked down slowly, looking around, the blood pulsing through his head.

Ox was sweating as he unlocked the door. The soft dust plumed as he walked and he could feel it clinging to his legs. He turned the flashlight beam round the area. He glanced back at the door again. He trained the light toward the far end under the altar. He moved forward until he was squatting.

When his head hit the rafters, he dropped forward to his knees. At two-foot clearance, he crawled, flashlight scanning ahead. The dust was so thick he closed his eyes to slits.

Should've gotten out of these clothes. Doesn't matter, they were covered anyhow.

When his shoulders hit against the ceiling, he didn't pause, but lay on his belly to crawl the last remaining feet.

Swimming in dirt.

His head emerged from the dust and he was hanging out over an area completely excavated.

Air clear here.

Something is down there.

He grabbed the flashlight and charged out the door. *Something is down there.*

He swung his feet around and jumped to the dirt floor. His shoes were full of dirt. He played the light round the area. It was much larger than the small excavation near the door. It was

THE HIDDEN CONGREGATION

oblong, running from one side of the sanctuary to the other. It was about fifteen feet deep and fifty feet wide.

He took a few steps and stumbled forward, catching himself before falling, almost dropping the flashlight. He stood in a small pit about a foot deep. The flooring felt firm. He squatted and ran his fingers over it. Hard. Greasy. The pit was a rectangle, seven or eight feet long and about four feet wide. In each corner, there was an indentation, like posts had once been there.

He scanned the light around the area. Another file cabinet, an old wooden one, stood at the far end.

"What on earth?"

He walked over to it and pulled open the top drawer. It was full of candles.

"I don't believe it. More candles, all black and tapered. Who stored these here? Nehmi? No. Ammahn? How?"

Ox knelt by the cabinet and examined the wood. Old. He took a candle out and rummaged around in the back of the drawer until he found a tin box of wooden matches, a really old tin box.

How long ago were matches invented?

He lit one. It spurted out a large yellow flame with a strong sulfur odor. Old—don't make them to smell that way today.

Let's just light a candle to see what happens.

There was a slight whispering sound and the pungent odor of wax. He blew out the match, pulled out another candle and lit it from the other. He dug the end of one into the embankment. He grabbed a handful from the drawer.

"Let there be light."

He lit another and dug it in about ten feet farther, then another and another. If the candles were the problem, they couldn't do any more damage than they already had. The dugout room got lighter and lighter. The row of sizzling lights cast halos through the dust.

Probably candles made with animal fat.

He turned off the flashlight and walked slowly to the far side, studying the floor, the ceiling, the sides, and back wall. There was no other way in—no other way out. Spooky. Looked like a medieval dungeon. Quiet, just the sizzling—and the odor. It was becoming thicker, sifting through his mind, like fog. And through the fog, he was rubbing against Cynthia's softness, feeling her body with his.

Dizzy, he knelt in the dust.

"I won't stop you."

Why had he stopped? If he could get to her now—maybe he should blow out the candles. There was something there in the dirt. Some kind of print. He leaned closer: a shoe print. He hadn't walked here. No, too round for a footprint. A horse, a small horse, maybe.

Ox closed his eyes and tried to push through the fog in his mind. *Have to be stronger than it, stronger than it.* He sat and took off his shoes and poured out the fine dirt. He leaned against the embankment across from the row of candles. He watched the pale wisps of smoke drifting from them.

"What is this place?"

He looked up at the thick ceiling. And upstairs in the sanctuary, there was a sub-flooring, and finished floor, and the rug on top. He couldn't guess how thick that was. Sound might get through, but just barely.

The candles' sizzling noise almost sounded like singing. He thought of Cynthia and her legs. *"I won't stop you. I won't stop you. I won't stop you."* He stood quickly and played the light through the dust toward the nursery. Someone knew. Someone had locked the door after they left.

My God, I could have done it to her. We might still be here in the dust.

He could feel her softness, and smell her sweetness.

THE HIDDEN CONGREGATION

My God.

"You did her."

It was like a whisper from the dark. He turned around. No one there. A whisper from the darkness all in his mind.

No. No. I didn't.

Ox left the candles burning, leaped up the embankment and crawled through the dust toward the door. Who knew? What was going on? He stopped just inside the door and stared around again. The candlelight at the far end wobbled reflections against the wall. He had to catch his breath. He could see Cynthia, vulnerable, waiting.

"*I . . . won't stop you.*"

He stepped outside and closed the door. He had to wash and go home and lie to Barbara.

In the sanctuary, he stopped. Pale light sifted through the stained-glass windows. The room took on a surreal quality as the colors muted to pastels in the dimness. Had he really thought that thought—*you did her*?

The dark wooden wall panels glistened. He felt the presence of their secrets.

Now they had another.

He retreated to the safety of his study. Ox's thoughts darted back and forth between Cynthia and Barbara, between lust and lies, between shock and remorse.

He could still feel soft flesh under him, and the odor filled his mind. And there was Barbara. *Now we all know what the mommy and the daddy and the little girl and the little boy all look like. We're a family.*

And he could still see Cynthia lying in front of him, exposed, vulnerable, calling. He forced her out of his mind. His suit was filthy. He had to shake it out. Unbelievably dirty after crawling all the way in. He had never had reason to lie to Barbara before.

What had happened to his soul? Cynthia had come to him for help. How could he ever think of himself as a minister again? But the candles were part of the problem and he had lit them and analyzed. He was stronger. But what if Cynthia had been there? How much analyzing then?

Best not to get washed. He would concoct a story about crawling under the flooring because of a smell or something. *Go home dirty.* Good God. How could he do this? *She's not stupid. She'll be hurt. Can't lie to her. Have to. Have to.*

The door was locked. Somebody knows. Who knows?

Walking home, he was glad it was getting dark. The dirt was a badge he didn't want anyone to see. He felt as though he were leaving a trail behind him. He paused at the front door, took a deep breath, and went in.

"What on earth happened to you?"

"Crawling around in the unfinished portion of the basement. Dirtier than I thought."

Barbara held his suit coat open and examined his shirt and tie. "Well." She let go of the coat. "I should say it was. That suit will have to be cleaned a few times. Take it off. I'll put it in a grocery bag." She called back on the way to the kitchen, "What were you doing, crawling around in the basement?"

"There was a pipe knocking. I was trying to figure out what it was."

She reappeared and dropped the bag on the floor. "Are the pockets empty? Maybe you should let Nehmi take care of the pipes. Good grief, even your underwear is dirty. Drop it in the bag. Don't worry, Martha's in her room drawing pictures of clouds and rocks."

Ox had to ask. "Clouds and rocks?"

"Get those socks in there, too. Yes, clouds and rocks. She likes them both, only she says the clouds belong on the ground and the rocks in the sky. Safer. So that's the way she's drawing them. Get upstairs and put something on. If she sees you, she may decide to draw something else. Dinner will be ready in five."

That night, in the bathroom he avoided the mirror. She had bought the story. *Easy to fool someone who loves and trusts you. Easy.* He felt as though he were leaving a trail of dirt through his soul. Cynthia couldn't compare to Barbara. Nobody could. *Clouds on the ground. Rocks in the sky. World upside down.*

CHAPTER TWENTY-ONE

When Angel opened the door to the church, she stepped inside then stepped back. The smell—faint, but it was there. Yes, she was certain. How could she ever forget? She had a sinking feeling, of drowning. She looked toward the double doors into the sanctuary, then at the rug. Yes. Yes. The dust was there. The dust.

It was early. No one else was in yet. She quickly got out the vacuum cleaner and began to clean up the trail from the steps upstairs through the sanctuary and down through the nursery. She opened the door to the dirt basement. The smell of candles was strong. She slammed the door.

Still holding the vacuum cleaner, she leaned against the door, remembering: the candles, the voices, the flames, the screams—the evil. She closed her eyes, but the sound was still there. Ox and Cynthia, it had to be. She wrapped the cord around the vacuum cleaner and hurried back upstairs. There was no hope. He was supposed to rebuild the church. And already, here it all was again. What was going to happen to them all?

She stepped into the Community Room and looked at Ethan's portrait. He gazed straight at her. Were his eyes pleading with her?

THE HIDDEN CONGREGATION

She wouldn't tell anyone. She would wait and see. But the screams, and the smell, and the odor of the candles. She would never forget. She stumbled up the stairs to her office. She had to sit. She had tried to get it out of her mind. And here it was again . . . the candles, the dust.

She recognized Ox's footsteps coming up the stairs. She could hear him unlocking his door.

"Good morning, Angel," he called.

"Good morning, Ox.

He sounded all right. But something had happened. She had to go see. But he came before she could get up.

"Angel, what do you know about Ammahn Laval? He used to come to this church before. Did he just quit when Dr. Petersen died? Has he been back since then?"

"No, not until now."

"What's he do for a living?"

"He's an archaeologist. He did some work at the University."

"You have an address for him? I'd like to know what he's up to."

"Up to?"

"Just curious."

"He used to have a place up near Conshohocken, a little house on a farm where he said he was doing some diggings."

She rummaged through her files. "This might have it." She laid a file folder on the desk and leafed through it. "Here it is. Twenty Foot Road, Cold Point, Pennsylvania."

"Thanks. I'll have to figure out where that is. I'm sure it'll be on a map." He had already started back to his study.

She took a step forward. "Was there something in particular he did, to make you curious?"

"No, just a few little things. Mary Jane seemed concerned about him. Said he was here when all the difficulty started." She felt his eyes on her.

She heard herself ask, "Has he done anything to you?" She had to look at him to see what his reaction to the question was.

"Not that I know of. Maybe."

She felt her stomach muscles tighten. "Has anything strange happened to you?"

Ox sat down in front of her desk. "Something almost happened. You might describe it as a close call. It was bad, but it could have been worse." He was watching her closely. "If I tell you what it was, will you tell me everything that happened before?"

Angel put her elbows on her knees and buried her head in her hands. He said nothing. "I can't do it."

"That dirt basement down beneath the sanctuary is a strange place."

There was no place to retreat to. "How?" She couldn't look at him. He knew.

"Have you ever been in there?"

There was no question. He knew. She thought of running to the bathroom, but she stayed glued to her chair. "I might have some time in the past."

"Was that in the past that we are talking about?"

She couldn't look at him—couldn't escape—didn't know what to do. "I can't talk about it." She couldn't look up. She knew he was staring at her. She could feel his eyes burning into her.

"When you walked in there, did the dust cling to you? Did the smell of candles make your brain—your whole body—vibrate?"

"Oh, my God." She swirled off her chair and stumbled against the wall. "Oh, my God." She tried to push herself into the wall. She had to get out.

"I really do think I need your help. I think there's some pretty powerful stuff going on, but I don't understand what."

She pushed past Ox, almost lost her balance down the stairs,

THE HIDDEN CONGREGATION

and stumbled into the bathroom. She crouched in a corner and cried. The pit, the screams, the flames. Oh, God.

I want to forget. Don't bring it back. Don't bring it back.

She leaned her head against the wall and closed her eyes. Her mouth was dry. She felt sick in the stomach. She tried to swallow to keep her stomach down. She lay in the corner and tried to relax. She took a deep breath. Maybe Ox could do it. Ethan couldn't control things. She knew Ammahn had controlled everything. It all got out of hand. She stood up, walked over to a stall and got some toilet paper to dab her eyes. Another deep breath helped.

I do need to help him. She remembered the morning when she had come to her senses. The horrible morning when she finally realized.

I will never forget.

The odor was back. The dust was back. It was starting over again. She had vacuumed up the dust, but she couldn't vacuum her mind. She wasn't going to be able to hide it. It would get worse.

In desperation, she ran over to Ethan's portrait.

Help me blot it out. Tell me what to do. We can't let it start again. You, of all people, know.

CHAPTER TWENTY-TWO

Ox sat in his study, being careful to leave the door open. He felt a little remorse for what he had done to Angel, but knew he was justified under the circumstances. Neither he nor Cynthia was promiscuous. Something very evil and very powerful had been taking place in that dirt basement and it was no longer a matter of the past. It was a matter of now.

He stared across the valley at the trees and the sky. Some of the clouds really could pass for rocks. He liked to have his sermon completed no later than the preceding Monday, and here it was Tuesday. He had to get busy. He tried not to think of Cynthia then realized the best thing for him to do was to force himself to think of her, but to do it objectively, to force the emotion out of it and analyze it.

More important than writing the sermon right now. He thought of her smell. Now analyze. What did it consist of? What could he compare it to? Nothing—the odor of every flower that grew. Everything. Was it the candle smoke? Was it the dust? Was it a combination? There simply was no rational explanation. It was powerful, no question. It was overwhelming, compelling, stimulating. He thought of every adjective he could to describe it. He leafed through his thesaurus saturating himself with

THE HIDDEN CONGREGATION

words to the point the smell became something he could think of analytically. Good. Now the softness of her, the wonderful softness of her. She was almost like warm liquid with body. She was sleep and love and comfort. He thought of "sponge" and "enveloping" and went to the thesaurus again.

"Ox."

It was Angel.

"Sorry Angel, but you know I had to. It's no longer history. Whatever it is, it's here now, in this building. It's not going to let us alone."

"I know that, now." She glanced around the room as she formed her words. "I saw the dust on the carpet and could smell the candles. We were all caught up in it. Everyone but Mr. Nehmi."

"Was Ammahn in back of it all?"

"I think he must have been. And after it started, he seemed to take over. Ethan didn't seem to have any control or influence over what was happening. Nehmi saw them together. He was just caught up in it. Completely. We all were. We were just carried along." She closed her eyes and shook her head as though to blot it out.

"What about the pit?"

She leaned against the wall and closed her eyes. "There was a kind of an altar there."

"Was it devil worship?"

"I'm not sure. We didn't think so then. We didn't think about that at all. We were just living each day, until . . . did you and Cynthia go in there?"

"Yes."

She came the rest of the way into the room and sat in front of his desk. "So did Ethan and me."

"What happened?"

"I suspect the same thing that happened to you and Cynthia. We went in there at five o'clock one afternoon and didn't come out until almost midnight. I just forgot that the rest of the world existed."

"What about Dr. Petersen? How did it affect him?"

She leaned back in the chair, shaking her head. She didn't try to stop the tears. "Please don't tell the bishop or let our secret out." She wiped her eyes with the backs of her hands. "I don't want Ethan's name muddied now. He went through too much. He was a good man. He really didn't have control over the things that happened after that." She leaned forward and covered her face. "We were weak."

"You and he were the first to go in there?"

"We were the first, but I just can't talk about it anymore." She got up to leave. "I'm sorry about what happened to you and Cynthia, because I know what's going to happen next. You will be the tool, just as Ethan was. You've got to watch out and not let it happen anymore. Although it's probably too late." She held a tissue to her nose and walked slowly toward the door.

"Before you go, Angel . . ."

She stopped.

"Cynthia and I managed to throw it off. It was a close call, but we managed to get back out before things went too far. But we both know the power of the force that was there, and we may not have the strength to throw it off next time. That's why I need to know everything before it's too late."

"Yes. Well, Ethan and I got out the first time, too. But we were drawn back. You will be, too."

"That evening, you mentioned wasn't your first time in there?"

"Second. I'm glad at least you got out the first time. Some of the others didn't."

THE HIDDEN CONGREGATION

Ox leaned back in his chair. He lightly drummed his fingers on the desktop. "You said Ammahn seemed to take over. In what way?"

"Apparently, he spent a lot of time with Ethan. He kept asking him what was happening, like he didn't know. Acted like he wanted to help, but we all knew better. Nehmi was on to him. He just wanted to know how much Ethan was under. Then after all the deaths, he left. Just vanished."

Ox wanted to ask what she meant about the deaths, but decided it might be more than she could handle for the time being.

"I'll talk to the group anyhow. There might be some hope. You did get out. Maybe you could again." But Angel's face didn't seem to carry much enthusiasm or hope. "I'll call the others. Maybe it's time we had a meeting."

"Angel, have it at someone's home, not here. And I want to be there."

"Well . . . I'm not sure. Well . . . Oh, we have to. I'll ask the others."

"Angel, I've a right to be there. I've been in there, too. I'm no longer the stranger here."

"Maybe the others will see it that way, too."

"Don't tell them what the meeting's for. Tell them it's an emergency meeting and they must be there. Tell them it will take the place of the planning meeting."

"All right. I'll do it. I'll call Hilda first to ask her if we can meet at her house."

She quickly left the room and Ox saw the phone light go on. She wasn't wasting any time.

Cynthia—she should be invited, too.

He waited until the light went off and got up, but Angel was already in the doorway. "Hilda said yes."

"Be sure Cynthia is invited. She should be there, too."

"Oh, yes. It's got her." And she was gone again.

He thought of the sermon he should be writing, but gave it up. He couldn't. The meeting was more important. It was the verge of a breakthrough. He would have to describe what he and Cynthia went through. Did he need to get Cynthia's approval? No. He would have to go ahead. There might not be time to talk to her ahead of the meeting, anyhow. He might be able to talk to her before then. How should he open the meeting?

"Hello, my name's Ox, and I'm a dirt basement junkie."

"I wouldn't have stopped you."

Her voice seemed to fill his head. *God. I really am a junkie. An addict. I can't get her out of my mind. This is really a sickness, a form of insanity, an invasion of the mind. I don't want to stop it. It's overwhelming, compelling, stimulating, exciting, wonderful. What else? Overpowering, overcoming, destroying. Destroy or be destroyed. Yes!* *"My name's Ox, and I'm a dirt basement junkie, but not for long."*

He swiveled in his chair and looked out over the valley. Sky full of clouds, earth full of rocks. This morning, he had thought he had no right to even stand in front of the congregation and preach to them on anything. Now he realized he was the best qualified. *Wait. Can't get too confident.* The fact is, he nearly violated her. He did violate her. She trusted him. Came to him for help and he rolled in the dirt with her. And he wasn't over her by a long shot. "I'm Ox, and I'm one of you." "Hi, Ox." "And so is Cynthia." "Hi Cynthia." Time for a clean breast of things. *Can't do the job unless I come clean or I'd be living a lie.* He thought of Scott Peck's *People of the Lie.* He didn't want to be one of them, sanctimonious and self-righteous.

He couldn't get her out of his mind. *Don't get her out of your head. Think about her and your sermon at the same time. Keep her there. She's a part of it.*

THE HIDDEN CONGREGATION

The sermon had to cover evil, the evil in the basement, without being specific. How could he describe so much evil, so much power? Good against evil, what an overworked idea, over simplistic. Was it a real battle after all, or just an illusion? *Cut the egghead stuff. This was personal—personal good and evil.* He began to type on his keyboard.

He stared at the sky, at the clouds. He thought of Martha, of Billy, of Barbara. *Oh, Lord!* He would have to tell Barbara what happened.

CHAPTER TWENTY-THREE

Jessie May switched off the headlights and pulled over to the curb a block away from the church. She and Emmett sat quietly for a while. It was after midnight and the street was empty. There was no moon.

"Let's go," said Emmett.

They got out of the car and shut the doors without slamming them. Rain was predicted, but it was a warm night, so they hadn't worn raincoats. Jessie May thought she felt a drop of rain, but it might have just been moisture.

They walked toward the church without talking. They followed the flagstone walk toward the back of the church, past the swing-set and on toward the back fence. In spite of the hour, there was still traffic on the parkway below.

The back of the building was dark. Other than the distant hum of traffic, it was quiet enough that Jessie May could hear her own breathing. They walked toward the other side of the church and stood outside the graveyard, looking at the overgrown mess.

"They've got this pretty much hidden, haven't they?" said Jessie May. *Who is "they?"* she wondered. She stepped over a tangle of weeds littered with trash.

THE HIDDEN CONGREGATION

Emmett pressed ahead with a small penlight.

Jessie May whispered after him, "Look for Lewis or . . ."

"I know the damn names."

Jessie May caught a briar on her arm. "Damn."

"Here's Petersen's grave."

Jessie May joined him. "Where's his wife's?"

"Don't see it. His was the only one not hidden under all this crud."

"She should be here somewhere."

"Maybe she ran off and joined that cult, like all the others."

"I don't buy that cult stuff, Emmett."

"Why not? This crazy church has its own belief. All the souls connected. Lots of crapola. Shit, why can't they be like other churches?"

"You mean like yours."

"Could do a lot worse."

"Here's something. What's this?"

Emmett peered over her shoulder. "A bone? Well what do you know? A bone in a grave yard."

"Awfully small. A finger?"

"Hell. Could be from an animal."

"I'll bag it anyhow."

"Let's go."

"There's something strange here." Jessie May kept poking at graves, reading the tombstones. "Lot's of single graves."

"I felt a drop of rain. Let's get out of here."

"Wait a minute. I'm looking for graves of couples."

"Jessie May, it's raining. I'm going to the car."

"A great backup you are."

"Crap on backup. It's raining. By the way, I'm not going to keep on calling you Jessie May. Makes me sound like I'm from the damn South."

"You are. You're from South Philadelphia."

"I'll call you Jessie or May. Which one?"

"Neither."

"Okay then. JM."

"If you're too lazy to say the name, just call me J."

"No, I like JM. Sounds like Jim."

"Okay, I'll call you M for Emma."

They ran for the car when the drops turned to drenching rain.

CHAPTER TWENTY-FOUR

Cynthia left the Institute early. She gave her students some independent work and sent them on their separate ways. She drove out East River Drive into Fairmont Park and pulled over along the Schuylkill to look at the water and think. She sat in her little Datsun and watched the Canadian geese waddling around on the bank. A slight breeze carried the odors and sounds of the park.

It was mid-afternoon and the area seemed filled with people running, riding bicycles, walking. Some were relaxed; some were intense; some looked unhappy in spite of the setting. There was a crew sculling along the river, the coxswain yelling something to the others she couldn't make out while they pulled in unison. Could be from Penn. She felt like an outsider, separate from them, from the runners, from the bicyclists. Everybody seemed to have purpose, even the geese. What was hers? How was it all going to end?

She couldn't get a grip on things. First, she was worried she might be gay, and now, Ox. Her emotions were running everywhere. She had no control. Worse, she didn't want to control.

That was the problem. She didn't want to control. Her whole body was on fire and it consumed her. She didn't want to stop it, but intellectually, she knew she had to. *If we were on a date, I would be doing naughty things.* She was about to slip into fantasies again. Delicious fantasies. She had to control. Had to. Then it hit her—music. She would compose it all. Some of it she had already . . . the church itself. But her feelings right now, and since Monday, were sporadic brush fires and her body was the grass and the fire. How could she compose it? It had no form. Yes, it did, but it followed its own form, changing course constantly, themes clashing, counterpoint upon counterpoint.

She closed her eyes and let it play freely in her mind. She thought of Ox and let the music flow. It was beautiful, exciting, compelling, and discordant. She wanted to slip her hands between her legs and squeeze herself into ecstasy, but she refused. She forced herself to think only of the music. It didn't sound like her other music, wilder with uncontrolled variations. She would write it that way and clean it up later. She picked up her music notebook and began to record, mindless emotion.

Then she decided to write a theme that was exclusively Ammahn. The theme was definite, heavy, and angry. It carried a sense of control and followed naturally after the confused flight of the unpredictable deer. And yet, there was something else in him she couldn't recognize.

Without thinking about it, she found herself bringing in the theme of Ox. She felt his strength. She felt his desire. She smelled his body. But she did not allow herself to be inundated. She scribed the notes quickly. There was a theme of complete determination, but there was something weak and lurking in the dark. Did he have his demons, too?

The church with all its beauty formed a thematic background, but the congregation arose lamenting the past, with no hope for the future. And there was Ox again, exciting, exhilarating, and there was Ammahn, or was that Ox, too? And trying to be heard was her own theme of loneliness.

THE HIDDEN CONGREGATION

She wrote it all down, scratching through a few notes that needed to be revised. She would do the whole thing over again later. She flipped through page after page.

She hadn't realized how long she had been there. The sun was shining in her eyes as it began its drop from the sky. There was a glare on the river, and more scullers. Two families were having picnics on tables along the river. One of the geese was challenging them. There were more runners, bicycles, cars, people going home from work. She closed her notebook and wondered how many of them were plagued with desire for the forbidden.

She knew something she couldn't explain had been at work at the church. Something had taken control of her, or else she had let it. But there was something there she didn't understand. It had seized Ox, too. It was desirable, undesirable, and sinister.

But she really wasn't sure she could. Maybe she should just leave. She could move from the third-floor apartment. She could join another church. She could simply not join any church. But she didn't want to run. She didn't want to leave. She wanted to be around Ox. She liked everything about him. Especially his smell and his taste, and his warm body.

There. She had to translate that into music. She got her notebook out and started writing again. A recurring theme she couldn't control—frontward and backward, a retrograde—all Ox. No more fear of being gay. At least that was behind her. Ox and Ammahn. Were they the flip sides of the same coin? And the congregation, and Nehmi.

Having it on paper helped her to get hold of herself. Maybe she could control it. Maybe. Maybe. She would analyze her music like a critic, later.

It was dark when she got home.

CHAPTER TWENTY-FIVE

The shadows were long when Ammahn put foot to the wooden porch. He paused, slapping the dust out of his trousers with his notebook. Tomorrow, he would spend the day at the University. Saturdays, Sundays, and Mondays were his. The other days, he shared knowledge with students and faculty. He lived in the fields of fossils. They lived in the dust of books.

He had been in the lower corner looking for hidden traces of the dirk-toothed cat or whatever creatures were preserved in the crevices of the earth-brain buried in the dark memory, waiting to be recalled. He jotted another note in the book.

He stepped inside and greeted the calf on the wall.

"You've joined our mother, little one. I saw you hiding in the rock and the sword grass. In the mind of man, you're still a reality, but there are those who lie far beyond our recognition—in the mystery of the long past."

He lit a lamp to chase the dusk. He climbed the stairs to the second floor and lay on the mat.

"It's all right. Humanity will follow you into the midnight world. Good and evil look the same in the dark."

He thought of Oxford Christie and Nehmi. Fighting in the

dark over a lost congregation. Mrs. Christie had better watch out. Marriages don't survive at One Soul.

He had to prepare some material he had found for the seminar tomorrow. There wasn't much to be done. He had always lived with bones and fossils from all over the earth, studying the dead. Parent of the living. He would merely translate what the artifacts told him. But he would study the remains of the One Soul. He would study the developing lines of battle.

His fingers scratched through the gray hair covering his chest. His gaze carried him beyond the walls. Who had brought Christie here? Nehmi?

Pinned by the wings—butterflies in the earth.

He thought of the skull Nehmi had left, the vacated duplexes of a cat's mind. Nehmi had left it there for a reason.

Did evil dwell there with the same ease as with the human brain? Does a cat instinctively stalk its prey or does it dream and scheme to wreak disaster on other creatures? Is there a boundary between the instinct for survival and greed? Are any boundary lines possible around evil? Maybe Nehmi and Christie would demonstrate the answer. Nature is reluctant to give up its wisdom and exacts a price.

He thought of the calf hanging downstairs. "You've guarded my little house for fifteen years. I would have taken you to California, but I knew I had to come back here."

It had been fifteen years. He remembered Petersen, strange in torment, eyes of pain, weak, but interesting. He hid his evil under the robe of the church; sanctimonious, self-righteous, like Nehmi. Too God-like, but the God-like, in the end, are dead fireflies in the shale. The human being was incredibly varied within the same structure. Fascinating—the archaeology of the human capacity for evil.

The efforts to conceal had served to fascinate more. It had been a hard day digging, and hot. He closed his eyes and relaxed. He could feel the earth turning. It would turn regardless of human foolishness. All creatures lived in the earth or on its cortex. They drew their food from it, their water. They scratched the surface of the rotating brain and were at last stored in its memory.

Lot of silliness existed in their rules, their conventions. There's an unlimited human capacity for rationalizing evil. Is evil the failure to do good? Or is good the failure to do evil?

How does the third layer of the brain compromise between the struggle to survive and evil? What would the remains reveal? They wouldn't be in the graveyard. He would search for them where roots descend like ganglia into the fossil cells of memory.

Nehmi splitting the skull was a pitiable effort to taunt anger. He had no respect for creatures of the earth. Nehmi was the enemy. He had to be circumvented. He would try to keep him from Christie and the new members. Oxford Christie didn't know what he was up against.

He would set up an appointment with him—see how much he knew, or suspected—size up what he could do about it. Nehmi had a strong influence, more like a controlling grip on the congregation. Would that change with the new minister?

Ammahn found it relaxing to sit in the excavation under the house. He set a fire at the entrance to the cave. Some kind of draft sucked the smoke underground and he wondered where it was going. The intricate network of connecting caves and crevices led to hidden areas; areas human eyes had never seen.

Once, walking through the surrounding woods, he thought he could smell the smoke. Maybe it was seeping up through the root system of trees reaching far down into the earth.

Once, he had crawled down the cave for over a mile to a point

THE HIDDEN CONGREGATION

where it branched off into smaller caves. He had shined a light into three of them. He was sure he had seen eyes reflecting back in the last one. He had felt he was in "their" territory and had crawled back all the way to his own place.

He respected them. He knew they had come up when he wasn't there—tracks, small tracks.

Respect—when did creatures develop respect in the ladder of evolution? Maybe it was fear.

CHAPTER TWENTY-SIX

Ox pushed the rice around on his plate. He had decided not to tell Barbara about the meeting tomorrow night, but now, he was having second thoughts. He would have to bring her in on it sooner or later, but how could he tell her about Cynthia?

"What's the matter, Babe? Something bothering you? Don't like my cooking? Got indigestion?"

"I got ingestion, too," said Billy.

Martha looked at Billy, indignantly.

"We have a meeting tomorrow night I have to tell you about," Ox said. There. The decision was made. But how far to go? How much to tell her? How could he not tell her?

"So what's the big deal? Have they all decided on their funeral arrangements?"

"What's a funeral?" Billy demanded.

"Silly, a funeral is for planting things. That's why they carry all those flowers. And they have a big party in a special parlor," Martha said.

"I think it would be better if I told you about it after dinner," Ox murmured.

"Must be bugging you. Getting a handle on their problem? Things coming down to the wire?"

THE HIDDEN CONGREGATION

"Yes, it's bugging me, and yes, I'm getting a handle on their problem, and yes, it's coming down to the wire."

Barbara nodded. "Okay, children, you've finished up well enough. Time to go upstairs and get into your PJs then come back down for ice cream and a story. Only you don't get the ice cream unless you move slow, very slow. Don't be back down here for thirty minutes. Martha, you get to be the timer. Here's my watch."

Part way up the steps, Billy asked Martha, "Why do we have to move slow?"

"That's what people do at funerals. Play like we are carrying flowers."

Barbara gathered up the dishes and clattered them into the sink. "Okay, Babe. What's bothering you?"

"You mind if we go sit in the living room? I want your undivided attention."

"My, this does sound serious."

"It's more serious than you can imagine."

In the living room, she waited for him to start.

"I have found out what happened. At least, I have found out a part of what happened. The purpose of the meeting is to discuss it and get the whole story. There's still a lot I don't know, and I don't know if they'll tell me everything. Only those who were involved have been invited. It's at Hilda's house." Ox fidgeted while Barbara waited.

"First of all, I've got to tell you that I have not been truthful with you about certain matters, which I will get to. You know that unfinished part of the basement off the nursery?"

"Yeah."

"There's something very strange going on in there." He stopped. "This is going to sound totally bizarre. I don't know where to start."

"Start with the part about telling me the truth."

"No. I've got to build up to that."

"This is sounding worse and worse."

"It gets worse and worse, and I don't even know the worst."

"Well, get on with it already."

"When Petersen first came to this church, there may have been a member of the congregation who somehow had a hand in messing up the minds of members of the congregation. As corny as it sounds, I think it may have had to do with the struggle between good and evil."

"You're right. It sounds corny, but go on."

"You haven't heard anything yet. I'll condense it. Petersen and Angel, for one reason or another, were in that unfinished section."

"The dirt basement?"

"The dirt basement. The air in there became something of a mental toxin or stimulus, or both. It was a combination of the dust and a special candle wax. At any rate, the best way I can describe it was that the combination became some kind of aphrodisiac."

"Oh, wow. You're going to tell me they did it, in there? And they blamed it on the dust and some candles?"

"Listen until you hear the whole story before you make conclusions."

"Oh, right. I can't wait 'til you get to the totally bizarre part."

Ox shook his head, searching for a way to start again. Barbara watched him and became quiet.

"They didn't just have an affair. They had an orgy that lasted for hours. They lost track of time. If I remember correctly, she told me it was in the neighborhood of four hours."

"She told you? Angel?"

"Yes."

THE HIDDEN CONGREGATION

"Well!"

"Petersen was married, and he and his wife were devoted to each other. As time went on, others got caught up in it. Apparently, in one way or another, they all got caught. I still don't know the whole story, but I can't think of a better word to describe it than trapped. They all did the same thing. There in that dusty room, they became initiated to the evil that might have been plotted by someone. It might have been a man who has recently come back to the church."

"Ammahn Laval?

"Maybe. I don't know yet how he did it. Or if. But everyone says it was him, somehow. For all I know, he's the devil's messenger. Apparently, he planted the candles there." The hardest part was coming. "I ask you to have a willing suspension of disbelief. It's necessary if I'm to go on with this."

"Okay. I'm suspended. Go on."

"I know this because I went into the dirt basement, breathed the candles and the dust and almost succumbed to the trap which I'm convinced someone set for me."

"You and Angel? Please. I would have thought she was all used up."

"No. Not me and Angel."

She waited.

"Me and Cynthia."

"Oh, my God." She stood up. "Why didn't I guess it?"

"You'll note I said 'almost succumbed.'"

"What about her?"

"She went through the same thing I did. We forced ourselves out through sheer willpower in spite of the drugged air. I know what it felt like and I can now understand what happened to the whole congregation. And they now know that I understand and so they're willing to discuss it. They know I'm not going to pass judgment on them because unless you have experienced it, you can't believe it. If Angel had told me without my going through it, I wouldn't have believed it. I would have passed judgment. She was a minister groupie and wanted to get into his pants, or he was a lecher and wanted to get into hers, or both. But it happened to all of them, and you know some of them. Think of Elmer. Do you think he was ever a lecher?"

While he rattled on, Barbara had settled down. She watched him and sat as though stunned, but the shock seemed to have subsided. She was thinking it through. He stopped and for a few moments, there was silence.

"How close did you two come to doing it?"

"Before we walked in there, there was no thought or inclination in either of our minds to do such a thing. While we were in there, neither of us could think of anything else. We were both totally consumed with passion and animal lust. When we came out, it stopped like a switch had been turned off."

Barbara was silent.

"I didn't tell you about it before because I didn't understand what had happened. I thought maybe I had become a lecher. I felt I had violated your trust. I felt I had violated Cynthia's trust. I felt I had violated my ministry and the faith of the entire congregation. I couldn't talk about it. Although we didn't do it, we both wanted to."

"This is such a crazy story, I'm beginning to believe it. It's not the kind of thing you could make up. Besides, you've always been a lousy liar."

"Let me give you some of the gory details. We went in there on Sunday afternoon. We had been talking about the music committee and I gave her a tour of the church. The door to the dirt basement was supposed to be locked. It wasn't, and since I hadn't been in there, I went in. She followed. I discovered an old

THE HIDDEN CONGREGATION

file cabinet full of candles, black ones. I lit one so we could see better, then it happened. We didn't even touch each other, but the feeling was so strong we both got out as quick as we could. It worried me so much that on Monday morning, I went back in there with a flashlight and looked around. Nothing happened. I knew I didn't have the hots for Cynthia. I couldn't explain it, but felt confident that whatever it was, it was gone."

"Okay, I believe you."

"Wait. There's more. Cynthia had set up a counseling meeting with me on Monday afternoon. After the session, we discussed the feelings, acknowledging that it had happened to us both. She was worried she might have become promiscuous. I told her I had gone back in and I was convinced there had been some influence, but that whatever it was, it was either gone or I was stronger than it. She felt the need to prove herself against it also and wanted to go back in. So I went down with her with a flashlight. We went in. We walked and crept in as far as the low ceiling would let us, and suddenly were overcome by the same feelings. This time we not only touched each other, we grabbed each other and rolled around in the dirt."

"So that's the pipe you were investigating when you got your suit so dirty."

"This time, we literally dragged ourselves out. And once again, the influence subsided. Although, I have to admit, it wasn't like turning it off all of a sudden as it had been the first time. It still lingered after we came out. The influence was greater. I'm worried about any third encounters. At any rate, I went back in to get my flashlight and her shoes. Then I discovered it."

"What?"

"Someone lit a candle, apparently with a short wick so the flame wasn't high enough for us to notice when we went in, but the fumes were there."

"Was it burned down? Had you left it there from the night before?"

"No, I distinctly remember putting the candle back in the drawer and slamming it shut. Someone else put that candle there and left it burning. It was deliberate. And that's not all. After she left, I went back down there again, and the door was locked. Someone had locked it within minutes after we came out. We were not the only ones in the church."

In the silence, they could hear Martha. "No, Billy. It's not time yet. Move slow. We have ten more minutes."

"Any of my friends would tell me I'm a fool, but I know you are telling me the truth. The question is, how do you feel about Cynthia, now?"

"Confused. There's a tossed salad of feelings. I've fought off the sexual desire by analyzing it to death. It worked. Now I'm worried about her going through the same process or not going through the same process. She's a nice person. She came to me for help, and I think I might have messed her up even more."

"Look, Babe, if what you told me is true, you didn't mess her up. Ammahn or someone else did."

"True, but I was the instrument."

"Maybe you're a stronger instrument than whoever it was counted on. You got out of there twice."

"Angel said the others didn't get out even once. That's why she feels there's some hope."

"This has been a lot for me to digest. Is Cynthia going to be there tomorrow night?"

"I hope so. I've not discussed it with her yet. I need to. She might just decide to walk away from it all. I wouldn't blame her. It might be the easy solution for her."

"She might be even more reluctant when she hears that I'm going to be there."

THE HIDDEN CONGREGATION

"I hadn't counted on that."

"Well, think about it. I'm involved. Someone tried to destroy my marriage and I'm going to get the son of a bitch."

Ox pondered the meeting between Cynthia and Barbara. Barbara could handle it. He wasn't sure about Cynthia. "Yeah, you're right. You should be there. You are among the initiated."

"Damn right."

"I need to go to see Cynthia to let her know the purpose of the meeting. She's entitled. She shouldn't be taken by surprise."

"I've got a better idea. You stay home and give the kids their ice cream and story. I'll go see Cynthia. I've something in common with her. Ammahn, or whoever, tried to screw us both."

CHAPTER TWENTY-SEVEN

Cynthia stopped playing to pick up the phone. Maybe it was Mom or Dad.

"This is Barbara Christie. I need to talk to you about a very important church matter, and I need to talk to you now. Can I come and see you for a few minutes?"

Cynthia held her breath. She felt her hand squeezing the phone. "Why, yes, of course."

She should have asked what it was about. What could it be? It could only be about her and Ox. Maybe she could call her back and tell her no. She wished she had moved, left, gone somewhere else. She stood, staring at the door. *Oh, my God.* What could she say to her?

She sat as though paralyzed. After a while, she went downstairs and waited. When the doorbell rang, she opened the door.

"Hi, Cynthia. Thanks for agreeing to see me on such short notice," Barbara said.

"Oh. Well, of course."

Part way up the first flight, Barbara said, "You and I need to do some planning." She put her arm around Cynthia's shoulder and squeezed. "I know you've been through some kind of hell. We'll talk about it upstairs."

THE HIDDEN CONGREGATION

Cynthia's throat grew so tight it was painful. She blinked back tears. She leaned against Barbara and held her head bowed as they walked the rest of the way up. Inside the apartment, Barbara steered Cynthia to the couch. They sat facing each other. Cynthia couldn't speak. Her hands shook.

"Someone set you and Ox up. You don't know it, but that's what he did to the entire congregation years ago. Only they didn't escape like you and Ox."

"The entire congregation?" Cynthia couldn't keep the tears back. She felt as though something tight round her chest had been removed. "How? I couldn't understand what happened. The entire congregation? All of them? You mean in the dirt—in the dirt . . ."

"Angel told Ox the whole story today. She and Dr. Petersen were set up in that same basement and had an orgy. They were in there four hours. They were the first. Then the entire congregation, except Mr. Nehmi, got trapped. It's some kind of aphrodisiac. You and Ox survived it."

Cynthia felt as though she was in a whirlpool. She covered her eyes and leaned forward. "You mean, maybe I'm not immoral after all?"

Barbara held her in her arms.

"It's okay. When you get a grip on yourself, we've got to talk about what we're going to do to get the bastard or bastards. No one's going to get away with it. If it had succeeded, it would have ruined my marriage. My kids would be without a father. Ox would have lost his pulpit and probably his mind. And you would spend the rest of your life thinking you were some kind of whore."

"Oh, my God."

"Thing is, that man will try again. He's probably gloating right now thinking he's got the two of you in the palm of his hand."

"What can we do?" Cynthia let out a long breath. "Oh, thank God you came." She wrapped her arms around Barbara's neck. "I've been going out of my mind."

Barbara gripped her shoulders and held her eye to eye. "I don't know what we can do, but I know we can stop him if we all work together. Ox thinks it could be the devil. I'm more inclined to think it's just an evil and vicious person."

Cynthia cried lightly. "I'm so grateful to you for coming to me. I wasn't trying to be promiscuous. I didn't have designs on Ox."

Barbara hugged her tight. "I know that. Now you've got to know that. And I know you have doubts about yourself. Think of the congregation. All those people you see, the old ones, succumbed. You are not alone, except you and Ox came through it. Not without some scars, but you came through it."

Cynthia got up for a tissue. She wiped her eyes and her nose. "I didn't expect you to be this understanding. I thought you would be angry, that you would accuse me of trying to wreck your home."

"That was my first reaction, but I know my husband and I realized what had happened. He spelled it out for me. I know he's right."

Cynthia sat beside Barbara again. She started to speak then hesitated. "I would be lying to you if I said I didn't feel an attraction for him now."

Barbara said nothing.

"But I'm working him out of my feelings. At least in any sexual way. I've been working on it."

"Yes, I know. Ox has been doing the same thing. And what you are going through is nothing compared to what the congregation is going through. We don't know the whole story, just the beginning. Tomorrow night, now that they are not alone, now

THE HIDDEN CONGREGATION

that you, Ox and I know, we might be able to get the whole story then do something about it."

"That's the meeting tomorrow night?"

"Yes. Angel confessed when she found out about you and Ox's close call."

Cynthia covered her face. "Oh, I don't know if I can face them and admit what happened."

"Sure you can. They've all been through much worse. They'll look on you as having more strength than they did. You and Ox will give them hope."

"Ox is the one who had the strength. I'll tell them. He pulled me out. Dragged me. I didn't want to leave."

"You didn't stop him from leaving. You didn't rip his clothes off. Don't underestimate yourself. Will you participate tomorrow night?"

Cynthia thought of facing that room full of people. She didn't know them that well, not even Hilda.

"We need you. Will you do it? Will you help us?"

Cynthia thought of Hilda being caught up in the horrible net. The poor soul. Poor sweet soul.

"How can I say no?"

CHAPTER TWENTY-EIGHT

The entire group was finally settled in a semicircle in Hilda's huge old living room. Ox stood and tried to conceal his nervousness. Elmer was not his usual patient self. He looked belligerent. It was obvious he thought this was another attempt by Ox to pry out information. For the most part, they sat as though waiting for some unwelcome announcement regarding a church matter.

"Are we going to get a sermon?" asked Elmer.

"This is not a sermon, and it's not rehearsed. I think the best thing I can do is to simply state a few facts and events."

The room was quiet and Ox wondered what music Cynthia was hearing at the moment. She looked pale and anxious.

"This past Sunday afternoon, Cynthia and I walked into the dirt basement at the church."

The same expression of alarm came over all the faces at once as though by the flip of a switch.

"We lit a candle, a black one, so we could better see."

"My Lord," said Mary Jane.

"We left there a short time later, because we knew better. Neither of us wanted to leave. If I were talking to anyone else, I would have to explain that."

THE HIDDEN CONGREGATION

No one said anything. It was as though the words were penetrating, sinking into the skin.

Cynthia stared at her feet.

Finally, Joe cleared his throat. "How long were you in there?"

"How long would you say, Cynthia? Ten minutes?"

"I don't know. I lost track of time."

"Ten minutes? Nothing happened?" asked Elmer.

"After we came out, we were worried about our feelings. We couldn't explain them. On Monday afternoon, we went back in, really to prove to ourselves that there was nothing wrong with us and that nothing would happen."

Mary Jane put both hands to her mouth.

"We were wrong."

"Dear God, not again."

"Shut up, Mary Jane," said Elmer.

"Go on," said Joe. "What happened?"

"Like two animals, we rolled around in the dust together, but we had the willpower to drag ourselves out into the nursery."

"You didn't . . ." Joe waved his hand in a circle.

"We didn't copulate like animals. But it's what we wanted to do."

Cynthia stood up. "I would have. I wanted to. Ox dragged us both out. I have never felt like that in my life." Her voice trembled, but she said it factually as though she were over the shame. Ox watched all the faces. They were digesting the news.

"I went back in to get her shoes and my flashlight and discovered someone had left a lit candle in there. The fumes and the dust were there waiting for us when we went in."

After a silence, Elmer said, "I have to admit, this does sound bad."

"Cynthia left, I went to my study. Then I decided I had to investigate and went back down. The door was locked."

This news sunk in with an impact.

"I don't know who's in back of this, but it has to be the same person who engineered it before. Angel, I didn't warn you I would call on you, but do you have something to say?"

Angel hunched over in her chair. "I knew, when I came in on Tuesday . . ."

"Angel, we can't hear you," said Elmer. "Stand up."

She did and started over. "On Tuesday morning, I smelled the odor when I opened the door from the courtyard. Then I found the dust on the carpet. I knew he had gotten Ox and Cynthia. She was there when I left Monday after work. I knew it had started again. I lost all hope. Then Ox came in and he asked about Ammahn Laval, then about . . ." Here she stopped, then resumed. "He asked about the pit in the dirt basement."

Elmer turned his head away as though to avoid seeing the pit.

"Then I knew. Ox was one of us and I told him all about Ethan and me. I also told him the rest of you had been caught up in it, too."

"Maybe you should have asked us about that first," said Elmer, but he no longer sounded sure of himself.

"Oh, Elmer, it's out," said Hilda. "He's one of us now. So is Cynthia. And I guess Barbara is too. Ox is her husband."

"Oh, my God," said Mary Jane. "I don't know if I can stand this."

"What can't you stand, Mary Jane?" asked Elmer.

"I had gotten over being ashamed."

"You don't have to be ashamed," said Ox. "You were tricked, trapped. You had no idea what he or it was doing. You thought it was your own idea. It wasn't."

"There's a lot more that you don't know, Ox," said Mary Jane. "After it got started, we kept going back to the dirt room. It went on and on. We knew what we were doing. Oh, I don't want to talk about it."

THE HIDDEN CONGREGATION

"All right everybody." Elmer stood up. "It's happening again. We've got to stop it. Ox, what you don't know is that it finally culminated in a number of deaths: my wife's, Mary Jane's husband, Hilda's sister's, everybody here, except Nehmi, lost someone. We've got to prevent this from happening all over again."

"Elmer, how did he kill them?"

Elmer bowed his head. "They were all . . . initiated, then . . ." He sat down, but then he stood back up. "I don't want to talk about it either, but now we have to, because it's obvious we have to do something about it." He sat back down then added, almost whispering, "My wife died because of me. There. I've said it. Cathy died because of me." He started crying. He bent forward and cried—shoulders shaking.

Mary Jane put her arm around him.

Ox realized they all were thinking the same kind of thought, blaming themselves. "Have you ever shared this kind of thought with each other?"

Hilda was crying. "No," she said. "It was . . ." she shook her head, "too horrible. The way they died."

Then it hit Ox. "The pit?"

He could tell by their expressions that it was.

"I think every one of you has got to realize you were under some strong influence. You were victims. What you were exposed to was powerful stuff. It carries over from the dirt basement. That makes it even more dangerous. And the poison could be planted somewhere else, too. We've got two things we have to do. We have to stop him. I keep saying 'him' because I don't know who it is, but I'm assuming it wasn't a woman. We all have to realize we're not to blame. We are victims."

Hosannah stood up. "I've got to tell someone. I've always blamed myself for Stuart's death in that horrible pit. I can only hope that wherever he is today, he knows I loved him." She fell back into her seat and the tears that were held back all those years suddenly erupted. Her shoulders shook. Her whole body shook as she wailed, "Stuart!"

"Ox," said Elmer, regaining control of himself. "I've been the one putting the brakes on talking to you about this. Now I guess I should be the one to speed up the telling. The sex was just the beginning. It broke down our inhibitions. It changed our whole set of values. Ultimately, we all participated in it. I can't think of any other way to describe it. We became a deviant society." He stopped to wipe his eyes. "There's just no other way to describe it. We all led two lives: one that was normal, the one upstairs; and the other, hidden away downstairs in the basement. Eventually, the hidden one became the normal one for us. I think we were all crazy. By our standards now, there's no question we were all crazy. Except the ones who died." He sat back down. "I'm sorry, Ox. I just can't talk about it anymore."

Joe stood up. "Ox, it was our fault. They were sacrifices. We needed the downstairs society to be the largest, not the minority. We needed it to be the majority. That's the bottom line. We are guilty."

"Joe," said Elmer. "I almost wish you were right. That would mean we were murderers and they could put us away and out of our misery. But we weren't fooling them. They all knew. They knew what was happening. Before Cathy drank the potion, she lifted her glass to me and said, 'Goodbye, Elmer.' She knew."

His eyes were wet. "They all knew." His voice cracked again as he almost lost control.

"I wish you were right," said Joe.

"I am right. Believe it. But it's no blessing. They wanted to die because of us."

"It's time," said Ox, "for us to lay some plans to rid ourselves of this threat and this guilt."

THE HIDDEN CONGREGATION

Nehmi stood up. "Tomorrow, let's you and me talk about what can be done. I agree the time has finally come." He moved toward the door. "Goodnight. You had a good meeting. Ox, I'll see you tomorrow."

When the outside door shut behind him, it served as a signal for the rest to leave. They looked at Ox in anticipation.

"I get the sense that everyone's kinda wrung out. This has been a valuable meeting." Ox looked at each of them in turn. "I want us to meet every Wednesday night from now until the threat is gone. This will be our planning meeting. The most important thing we can consider is our own future. Okay?"

"I volunteer this room for the meeting," said Hilda.

The meeting was over. Elmer shook Ox's hand. "Thank you." Then he wrapped his arms around him, laying his head on his shoulder for a full minute. "Thank you."

The rest filed by, each shaking his hand then hugging him. They all looked their same tired selves, but there was something different. There was a sense of relief, and maybe even a sense of hope. Then, everyone was gone except the four of them: him, Barbara, Hilda, and Cynthia. Ox felt a need to talk to Cynthia.

"Are you going to be all right?"

"Yes. Barbara helped, and this meeting helped. I'm okay. How about yourself?"

"I'm okay now, after considerable self-analysis and after realizing what had been done to us."

"Thank God you're here," said Hilda. "And thank God you're so strong." She wrapped her arms around him. "I need you."

Walking home, Barbara said, "Ox, I want to attend all the meetings. There are going to be times when they're really going to amount to group therapy. They're going to need some facilitating."

"You ought to be there anyhow. Better line up a standing babysitter." They walked past the church.

"He, no doubt, has a key. We need to change the locks, but it's expensive."

"What the heck, Ox. Locks don't make any difference. He could probably pick any of them."

"Maybe you and I ought to go in there and smell the roses."

"Since when do we need any dust and candles to give us a jump start?"

Ox smiled. "I have to admit, I haven't a notion as to what to do. Not a clue. Maybe Mr. Nehmi will have some ideas. Apparently, he did something in the past. We need to do something." Ox looked back at the church. "To do anything openly means exposing these people to the world."

They walked on in silence.

"There have been a number of church burnings in Philadelphia. Maybe that's the answer." He remembered the newspaper article he had read the morning the bishop had called him. Was there some kind of divine providence at work?

"If you're going to burn the church, make sure we know who did it and that he is in it at the time."

"No, it might be like throwing a rabbit into the briar patch. He'd probably roast hot dogs."

"Ox." She grabbed his arm. "Are these people guilty of murder?"

"Right now, God knows."

They turned and looked back at the dark church. The structure was accentuated by the dim shadows of moonlight.

"For all I know, he's in there right now."

"Well, for all we know, Mr. Nehmi could be in there, too." Then it struck him. Could Nehmi have anything to do with it?

CHAPTER TWENTY-NINE

Elmer closed the door and leaned back against it. He stared at the empty hallway. The house was quiet. He was alone. He kept thinking she would come down the steps or walk in from the kitchen. But she wasn't going to appear. After all this time, she was still there somewhere. Only she wasn't. She never would be. He had killed her. Did she know why? Did she die thinking he hated her?

He had become an old man without her. He put his hands to his face and cried. "I'm sorry. I'm sorry. I took your life away from you." He played the scene over and over. *Goodbye, Elmer.* There were tears in her eyes. "Oh, God, bring her back." *She looked at me as if she adored me.*

He stumbled out to the breakfast nook where they used to eat together. He sat and leaned forward on the table. He didn't deserve her. He didn't deserve to forget. He looked around in the kitchen. She had been so loving. She deserved better.

He was a different person. His life was gone, too. Now, he just went through the paces. He lived out of cans or frozen food or ordered out. Alone, forever alone. He was getting thin, and being tall accentuated it. If she did somehow appear, she might not recognize him. But she would never change. He would never forget her—and those last moments.

CHAPTER THIRTY

Nehmi was waiting for Ox when he came in. They walked up the steps to the office. "I've been inspecting the building," said Nehmi. "Now that you're on to him, he'll become more devious. Watch for traps."

"How would he know we're on to him, and who do you think he is?"

"He knows you aren't stupid, Ox. He's put you through hell and knows you had the presence of mind to escape. And he knows you can spot a setup."

They sat in the study.

"Mr. Nehmi, who do you think he is?"

"I'm certain it is Ammahn Laval. I've been certain all along. You heard a good bit about what went on from the meeting. And you had been piecing things together anyhow, even before the events of Sunday and Monday."

"Mr. Nehmi, stop right there. I've got a burning question. Assuming it was Ammahn, did you know he was setting us up?"

"Of course."

"And you let him?"

"Had to. I had to know how strong you were. Had to know if you could defeat him."

THE HIDDEN CONGREGATION

"And if I hadn't been strong enough, would you have just let us go on?"

"If you weren't strong enough, I couldn't have stopped you anyhow. You would have done it later if not then. No, I wouldn't have stopped you. I would have felt sorry, but I would have just started looking for another way. I'm glad you were strong enough."

Ox digested that for a moment. "You got here about—what, twenty-five, thirty years ago? Was it basically over by then?"

"Actually, it was happening then, but I didn't know what was going on. I was just the caretaker. But the killings were over about fifteen years ago. Ammahn then only had to walk in and take over. My role became to stop him."

The two men sat facing each other for a few moments without talking. Nehmi broke the silence.

"Let me give you a thumbnail sketch of the entire situation. He had to get Petersen first. He was the key, the spiritual leader. He and Angel were the initial victims. He let it go that way for a few months. Petersen was a young man then and Angel a very young woman. He hadn't been married all that long. I won't go into what it did to their personal lives. You can imagine. Then he set up a second pair, and after a short time, a third. Then he engineered it so they came in on each other. In that room there were no inhibitions. An orgy resulted, and each week he added another pair, making sure one spouse of each marriage was omitted. Group orgies were common. After a while, they all participated in enticing others in.

"The network of lies about meetings at the church was incredible. In a strange way, the activity of the church increased because they had to be doing something legitimate with all that time at the church. No spouse can remain that trusting for such a length of time without some kind of tangible results."

"Any pregnancies?"

"No, strangely enough. In the beginning, there might have been a few abortions. With the extreme exertion involved and their advancing years, there could have been a few coronaries. But that didn't happen."

"Mr. Nehmi, why did you feel it was your responsibility to help? You weren't really close to them, were you?"

Nehmi seemed to be selecting his answer. "Actually, when I was a lot younger, I was a member of the youth group—for about a year. I knew some of them remotely. I felt a responsibility."

"I'm glad you took it so seriously."

"I haven't told you the worst part."

"The deaths?"

"Joe touched on it last night. They built a counterculture, complete with a counter religion that eventually included animal sacrifices in that pit. Ammahn provided an elixir for the animal to drink first. Then there was no pain. Not even when they started burning the animal. Ammahn was simply a facilitator in all this. He happened to have all the props they needed. He had a paint substance that included a flammable mixture. They painted the animals then burned them. Ammahn always got rid of the bones for them."

"Who provided the animals?"

"In the beginning, Ammahn, but as time went on, they all brought them in. Chickens, dogs, cats. Ammahn brought in a goat once, and that time, they cut out the organs first and passed them around, squeezing blood on themselves."

"And Lawrence Pregle?"

"Oh, yes. He's buried himself at playing the organ since then."

"And the spouses didn't know?"

"Some might have begun to have questions, but none suspected the magnitude of it. It had divided the congregation into an in-group and an outsider group. Only the outsiders didn't know that's what they were."

"This is just beyond belief. How could Ammahn or anyone have that much influence? Wait a minute. How did they explain being covered with dust? The spouses had to notice that."

"I don't know what Dr. Petersen and Angel came up with to explain it, but later, Dr. Petersen had tarps laid down. Then they expanded out into the nursery. It was night and only the participants were around. Eventually, it was the entire choir and various committees."

"This is bizarre. Wasn't there the chance someone would chance in?"

"They locked the nursery door—private committee meeting. There were mats, supposedly for children."

"I just can't imagine it. How can that kind of evil influence continue without detection?"

Nehmi leaned back in his chair and surveyed Ox. "It's easy to fool someone who trusts you."

That struck home to Ox. He had fooled Barbara because she trusted him.

Nehmi continued, "You certainly know that humans are far from perfect. Ammahn knew that and played to their weaknesses. He had that much influence because they let him."

Ox was finding it hard to believe Nehmi could have known all of what was happening. "When did the human sacrifices begin?"

"It wasn't long before they had a few sick members, terminally ill. They brought them in after an orgy, gave them the elixir, painted their bodies, tied them and stretched them taut over the pit and set them on fire."

"They murdered them?"

"Oh, they were terminally ill and in great pain. You talk about powerful compounds, that elixir was something. They were actually smiling until their faces were burned away. Oh, they were convinced it was the humane thing to do, and today, there are many who would agree with them. But not the next step."

"This is the part I'm really dreading to hear."

"For good reason. Their counterculture had been years in the making. It finally became established, and in their minds, nothing was more important. Nothing else mattered. It was so important, they decided it was time for their now true religion to be out of the closet. They knew their spouses would not approve, and their marriages, not too surprisingly, were no longer strong. They were as misled as severe drug addicts in complete denial. There was nothing to do but to get rid of their spouses. It was the only thing to do." Nehmi paused as though for dramatic effect. "One by one, they brought them in to a party or meeting or whatever, gave them the elixir, took them into the dirt basement, stripped them, painted them, and burned them."

"Over what period of time?"

"Less than a year."

"Didn't people wonder where they had gone?"

"There were a number of missing persons. There was talk about them running off to join a cult. In fact, one of Ammahn's friends from the choir was accused by the police of leading a cult and influencing the spouses to leave. He disappeared and more church members kept disappearing, and they were never able to trace him or them. It's still an open case, I'm sure. But the police never suspected what was going on in the dirt basement.

"They finally got rid of all the 'non-members,' but Ammahn threw them a final twist that set them back and, in a sense, placed them in their own permanent hell. The last one burned was Petersen's wife. Ammahn made sure that the elixir would give out at about the time she was burned."

THE HIDDEN CONGREGATION

"This is just unbelievable."

"Exactly. Her screams were horrible enough to jolt them to their senses, whatever remained, and they realized they were twisted and now had nothing. That ended the whole thing and they've been zombies ever since. The church became worthless, and that's what Ammahn wanted from the beginning. Petersen was a wreck. He threw himself into prayer and philosophizing. He was a lost soul groping for his way and had an appeal to other lost souls, which is what they all were at this point. The church was a great prize for Ammahn, a great accomplishment."

Nehmi took a deep breath and studied Ox.

"So you are saying they were sacrificed by the minority that wanted to be the majority. Aren't they all guilty of murder?"

"I've thought a lot about that, but it's not for me to say."

"It's hard to believe any of this, but if this really happened. I guess I could think of them as insane. But to do what you say they did, they would have to be totally insane."

"What happened to your mind when you were in that basement?"

"While I was in there, I just about lost it. But I got my senses back when I came out."

"Did you feel any influence at all when you came out?"

"The second time, noticeably. I had to really work at purging my mind."

"Multiply that by hundreds of exposures and the total loss of guilt. Powerful stuff. Extended beyond just sexual urges. Extended into all their actions."

"Well, I've no doubt they were victims. I felt like one and my exposure was minimal by comparison. I hate to even think about what could have happened. I could have lost my family, everything. I can't imagine doing such a thing to Barbara."

"I don't think Petersen could have either, in the beginning."

Ox envisioned the scene of Petersen's wife burning alive, stretched between four posts. "My God."

"Exactly."

"Mr. Nehmi, who provided the elixir and the potion, and any other supplies or props?"

"Petersen brought them all in, but Ammahn was the supplier"

"What did you do to drive him out?"

Nehmi smiled. "A little bit here, a little bit there. Did some things at his house. That was an invasion of his territory. Split the skull of a goat he had hanging on the wall. Dug up animals he had buried on his farm, an invasion of the ritual area. Split their skulls. Left them scattered around his place."

"He buried the animals there? What about the humans?"

"He was smart enough to dissolve those."

"That accounts for the missing graves in the graveyard."

"I continued to watch him here and intercept his attempts to drag others in. He invited some new visitors to his farm. I appeared also. I became his shadow."

"Some of the congregation have indicated to me they weren't sure Ammahn had engineered it. How could they not know and how can you be so sure?"

"First of all, when he trapped the first few, he was nowhere in sight. Petersen became his tool. He would make suggestions, give him the animals, provide him with the elixir, everything. It wasn't necessary for him to even be there. He controlled through Petersen. And after Betty Petersen's agonizing screams, they dwelled on their own spouse's deaths and imagined them doing the screaming. They realized their partners had died for nothing but their own twisted pleasure and they had thrown away their entire lives."

Angel came in with coffee. "I know you have a lot to discuss." She left quickly.

THE HIDDEN CONGREGATION

"There's really not that much more to discuss," said Nehmi. "We've covered the highlights of the history. You'll find out more as you interact with each of them in private or in future meetings."

"One more thing," said Ox. "I still don't know how you can be so certain about this. You didn't actually see Ammahn doing any of these things, did you?"

"I'll have to admit, it is all suspicion, but I just thought his behavior was strange. I'll try to think of some examples to give you later."

Ox had hoped for something more definite in response. Hilda and others suspected Ammahn, too.

"We've got to figure out what to do to stop him," said Ox.

"He knows he's got opposition. He knows you're not a weakling, but he also always overestimates his strength. And if you have any real weaknesses, he'll find them. I left him a little plaque on his house, a present to remind him that he was going to have a shadow while he was here. That won't be enough. With a new minister, he's got to reestablish himself. He'll be determined. You're his primary target."

"Okay, what do I do?"

"That's what you've got to figure out."

CHAPTER THIRTY-ONE

Martha and Billy skipped along ahead of Ox and Barbara on the way to church. It was going to be a hot day. There was a breeze, but the air was already so hot it smelled baked. The heat of the sidewalk came through his shoes. He could smell the grass drying—like St. Louis.

"Daddy, what's this?" Billy had found the discarded skin of a cicada.

"Silly, it's a June Bug."

Close enough. Billy jumped a few times then stared into the face of the bug.

"What are you doing?" asked Barbara.

"Looking at his insides."

"Silly-Billy, he doesn't have any insides. He took them with him," Martha proclaimed.

"No he didn't. He left a few."

Barbara spoke softly so the children wouldn't hear. "Reminds me of a few individuals who are just shells with a few insides."

Outside the church, they met Tom Fitzgerald, Chris Frankle, and their wives. Sarah Fitzgerald was carrying a squirming one-year-old in her arms. Chris was holding the hand of his three-year-old daughter, while Amanda Frankle adjusted the patient little girl's hair bow.

THE HIDDEN CONGREGATION

"We'll invade your nursery this morning," said Chris.

"And I'd be glad to help out," said Sarah.

"Just what I was hoping for," said Barbara.

As Ox headed for the chancel, he realized he just had the necessity reinforced for getting rid of Ammahn. He could see not only his own home destroyed, but the Frankle's and the Fitzgerald's, and others to follow as well. He had to come up with a plan.

Ox sat behind the pulpit waiting for Larry Pregle to finish his prelude. He looked at the congregation. There were a few more newcomers. Tom Fitzgerald and Amanda Frankle sat in the congregation. Chris and Sarah were obviously in the nursery with Barbara and the kids. Ammahn sat in the back row. Some of the old members turned to look at him, and Ox could sense a changed attitude, one of challenge. Was it too soon for that?

Elmer stood up and whispered something to Angel. He left the pew and ran out of the church. Ox scanned the congregation again and realized Hosannah wasn't there. Could that be what caused Elmer to rush out? He rose as the prelude ended.

"My sermon this morning has to do with personal good and evil. Martin Buber said the churches harbor hypocrites. Of course, we all have our darker side. There's nothing new about that. If we were perfect, we wouldn't need churches. We don't tell people about our goodness, because it sounds self-serving and because they would be more likely not to believe it coming from the personal source. We don't tell people about our evil for a different reason. They might believe it."

Ox kept his eyes focused on Ammahn, who sat quietly watching, but every now and then, he diverted his gaze from Ox to the members of the congregation.

"There is good and evil in each of us. We view God as all good, just as we view the devil as all bad. We are, in fact, a combination.

We aren't one or the other. We are both. Do we cast out the evil in ourselves? We know we can't. We're human. Each of us carries potential evil inside. Each of us who can analyze with any degree of objectivity struggles with it to prevent it from influencing our lives. But we must be realistic enough to recognize that we cannot be pure. We cannot be God. Not even the saints were free of evil. They had to grapple with their own demons also."

Ammahn seemed to be watching the members of the congregation. Ox continued to talk directly to him.

"Our mission is to understand our evil. Even more, we must draw strength from it. To understand is the beginning of influencing ourselves to avoid harm to ourselves and others."

Nehmi came in and sat at the opposite end of the back pew. Ammahn turned to look at him and Nehmi smiled at him. Ox restrained a laugh at Ammahn's obvious annoyance.

"We don't cast out evil; we embrace it; we draw it in; we absorb it; we make it ours; we stand straight in the knowledge of righteousness. Not our righteousness, for we do not own it. It is loaned to us for our use."

Ammahn gave a long look at Nehmi and stood to leave.

"We don't let it pull us down; we recognize our humanity, rely on our consciences, understand our evil, accept the good in ourselves and draw from it."

Ammahn stepped out through the doorway.

"We try to determine the reason for the evil and satisfy that need in some constructive way. Don't be ashamed of who you are. Simply learn what your drives are; strive to control them rather than to allow them to control you. You won't always be successful. It may be a gradual process. It may be a lifelong endeavor. Consider your evil as an opportunity for learning and development."

In the dining room after the sermon, Ox had just finished

THE HIDDEN CONGREGATION

talking to Tom Fitzgerald when Elmer came rushing back in. "Ox, it's Hosannah." He could hardly talk, not like Elmer at all.

"What's happened?"

"Hosannah. She . . ."

Ox put his arm over Elmer's shoulder as Angel came running over.

"Hosannah's gone. She committed suicide."

Angel covered her mouth.

Elmer headed for a chair. "I have to sit."

He fell into a chair and Angel started crying. Soon the whole congregation had formed a semicircle around him.

"Elmer, what happened?" Ox crouched beside them.

"She hung herself. She left a note."

"Why did she do it? What did the note say?"

"I called the rescue squad. The police took the note."

Nehmi pushed through carrying a cup of water. "Here, Elmer."

Hilda knelt beside him. Tears filled her eyes. "Oh, Elmer."

Elmer propped his elbows on his knees and held his head. "The note. The note."

"This is awful," said Ox. "Did she say why?"

"She said . . . she said, she was going to join Stuart if he would have her after what she had done to him. She said her soul might be destroyed, but she didn't care anymore."

"And the police took the note?" asked Ox.

Elmer seemed to realize the significance of that for the first time. "Oh." Then he remembered something else. "She left a will, dated Friday. She left everything to the church." Elmer stood and Ox stood with him. "Ox, she left everything to the church because she believed in you. I know she wouldn't have done it otherwise."

Joe nodded his head. "Makes absolute sense. You know what happened."

WILLIAM T. DELAMAR

Elmer had tears in his eyes. "I think we are going to fix things for the future in this church. I wish you had been here years ago. Things might have been different. Hosannah would still be alive."

"A lot of people might still be alive," said Joe.

Ten feet away, in back of the older members, Jessie May and Emmett stood listening.

"I hope I can meet your expectations, Elmer. If we all work together, maybe we can do it. But we can't be overconfident. We've got to recognize the power we're up against, whether it's Ammahn or someone else."

"Oh, it's Ammahn. Who else could it be? Where is he, by the way?"

"He left before I finished the sermon." But then, Ox saw him coming in the door. "He must have changed his mind. Here he comes."

Ammahn walked over to Tom Fitzgerald and Amanda Frankle, shook hands with them, and gave the appearance of welcoming them to the church. Then he moved on to the other new couple whom Ox hadn't met yet. As he did, Nehmi strode over and introduced himself, turned his back on Ammahn and ushered the couple over to Angel and Hilda. Ammahn stood in front of the portrait of Petersen as though studying him. He turned and left, passing Cynthia and Barbara as they came in.

Cynthia stood still and gave him a quizzical look as though she were trying to understand what went on in his head. Ox was surprised to see Barbara stare into Ammahn's face as though she were ready to hit him. She didn't move aside for him, and for a minute, it looked as though she were going to push him. Ammahn sidestepped her and moved rapidly on.

"You're looking pugnacious." Ox put his arm around her.

She pushed away. "You know what he just tried to do? I know

THE HIDDEN CONGREGATION

it was him. Chris Frankle and Sarah Fitzgerald walked into the dirt basement together. I pulled them out right away. No damage done."

"Let's hope not. What were they doing in there? Why did they go in?"

"Chris said someone told him that was where the treats were for the kids. He doesn't know everyone in the congregation, but from what he said, it had to be Ammahn. And there was the distinct odor of candles."

"Tomorrow," said Ox, "I'm going to get rid of all the candles. I'm going in down there to pull them out of both cabinets, tie them together, take them out to the courtyard, and light them out there. We'll have a noonday mass in the open air. We'll get rid of the candles. Then we are going to padlock the dirt basement. Off limits until we think of something to do with it. It can't stay the same."

Elmer nodded. "I'll come and watch."

"So will I," said Barbara. "You should, too, Cynthia."

"No, I don't want to ever smell those candles again."

"They'll be harmless in the open air," said Barbara.

"I don't want the slightest reminder."

"Cynthia, it would be a mistake to try to blot this out. Analyze it and think it through, but don't forget it."

"Don't worry. I'm not likely to forget. No. I'll be here, though, at four, if we're still scheduled. I'll feel safer knowing they're gone. No more booby traps. Maybe you ought to sprinkle some holy water around, just in case."

Ox worried about the idea of other booby traps—holy water versus fire.

Elmer stood beside Ox. "I don't think there's one of us who hasn't thought of doing what Hosannah did. Maybe we ought to make her house the parish house."

Ox thought about it for a moment. "That would be nice, but I think the church could use the money if we sold it and everything in it." *Hell of a way to build the finances*, he thought.

That night, Ox pondered over what to do. Throw Ammahn out? Why not? Just tell him to leave. But he knew that so far there was no real proof he was the instigator. Everyone thought he was guilty, but no one had actually seen him do anything. How could he confront him without any real evidence?

Besides, to incriminate Ammahn would be to incriminate the entire congregation. And Ammahn would know that. He could walk in any time he chose.

CHAPTER THIRTY-TWO

The morning light filtering through the stained-glass windows had the strange effect of projecting the images from the windows across the chancel rug. It looked as though the windows themselves were laying across the floor.

Ox wondered if he should call Elmer to see if he wanted to be on hand for pulling all the candles out of the basement. He decided against it—it was probably not a good idea. The dirt basement was a place to evoke painful memories. Maybe Nehmi? No, if he had wanted to, he would have volunteered. Nehmi . . . It was a strange formality. Always mister. Nobody called him by his first name. Of course, he was the caretaker, not one of the congregation—but still, those who had known him for a long time might have broken through the formality. Maybe he didn't want to get too close because of what they had done.

Ox had dressed in old dungarees and tennis shoes for crawling round in the dirt. He paused inside the nursery and looked at the door. The entire building was still. It would be an hour before Angel came in. So much had happened beyond that door. He envisioned the orgies, the ritualistic ceremonies, the human sacrifices, and the final chapter.

If Ammahn was, in fact, the instigator, he seemed vulnerable nonetheless. His annoyance with Nehmi's smile indicated at least one chink in the armor. But how to cope with him? He had, some sort of sorcery on call. Ox prayed for strength and more knowledge. He was beginning to think it was Ammahn, simply because everybody else did. Actually, he had to respect their viewpoint. If anyone would know, it would be them. Okay, so it was Ammahn. He felt relief with the acceptance.

He opened the door and turned on his flashlight. Now that he knew, images of past events seemed to crowd the space. He wouldn't want to be in this place of memories if he had been part of the caravan of disasters. The echo of that poor woman's burning screams must still be vibrating in some of the corners.

He opened the file drawer. It was empty—nothing there. Ammahn must have come in during the night and removed them. He slammed it shut and opened the other drawer. Empty. Not even a trace. Ox nodded. He should have known, should have anticipated. Of course. And he knew the cabinet in the excavated area would be empty, too. But he would have to check it anyhow. There was no choice.

Crawling through the dirt, he realized the dust was part of the initiation. You had to get a face full just to reach the pit. He crawled the last few yards. He dropped into the pit area. This was where the horrible ceremonies took place all those years ago. Now the pit was empty. No burning bodies stretched taut between posts. Only the oil from their bodies remained, etched and projected into the ethos and into the dust. He looked up at the ceiling. Scorch marks. He hadn't looked there before. He felt mesmerized. The marks seemed like the final exclamation to what had happened. He could see the flames that made them. He could hear the screams. And he could envision the horrified faces and the desperate face of Petersen.

THE HIDDEN CONGREGATION

He turned away from the pit and played his light on the file cabinet at the far end. Both drawers were open. Damn. Well, no surprise. So Ammahn was a step ahead. What would be his next move?

Ammahn had to be a demon of some sort, and he had to be stopped. He seemed to know what the next step would be. Ox played his light on the cabinet as he approached. He could see there was something in the top drawer. He focused the beam into the drawer. There was a covering of dried leaves. Aspen? Cautiously, he scraped the leaves aside with his flashlight.

Underneath, there was dried grass, matted and tangled into another layer. He lifted it out of the drawer and dropped it on the dirt floor. He stared at the next layer before it dawned on him what it was. Hundreds of dead moths. How did he manage that? Then he figured it out. They're attracted to light at night. Easy. He scooped them aside and discovered a dried snake skin, a long one folded crisscross into another layer. He lifted it out with one hand and discovered a snake head looking up at him. He dropped the skin and stepped back. The head didn't move. He couldn't see its body. There were a handful of cicada shells, a few dead butterflies, a split skull— the one Nehmi had left by the swing set? He moved closer. The head stayed the same. At the front of the drawer was a dead bird, a sparrow. He poked at the head with the flashlight. It fell over. Severed recently—not dried out.

There was something under all this, papers of some sort, or a booklet. He lifted it out and poured the whole collection onto the dirt. Holding the booklet, he continued to stare at the mess at his feet. Was there a message here? What was it all supposed to mean? Moths attracted by the light. The congregation attracted by the candles. Humans and moths.

He shined the light on the object in his hand. It was an old listing of names bound together on the left by string. It was alphabetical. He recognized some of the names: Mr. and Mrs. Anthony Bannister, Mr. and Mrs. Elmer Weiss, Miss Hilda Danziger, Mr. and Mrs. Stuart Lewis. It was an old church directory, the congregation before all the black magic. The names of the survivors and the dead—the murdered.

Ox pondered again over what to do. Technically, they were guilty of murder. But Nehmi was right. They were all victims. If there was ever a justifiable case by reason for insanity, this was it. If he exposed them, it would destroy the church and they would be victims again. The courts would never believe their story. And they had never stopped being victims. No, he wasn't going to blow the whistle.

He pushed the drawer in carefully and looked into the second drawer. There, lying in the center of the drawer was a photograph. It was a picture of him and Barbara. *Damn him.* He turned off the light and stood there in the darkness, the only light now coming from the door at the far end into the nursery. *Damn him.* Clicking on the light, he knelt in front of the drawer and studied the picture, the sound of his heart thumping in the back of his head. They were standing on the street a few blocks down from the church. They were half turned around, looking back toward the church. Was it the day they saw the black limousine pull away from the building? Did Ammahn take the picture before he stepped out, or while he drove away? Had he been watching them all the time? Ox had the sense of being watched now in the dirt basement. He picked up the picture and began his return crawl through the dust.

He walked home to shower and change. Maybe he should spend more time at the house. Was Barbara in danger? For a moment, even the cost of incriminating the entire congregation to get rid of Ammahn seemed justifiable. But he couldn't do that. The church had to remain a sanctuary. Damn.

CHAPTER THIRTY-THREE

Ox filled Barbara in on the missing candles and the file cabinet content. "I tell you what. This man is a sicko."

"Barbara, I'm worried about you."

"Don't worry about me, Babe. Worry about him."

Angel's reaction was different. She looked around the office as though she was trying to find a place to hide. "I don't know what he's going to do next."

Ox called Elmer.

"Ox, I tell you, we've got our hands full. But when you get down to it, there's not much he can do to the rest of us. It's you I'm worried about."

"Me and Barbara and Cynthia and the Frankles and the Fitzgeralds and every new member who joins." Angel called those who had planned to attend the noon candle burning to tell them not to come. Ox could hear her lamenting the story to each of them.

She had seemed a little on the upside when she first came in, but now it was all downside again. He imagined the others were having similar responses—even Elmer, who seemed to vacillate between aggressive and fatalistic as though nothing could be done.

He stared out over the valley. What could be done? Nehmi could be Ammahn's shadow. He and the congregation, the older congregation, could hold him at arm's length and try to intervene with the new members. Ox could confront him and warn him, but he knew it would be an empty threat. What might he do to Barbara? Would he try to abduct her? Not his style. Ammahn would want her to compromise her integrity just as he and Cynthia had. He had the feeling that face-to-face, he could lose his effectiveness. Ammahn was a manipulator, a trapper—and what a trapper.

Ox spent most of the day working on a sermon. He knew from now on, he was going to have to constantly address the struggle between good and evil. And he knew it wouldn't be boring because there were so many variations. Not only that, this congregation had more experience than most in the forms and consequences of evil, and had also had the time to think about it—and think about it and think about it.

He found himself frequently staring out the window, trying to come up with a plan, any plan, to thwart the devil.

At four o'clock, Cynthia arrived.

"He removed all the candles?" She dropped into a chair and leaned her head back. "This has been a busy day, and I've not had too much time to dwell on what's going on. Actually, I was beginning to feel hopeful." She stared vacantly at the ceiling. "But he always seems to know what we're going to be doing. He's always a step ahead."

Ox sat facing her. "I'd suggest we not talk about Ammahn this evening." He didn't want her to know how worried he was. "What's really important right now is how you are feeling."

"I'm over my self-doubts. If nothing else, I can thank Ammahn for that. I'm sure he didn't know he was doing me a favor." Cynthia sat up straight in the chair and took a deep

THE HIDDEN CONGREGATION

breath. "This is the first time I've had a chance to relax all day." She smiled. "He did me another favor. I've got to know you better than I would have thought possible. And while that's something I have to work on to control, I'm glad we had the opportunity to use our will power. Well, actually, it was your will power. But I feel stronger as a result and I like knowing you on more than a casual basis." She rolled her eyes toward the ceiling. "Oh, boy. That probably doesn't make any sense. Anyhow, thanks to Ammahn, even if he is a monster."

Ox made no response for a moment. "We've lapsed back into talking about Ammahn. But for the record, I understand what you are saying, and I agree."

"Thanks. I was beginning to feel like a fool." Cynthia stood up and walked to the window. "I hadn't realized what a view you have from here. The late afternoon traffic is building up. I'm glad I'm not in it."

Ox waited.

After a bit, she turned and leaned back against the windowsill. "Intellectually, I've processed it. I feel confident I'm past it emotionally. Do you think it would bother Ammahn to think he had done someone some good?"

"Probably not. He would see it as temporary."

"You're probably right," said Cynthia, crossing the room and sitting back down. "But right now, in spite of everything, I'm feeling just a little bit better about myself than I have for several years."

"Well, that is something to be thankful for. Now it sounds as if I'm the one thanking Ammahn." Ox thought for a few minutes. Had they reached a point where she no longer needed any counseling from him?

She answered his unspoken question. "It's not Ammahn I should thank. If he had been successful, there wouldn't be anything to be thankful for. It's you I should thank. And I know that if I have any problem, you'll be there for me."

Ox nodded. Still, he wasn't sure.

Cynthia leaned forward. "Ox, I sound like I'm in love with you. And I may be. I feel addicted to you. I may be a recovering Oxaholic for the rest of my life."

Ox remembered his making a similar analogy. A dirt basement junkie. "What have you done to work your way out of it?"

"Composing."

"Composing?"

"I've composed a concerto of The Church of the One Soul."

"That sounds ambitious."

"Actually, it's therapy, but I like what's coming out." She smirked. "If it turns out to be a hit, I can thank Ammahn again."

"I'm beginning to think Ammahn is just a sweetheart. A lovable old rattlesnake."

"Seriously, what are we going to do?"

"All I've got is some bits and pieces of a plan. It's all long range like the Wednesday night group. Not an offensive move to get rid of him. Just defense. I just don't know."

"I want to play my concerto in the church."

Ox was surprised. Maybe it wasn't a bad idea. Again, just a defensive measure, something to stir the congregation and maybe Ammahn. "When can you be ready?"

"In a couple of weeks. I'm still working on a part of it."

"I like the idea."

Angel slammed open the door. "Ox, oh, my Lord. Candles! Candles on the altar."

Ox jumped up and followed Angel down the steps. Cynthia followed as they all ran into the sanctuary. Angel pointed to the altar. There were two black candles about a foot apart on the altar, their flames bright in the dim light.

THE HIDDEN CONGREGATION

"I went up to put them out, but there's . . . there's . . ." She hid her eyes with both hands. "I couldn't." She backed toward the doors.

"Cynthia, stay with Angel." Ox was afraid to get near the fumes with her. Already he could feel the effects. He walked toward the altar. Something in addition to the candles. What could be worse. He felt like he was defusing a bomb. Then he saw it. A color photograph lying on the altar between the two candles. "Oh, my God." A woman burning in the pit. Stretched between the poles. Mouth frozen open in a scream of agony. Eyes wide in pain and terror. Flames leaping out of her body. "Oh, my God." He knew who it was. He blew out the candles and two plumes of smoke rose upward. But they didn't smell like candles. They smelled like Cynthia. Sweet. Enticing. "Oh, my God." He had the presence of mind to grab the candles and the picture before running out of the sanctuary. Cynthia and Angel were standing in the doorway to the courtyard. They all three stepped outside.

Ox took a deep breath. He had to clear his senses.

"Ox, that didn't smell like candle wax to me. It smelled like you. Just so you know." She touched his arm and her hand felt warm, almost hot.

"I do know. And I know we still have a problem. A big one. It smelled like you, but he left us something else, too."

Angel was leaning against the wall. She seemed to have grown smaller.

"Angel, the photograph. Was that Petersen's wife?"

She nodded, unable to speak.

Cynthia looked over his shoulder then turned away. "Oh, how horrible."

Ox had to force himself to study it. He felt sick. He could imagine being there. No wonder the whole group had been crushed by it. A real monster did this.

CHAPTER THIRTY-FOUR

Ox watched the sad group filing into Hilda's living room for the second meeting. They had all arrived on time, but none had gotten there early. They came in as a group. He wondered who had coupled with whom during the orgies, but it didn't matter anymore. These were the survivors. They weren't couples anymore. Larry Pregle came this time at Angel's prodding.

Cynthia and Barbara sat together, and when Cynthia leaned her head on Barbara's shoulder, Barbara wrapped her arm around her. Ox could feel himself drawing strength from his wife. It was a good marriage. They supported each other. Ammahn wasn't going to destroy that.

Nehmi was the last to come in. He remained standing just inside the sliding doors. When Ox stood to begin the meeting, Nehmi stepped forward.

"Ox, I think I'd best go back over to the church, just to keep an eye on things. Especially when everyone else is over here. I thought I got a glimpse of him passing the church earlier. I don't like giving him free access."

"You sure you don't want to stay to contribute ideas to our plans, to our approach?"

"Not this time. I'm sure whatever you come up with, it'll be

THE HIDDEN CONGREGATION

the right thing." He slipped back through the doorway. Ox felt disappointed. He almost went after him to ask him to stay, but the group was now quiet, waiting for him to begin. He would talk to Nehmi later.

"Mr. Nehmi filled me in on some of the things that happened to you that we didn't discuss last Wednesday. I wouldn't believe it if I hadn't been through something of an initiation—Cynthia and I."

Cynthia leaned back against the couch. She looked exhausted.

Barbara spoke up. "Ox, does everyone know what happened to Chris Frankle and Sarah Fitzgerald on Sunday?"

"No. Not the dirt basement," said Joe.

"Apparently, he set them up, but Barbara pulled them out almost as soon as they got in there," said Ox.

Joe became agitated. "Did they smell the candles?"

"Yes," said Barbara. "But they were in there less than a minute."

Joe shook his head. "Doesn't matter. If they even got one whiff, it'll start working on them."

"He's right," said Elmer. "We all know once you're exposed, it keeps working on you." Ox noticed Cynthia nodding. "Yes," she said, quietly. She closed her eyes and bit her lip. "We've got to stop him," said Hilda. "He's going to get Cynthia and Ox and all the new people."

"Oh, Lord," said Angel. "But what can we do?"

"Let me ask a question of all of you," said Ox. "You are concerned about Cynthia and me, and the new members, but what about yourselves? Will smelling that mixture pull you back into his grip?"

"No, not ever," said Elmer. "The memory of Ingrid Petersen screaming and burning alive is all that odor brings to me or any of us who were there." His shoulders shuddered as he said it. "I'll never forget my Cathy burning and looking up at me."

"How can any of us forget," said Joe. "We don't count anymore. It's the new members he's after. He doesn't want the church resurrected."

"He knows he's already destroyed us," said Elmer. "There's nothing left of us. Just horrible memories."

"We've got to do something after what he did on Monday," said Angel.

"You mean removing all the candles from the basement?" said Elmer.

"Yes, and leaving two lit on the altar." It was the first time Ox had seen Angel angry.

"What?" said Joe. "I hadn't heard about that. What did you do with them?"

"Ox removed them."

"Oh my Lord," said Joe. "Did you breathe that stuff again?"

"Yes," said Ox. "It was pungent."

"And did it smell like Cynthia to you?" asked Elmer.

"Yes."

"Angel," said Joe, "you should have removed them. He can't hurt you anymore." Joe couldn't sit any more. He stood up and moved around.

"I couldn't. I . . . I just couldn't," Angel said.

"Why?" demanded Joe.

"It was the picture. I ran away. I just couldn't look at it."

"What picture?" asked Elmer.

Angel was silent.

Ox responded. "He left a photograph between the candles. A color photograph of Mrs. Petersen—stretched across the pit, burning."

"Oh my God. He even took pictures." Elmer seemed to grow limp and dissolve into the upholstered chair. "I don't know if I can fight this anymore."

THE HIDDEN CONGREGATION

"Oh, Elmer, you have to," said Mary. "None of us can fight if you don't."

Elmer just leaned back into the chair and said nothing. He started to say something then seemed to think better of it. Then almost under his breath, "He just seems to be everywhere."

"Yes," said Ox. "He does seem to be everywhere, but as Mr. Nehmi says, he overestimates his own strength and underestimates ours. We can beat him and you can regain your lives. You've been living through your own hell. It's time you took charge."

"Yes, but we can't without Elmer," said Mary. "We need Elmer."

Ox nodded. "Elmer's important to all of you, but you've all got to take a turn leading. If you always follow, you can be led by anyone. Think about it."

Without moving, Elmer said, "Ox is right." Then he leaned forward. "We've all got to do it." He stood up. "I'm just tired of being beaten so badly. But we all are. He made us do horrible things. Now we've got some hope and we've all got to pull the load." He seemed to develop a second wind. "I say we declare war on him."

"What can we do?" asked Hilda. "I'm ready." She shook her fist, and for the first time, Joe and Elmer laughed. The tone in the room changed.

"I'll tell you one thing we can do," said Barbara. She stood up. "Let's treat him like he's dirt. Don't just ignore him. Confront him. Let him know we are the enemy. Make him unwelcome." She sat down.

"That's a start," said Ox. "We can all be aggressive. We have our own private war with him."

"That's all right for us," said Joe. "But what about the Frankles and the Fitzgeralds, and other new folk? How do we convey this to them without telling them why?"

"The answer is, we don't," said Elmer. "We lead interference and protect them."

"Right," said Barbara. "Don't let him be alone with anyone."

"Whether new or old," added Joe.

Ox waited a few moments to see if anyone else was going to add anything. "Larry? Have you got any ideas?"

Cynthia stood up. "I . . . I just have to leave. I'll try to be back." She crossed the room to the door. "Please excuse me."

No one talked and Cynthia could be heard going up the steps. Ox exchanged glances with Barbara who then got up also.

"I'll be right back," she said. And she left to follow Cynthia upstairs.

"Larry, were you going to say something?"

Elmer interrupted. "That girl needs protection. She's fragile, a pawn to get at you, Ox. You're his main target now."

"That's what Nehmi said, too. And there's no denying she's suffering right now. Larry?"

"Well, I don't know that I've got much to add. I just play music and mind my own business."

"That's the problem, Larry," said Hilda. "You've withdrawn. You just act like nothing ever happened. The rest of us are living in hell, as Ox says, and you're just oblivious to it all."

"That's not true. The rest of you are living in hell, but I'm trying not to."

Ox watched the others as they sat looking at Larry. There was crying coming from the steps. Everyone turned toward the door. Barbara came in with Cynthia sobbing on her shoulder. "Some of you go up to the third floor and get those candles out of her bedroom."

"Oh, my God." It seemed as though everyone said it at the same time. Joe was the first to get up.

"I'll get them."

THE HIDDEN CONGREGATION

"I'll go with you," said Elmer.

The two men ran up the steps.

Angel ran out into the hall and called after them. "Open the windows and let in some air." Cynthia sat on the couch between Barbara and Hilda, both of whom put their arms around her. Hilda stroked Cynthia's hair like she was a child. "I have a double bed, and this young lady is going to sleep with me tonight."

Ox knew the meeting was essentially over. He also knew he couldn't go over to help at that moment. He knew all too well what Cynthia was feeling. Best if he stayed away for the time being. Barbara was the best medicine.

He talked with some of the members he had not yet visited and who hadn't participated in the discussions. He set up times to see two of them, Sam Cheek and Patricia Stallings, later in the week.

Joe and Elmer came back carrying two black candles.

"They were sitting in her bedroom, but the whole apartment is filled with the smell," said Elmer.

"We opened the windows and shut the door to keep it from the rest of the house," added Joe.

"You have back stairs, haven't you Hilda?" asked Elmer.

She nodded.

"Nervy devil," said Joe. "While we were talking."

"Well," said Elmer. "We know what we are dealing with."

On the short drive home, Barbara told Ox, "She was just standing in the middle of the living room crying. She looked totally defeated. The place was reeking with fumes and she was just standing there breathing it. I don't know, Babe. You've got a problem on your hands."

The war had just begun, and it was a personal war.

CHAPTER THIRTY-FIVE

Cynthia was too tired to stay awake, but her fantasies kept intruding, rampaging through her mind, crashing through her sleep. Just as the half dreams gained control of her will, a gentle hand would squeeze her shoulder and bring her back to Hilda's bedroom, to the real world, the solid world.

She imagined arpeggios of leaves fluttering across a moonlit path through the woods of her childhood. She drew strength from the music that came from her soul, only to suffer another invasion of frantic lust; then the gentle hand once again bringing her stability.

In spite of the symphony of conflict her night had become, she awakened in the half-light of morning, her favorite time for renewing her own spirit and creativity. She lay in bed with her eyes closed and played the Concerto of the Church of the One Soul with the notes rising and falling. The soft spring air of her memory swept across the James River and carried the voices of her mother and father more like violin tones than words.

She quietly arose before six and found the clothes Hilda had retrieved from her room. They were airing in front of a fan. She sniffed cautiously, then showered and dressed. She was grateful and felt Hilda and the others had saved her. Now she had her

THE HIDDEN CONGREGATION

strength back. She was Ammahn's target. She had been defeated, but now she was resurrected.

The church members had declared war. They were going to be aggressive. Could she be aggressive? Not in a belligerent way. She couldn't. She couldn't hate enough to do it. How could she make him a target without hate?

She knew—the concerto. She would call Ox and ask him if she could play it this Sunday. She would be ready.

CHAPTER THIRTY-SIX

As Ammahn's limousine entered the farm, he sensed something was different. He emerged from the heavy car, letting his feet feel the uneven earth as he slowly approached the old house, searching for what bothered him. Then he saw it above the door. A golden cross glistened at him, recently painted. There was blood on it.

He looked at it and shook his head—more of Nehmi's games. The man would have to be dealt with. He could either put up with it or take it down and ignore it. He chose to do the latter. He sat on the edge of the porch and thought about what he needed to do with Nehmi. He thought of the new minister, Christie, and wondered how he was doing. Had he been hooked yet? His wife looked like someone to avoid. And he had seen them with their two children. The man could deliver sermons and they seemed right on target. Petersen had been a confused old man. Nehmi had played the role of protector. He remembered Nehmi well.

After Petersen's wife disappeared, Nehmi became the care-taker of both the church and the remnants of the congrega-tion. That was the time California called. Ammahn was sorry to leave. He had wanted to take Nehmi on. The man was too perfect. And he had no doubt cast suspicion on him regarding

THE HIDDEN CONGREGATION

the things going on. He owed him for that. The church had an appeal in those days. It was strong, even famous. With Christie, that potential arose again—unless he succumbed to the same forces.

Nehmi. What to do about Nehmi?

CHAPTER THIRTY-SEVEN

In the half-sleep hours of the morning, Ox always experienced a free flow of thoughts and images. It was a time when ideas fell into perspective and pressing actions took shape, a time when, half awake, his dreams projected happenings from the past and placed them in the present. This morning was no different. The sizzling of candles with the sweeping sound of rising dust foreshadowed an emerging threat.

From dust thou art; to dust thou returneth.

He opened his eyes and stared at the ceiling in the half-light. Dust and candles. Had it really been the candles or was it his own lust? Maybe there was a reason for lust rhyming with dust.

From lust thou art; to lust thou returneth.

Our minds and spirits have the task of controlling and harnessing the body to carry us through life. He couldn't let the body control him. There was no telling where it would take him. Ammahn understood the vulnerabilities of the body and mind. He used his aphrodisiac knowledge to take advantage of it. He counted on the influence of the body to overpower the mind and spirit. Well, it wasn't going to work this time.

What was Ammahn's motive? Was he the devil? Was that a silly question? Did anyone believe in the devil? Was he human—a

THE HIDDEN CONGREGATION

warped human? He was good at getting through doors—doors to buildings, doors to humans. Hormones were keys and he was good at unlocking those.

Ox had to defeat him, to block him out. He had to be a fortress with all doors bolted.

He got out of bed. How could they defeat Ammahn? Ammahn was on a seek-and-destroy mission, and Ox was the main target, maybe through Cynthia. He was after the new members, too. Those new members had to be warned somehow. Ammahn didn't appear sinister to them. And Ox couldn't just tell them to watch out. Maybe he needed to goad, to provoke Ammahn into building a more negative image so he didn't look like Mr. Nice Guy to the unsuspecting. But how?

Ox dressed quickly and walked slowly to the church, listening to the cry of the cicadas sawing through their final summer ritual. Across the street from the church, there was a mimosa tree still filled with its delicate fairy blossoms. They looked unreal, fantasies. He stood staring at the tree. This whole mess seemed like a dream. Total evil in a dream world. An illusion. And he thought of the book on his shelf—*The Conquest of Illusion*—the one that had the note in it.

Angel hadn't come in yet. He opened the door cautiously and switched on the hall light. There were no smells other than the usual odor of still air.

In his study nothing seemed out of place, but he didn't feel comfortable without checking around. Angel's office seemed okay. He walked down through the sanctuary then the nursery, and the dirt basement. Nothing. How paranoid his actions would appear to others, but for a good reason. He was glad Nehmi would be in soon, and Angel.

On the way back, he paused to look at the portrait of Petersen. Maybe he ought to be back in the basement as a reminder to anyone not to go in there. Obviously, that was why he was there to start with. Just as he got back to the study, the phone rang.

"Ox. This is Cynthia. I'm ready to do the concert. I want to do it this Sunday."

She was so positive and sounded in such contrast to last night he would have said yes even if he hadn't liked the idea.

"If you're ready, I think it would be a great idea. But are you just pushing because of what happened last night?"

"Certainly. But I'm ready and I think it's time. If nothing else, it will help me get a grip on things."

"How much time do you need?"

"I think it will take about forty-five minutes."

"Good. That'll give us time for the offertory and a short homily by me. From what you've told me about your theme, I think my few words will tie in."

After Cynthia hung up, Ox felt reassured by her recovery. Ammahn hadn't gotten her yet.

Good Lord! If the bishop only knew what had gone on here. Maybe he did. And Ox realized if he did, it would be through Nehmi.

He wheeled his swivel chair over to the bookcase to retrieve *The Conquest of Illusion.* It wasn't there.

CHAPTER THIRTY-EIGHT

Ox gave a short homily on Sunday morning, then turned the program over to Cynthia. She stood in the center of the chancel with her violin. She closed her eyes and began to play her concerto, The Church of the One Soul.

She made the violin sing. It filled the sanctuary with sounds ranging from deep vibrating chords to sharp notes to shrill jabs. Ox remembered his first impression of the building from the outside: a castle, then a sanctuary, the high ceilings, the frescoes, the angels and bearded old men ready to throw thunderbolts from the arched ceiling.

Cynthia made the violin talk, sing, scream, and cry. At one point the chords seemed to roll and tumble. At another, they danced. Ox wondered if others saw the same scenes he associated with the music. They were all listening, leaning forward as though they might miss a note. Ammahn was sitting in the back in his usual spot. Nehmi had situated himself at the other end of the same pew, but both men were watching Cynthia. Ammahn seemed to be completely fascinated—Nehmi, totally surprised.

In the beginning, Cynthia was the center of attention, beautiful—even radiant—but soon it was the music, only the music.

It engulfed, danced, glided, soared, whispered and called. At one moment there was human trauma, heartbreaking and sad. At another: insanity, anger, hatefulness. Then lust. Then love and hope. Then fear and despair. It was as magic as moonlight after a storm.

Ox looked at Ammahn and was surprised that he seemed so absorbed by the music. He had expected more of a reaction. Was he fixating on Cynthia? Even more surprising was Nehmi. He seemed to be astonished.

Ox knew when the music hit the dirt basement. It became sinister, mean. The screaming violin jolted the entire congregation and Angel covered her mouth. Elmer almost stood up. Angel leaned forward, placing her head on the back of the pew in front of her. This music was more than a concert. It was an indictment.

Silence fell for a moment, then sounds of war and struggle. And then victory. Finally, the music swept into slow arpeggios with a sense of peace. Ox was surprised to see tears on Cynthia's face.

She opened her eyes and held the violin by her side. She smiled at Ox and stepped down to the first pew and sat.

Ox stood. "What you have just heard was an ending and a beginning. Cynthia has captured the essence of the Church of the One Soul and its future."

At the coffee hour, Elmer wrapped his arms around Cynthia. "You are taking care of us and we will take care of you. You have an amazing talent. We are lucky to have you with us."

"Nobody is going to hurt you," said Hilda.

Ammahn approached her. "Miss Neal, you are destined for greatness."

Elmer pushed in front of him. "Keep away from her. You aren't welcome here. You harm her in any way and you'll discover how

THE HIDDEN CONGREGATION

much life there is left in this church." He glared at Ammahn who could have easily tossed twice his weight aside.

"I understand your concern, but there is much you don't know."

Ox grabbed Ammahn by the shoulder. "It's time you and I had a discussion."

Ammahn slowly turned to him. The congregation had formed a circle around him. "You are right. It's time."

Ox held Ammahn's shoulder. "Let's go up to my study."

Ammahn looked at Ox then Elmer. He studied the congregation, returning their looks matter-of-factly. He nodded.

Ox saw Nehmi coming through the door from the hallway. "Mr. Nehmi. Would you get a padlock on that dirt basement door and double lock it. No one is to go into it for any reason."

Ox and Ammahn proceeded up the steps to the study. Elmer, Hilda, and Angel followed to the foot of the steps, but came no farther.

Ox closed the study door.

Ammahn turned to Ox. "I think I might be able to guess who was in back of that confrontation. I know something is going on—has been for some time."

Ox decided to play along. "Is this something that was going on when you were here before?"

"I've always known there was something terribly mixed-up going on when I went back to California."

"When was that?"

"I guess it was fifteen years ago. In a sense, it was earlier, but I was less aware because of my work at Penn."

"What was your work at Penn?"

Ammahn answered Ox's question with a question. "Did you ever read Scott Peck's *People of the Lie*?"

"Yes."

"Then you might have some idea of what I was concerned about."

"You think there was some hypocrisy taking place."

"I think it was—on a large scale, but I hadn't been able to put my finger on it. There seemed to be strange things happening. Little things, clandestine things. I sensed a lot of tension and conceit. It was getting worse by the week. But now, I would like to ask you, what's happening?"

"Strange things were going on. People were disappearing. Is that what you were referring to?"

"I noticed some people weren't around, that some were less involved than in the past. I wasn't that close with members of the congregation. I was interested in singing in the choir and attended a few rehearsals, but they began to act strange and I stopped going. I was intrigued with Petersen. It's hard to put my finger on it, but I sensed something both good and evil. You understand that my whole adult life has been wrapped up in the results of behavior. I'm an archeologist and anthropologist. I've studied the evil that hides in the rock and sand, waiting for the right moment—the moment of weakness. Things here pricked my instincts. There was an accumulation of little things.

"For one thing, Nehmi, always meddling. At one time, I saw him going down the steps toward the nursery with Angel and Petersen. He came back up alone. Nothing wrong with that, except for some reason, he looked guilty when he saw me looking at him. A strange look. Changes in behavior in the congregation. Nehmi had been the caretaker and yet he seemed suddenly to be, well, almost running things. I left with the feeling there was a rock that needed turning over. I have always felt there was some unfinished business."

"You were in college at the time?"

"I was a graduate student assistant in two departments.

THE HIDDEN CONGREGATION

Either one of which was enough to keep me fully occupied. I've done a lot of talking. What has happened?"

"Cynthia's concerto was a recapitulation of it all."

"That was an amazing piece of work, but please explain the congregation's attitude of accusation toward me."

"They hold you responsible for all the problems."

Ammahn nodded. "Carefully orchestrated over a long period of time, no doubt."

"And you hold somebody else responsible for all the problems."

"I don't even know what all the problems are, but yes, I do. And there's no doubt in my mind as to who."

"Mr. Nehmi."

"Yes, Nehmi."

"Well, you see there's nothing to prove he's guilty of anything."

"Is there any proof that I am?"

"No, but right now the smart money lies that way."

"So, I've got to prove my innocence."

"Seems that way. I think everybody would feel better if you weren't around."

"Hard to prove my innocence if I'm banned."

"The problem is things started again at the same time you reappeared."

"Now you've really got me. What started again? Nehmi controlling things? People acting peculiar? Clue me in."

Ox opened his middle desk drawer and pulled out the picture of Mrs. Petersen. He handed it to Ammahn and watched his reaction.

"God in Heaven." Ammahn stared. "She looks familiar. Who is this lady?"

"Mrs. Petersen."

"Is this the problem you were talking about?"

"Part of it."

"And this is what I'm accused of? There are some insane people here. How long has this been going on?"

Ox decided to tell the entire story from the beginning right through Cynthia and himself.

He left out no detail, including the potions and the elixir. He told it as though Ammahn knew nothing.

CHAPTER THIRTY-NINE

Ox and Barbara walked toward their house. Martha was skipping and Billy skipped along behind her.

"How did your meeting go with Ammahn? Is he out of here?"

"Interesting meeting, and no he isn't out of here. He said he wasn't leaving. He had to prove his innocence. Said I couldn't make him, and if I called the police, it might be hard to explain all the deaths."

"So we've still got him to put up with. He might live to regret that."

"He pointed fingers at others. Nehmi primarily, but also Elmer. He said Elmer was always the informal leader of the congregation."

"It seems to me he came back to make sure you didn't save the church. We better get the group together again to head him off at the pass. By the way, Mr. Nehmi came down to the nursery and put a hasp and padlock on the dirt basement door."

"I know. He gave me the only key."

"If Ammahn came back to get you, he's going to get got."

"He says he came back because he had an invitation to conduct an eight week-seminar at the University of Pennsylvania, and also because he wanted to look at some diggings he had started on his land in Cold Point—and because he always had an uneasy feeling something wrong had been going on. He wanted to poke around."

"Do you believe him?"

"At this point, I don't know what to believe. We have no proof of anything. But I did get an idea for my next sermon. If he's guilty, we'll get him. There's more than one way to skin a cat."

CHAPTER FORTY

Ammahn sat in the dormer of his little house, facing southeast, the direction of the Church of the One Soul. He had been unwelcomed at other places, but not on the outside of the earth. He remembered crawling in the dark through a series of tunnels in Kansas. He had lost his direction and his light had gone out. He thought he had seen a glimmer of light, but it was something else, a flash of something, then his instincts had set in. Or it was an odor or a sound. He had felt a presence, something didn't want him there. He had crawled backward, must have been yards. The tunnel was too tight for him to turn around. He was certain he was going to die. Then the tunnel linked with another and widened. He felt an air current and knew he had a chance. It had been a strange feeling.

But this was different. This was above ground, but in another sense, it was below ground—a tunnel of deceit. People should know things are not always what they seem. And that dirt basement was a hidden world—dust of creation, dust of procreation—with candles to match. Evil lurks like a shadow. There were enemies at that church. He gazed in its direction. When he had left, there were none. He hadn't anticipated the welcome he received. Considering everything, it's amazing the church still existed. But everything had not been considered yet. And they didn't have a handle on the situation.

They will remember what happened to them until they die, then who will remember? The dead are gone, but the great social brain records and doesn't forget. The final book is one of dust and stone, but someone or something flips the pages in the dark. The book of the gone and the never gone.

Who will write the next chapter?

CHAPTER FORTY-ONE

At the police roundhouse, Sergeant Oster laid the suicide note on the table and pushed it over to Jessie May and Emmett, who picked it up. "It sounds like this woman did away with her husband. I consider this a confession. She was a member of that church. Something crazy going on there?"

"Can't arrest anybody for being crazy. We'd have to arrest the whole city. That all you got?" Jessie May picked up the note. "Interesting meeting at the church after her suicide."

Oster waited.

"One of them said she might still be alive if Dr. Christie had been there years ago. Another one said, a lot of people might still be alive."

Emmett piped up. "Apparently, it's some guy named Ammahn."

Oster rolled his eyes and said, "Well, I guess we can add another name to the list. So far we have Elmer Weiss, this Nehmi guy, the new minister who was sent in to cover things up, and now somebody named Ammahn."

"Mr. Weiss was the one who mentioned Ammahn, but the others seemed to agree."

"This could be a break in the case or just another complication. I expect you two to get to the bottom of it. I think the new minister is the key."

"Funny thing about that graveyard. No couples buried there. None of those people who disappeared are buried there."

"Well, maybe they aren't dead. We don't know. We don't even know for sure about this Stuart Lewis. What did his wife do to him? Burn his toast? Or maybe they were all cremated and their ashes are on mantelpieces all over the place. You guys get busy. My money's still on the minister."

CHAPTER FORTY-TWO

Ox had prepared a sermon to make a statement and a challenge. Ammahn and Nehmi were in their usual places. This time, Ammahn stared at Nehmi off and on. Nehmi kept smiling. A new couple dropped in. Ox directed his sermon at the back pew.

"Did God create good, and the devil evil? Do we believe Lucifer was an angel that fell from grace and became a minor god? Or did God create both good and evil and leave us to sort out the difference? Is it our lot to eradicate evil? And if so, where should we start, but in ourselves. In the marriage of good and evil, we like to think good wins. In the separation of good and evil, does evil survive and constantly work at undermining good?

"Sometimes things happen that make us think so. Beauty and evil dwell together in nature, one beautiful species living off another. Emerson said, 'There's a crack in everything God made.' And in the scientists' book of DNA, there are useless pages—DNA that does absolutely nothing. One scientist stated God could have done a better job. On the other hand, maybe there's a purpose for those pages and we haven't figured it out yet. Maybe we never will.

"Is there a devil? Maybe there is inside of each of us, and maybe in some of us it takes over for a moment then we shift to the good side. There may be some strange individuals who never shift to the good side. They prefer the evil side. Have you ever known anyone who seemed like the devil incarnate? Pure evil? How do you deal with such a person?"

Ammahn looked at Nehmi and raised his eyebrows as though to ask that question. Nehmi looked the same question back. Hilda, Elmer, Angel, and some of the others looked back at Ammahn.

"It's important that you not let hate take over. Hate is the tool of the devil. Let us consider this church a hate free zone. In fact, I'd like to put a sign out front saying that. This is a church that welcomes all people, good and bad."

Now heads swiveled back at him, distinctly surprised, Nehmi included. Ammahn seemed to be pondering that statement. Maybe he didn't accept it. But maybe he would realize it would be better for him if the congregation did believe that. Ammahn looked at Nehmi and shook his head. He stared at Nehmi and Nehmi gazed back.

"I'm not one who believes in turning the other cheek, especially when there is an obvious plan to do harm," Ox declared. "I do believe if you are struck, you strike back. But never strike the first blow. Your strength must always be in being right. Evil is too weak to be open. Evil must sneak, hide, misrepresent."

Ammahn kept starring at Nehmi. It was like a confrontation. And Nehmi actually looked angry—something Ox had not seen before. But a staring contest wasn't going to do it. Ox realized Ammahn had actually made him wonder about Nehmi. The man really was skillful.

"At this time, I want to initiate a new custom, something I would like to see become a tradition. I'll call it 'pass the peace'. Please stand and greet your neighbor. Hug, shake hands, whatever. Let's take the next five minutes for this."

THE HIDDEN CONGREGATION

Ammahn stood up and walked to Nehmi with his arms outstretched. Nehmi backed away. He walked toward the front of the church and greeted the new couple.

Ammahn disappeared out the back double doors.

In the dining room, Elmer came over to Ox. "We've got to talk. Hilda, Joe, and all of us agree we can't welcome Ammahn."

Hilda joined in. "We can meet at my house. I think we should all meet right now."

"Why don't we just go up to my office? It's large enough if we all stand," Ox said.

Barbara had Martha and Billy in tow. "I'm going to have to take the kids home."

"They can play in my front hall," said Hilda.

Ox was secretly glad to see them becoming more aggressive, no longer defeated. "Round up the rest and let's go."

All of the group was there.

"Where's Nehmi?" asked Ox.

"He said he wanted to stay at the church just to watch things." Elmer glanced round the room. "We are deeply concerned. The idea was to make him unwelcome, push him out. What's this pass the peace thing? Is that going to make him unwelcome?"

"I was watching Ammahn while I was giving that sermon. He and Nehmi were sitting in the last pew. And they kept interacting to the sermon and to each other. I have to say, at times they both looked guilty, and at times they both looked innocent. I'm not at all sure Ammahn did it. It could have even been both. It could be neither."

Elmer looked completely flustered. "You can't think Nehmi did it."

"At this point, I just don't know."

"We all know it was Ammahn."

215

Ox realized they were all adamant about it. "Do you really feel the right approach is to tell him to leave? Will that solve the problem?"

Hilda said, "Ox, he can't hurt us anymore. It's you he's after. He can hurt you and Cynthia and Barbara, and those two wonderful children out there in the front hall. And he can finally destroy the church. We've just got to get him out of the way. Tell him to leave."

"And if he refuses, do we call the police?"

"Oh, I hadn't thought of that. Well, at least we could try."

"I agree," said Elmer. "We all agree. I think we should go right back downstairs to see if he's still there and tell him to get out and never come back. If he says no, we'll have to think of something else."

"If that's what you want to do."

They moved as a group back to the church and into the dining room. They found Tom Fitzgerald and Amanda Frankle sitting over to one side. Their children were sitting on the floor, quietly playing.

Barbara looked alarmed. "Where are Chris and Sarah?"

"They were here a few minutes ago," said Tom. "Maybe they went back down to the nursery."

Ox led the way, the whole group running behind him. Cynthia, Barbara and the kids stayed with Tom and Amanda.

They ran into the nursery just in time to hear Ammahn. "The key. Give me the damn key. I hear voices in there."

He had a firm grip on Nehmi's arm.

"I don't have the key. Ox has the only key."

"You've got it on you and I'll take your arm with it if you don't cough it up. Now!"

"Good God," said Elmer. "Someone's locked in."

Ammahn jerked Nehmi hard enough to pull him off his feet.

THE HIDDEN CONGREGATION

"That door had to be unlocked for anyone to get in there, and this creature was over in the corner when I walked in." He let go of Nehmi's arm and wrapped his big hand around his neck. He plunged his other hand into one of Nehmi's pockets with such force, Ox thought it would rip the pants off. "Aha." Ammahn held up a key.

Nehmi was frantically pulling at Ammahn's grip on his neck. Ammahn threw him to one side and Nehmi sprawled on the floor. He shouted, "Ammahn locked them in!"

Ammahn opened the door. The odor of the candles made it clear what was happening. Elmer grabbed Ox. "Get as far away from this as possible. You are still vulnerable." Ox watched Elmer and Ammahn go in. In less than a minute, they pulled Chris Frankle and Sarah Fitzgerald out. They were covered with dust and looked confused and embarrassed. "Oh, my God," said Chris.

Sarah was on the verge of tears. She buried her face in her hands. Ammahn went back in. He came out carrying six candles, still smoking from being extinguished.

"Close the door," said Elmer.

"I'm so sorry," said Chris. "I don't know what came over us."

"We know you don't know," said Elmer, "but we do."

"Yes," said Hilda. "What happened in there was done *to* you, not *by* you."

Sarah was crying. "I don't understand. I'm so ashamed."

"We need to all get out of this area," said Ox. "Let's all go up to the dining room."

"I don't know if I can face Tom," said Sarah.

"Trust us," said Elmer. "It will work out. There was something going on you don't know about."

Ammahn padlocked the door and handed the key to Ox. "You better hide this somewhere."

"I still have the only key Nehmi gave me. Only it wasn't the only key, was it Nehmi?"

"As caretaker, I felt I should keep a key just in case."

"Just in case of what, Mr. Nehmi?"

"Just in case someone got locked in there, like just now, so I could let them out."

"But what we saw as we came in was Ammahn trying to get the key from you to do just that. Why weren't you trying to let them out? Why did you tell him you didn't have the key?"

"My God," said Chris. "There's something sick going on in here."

Sarah blurted out between sobs, "We went back in to see why it had such an effect on us before."

"You are not the only ones this has happened to," said Ox. "And now we are trying to find out who has been in back of it. And that person is right here in this room."

"Speaking of this room," said Elmer, "let's get up to the dining room, away from here and this odor."

"Mr. Nehmi," said Ox, "you can answer my question upstairs."

When they entered the dining room, Sarah ran crying to Tom Fitzgerald and wrapped her arms around him.

Tom raised his eyebrows and looked around. "What's wrong?"

"Sarah and Chris got locked in the dirt basement," said Ox. "We are going to have a discussion about how it happened, who did it to them."

Chris walked over and stood by Amanda. It was obvious he was shaken. "Mr. Nehmi?" said Ox.

Ammahn stood like a guard beside Nehmi.

"Mr. Nehmi, why weren't you letting them out?"

"They went in on their own volition."

"Why did you prevent them from coming out? Why did you lock them in?"

Nehmi was getting angry. His face turned red like a rash. "Who said I locked them in? Anyone can snap a lock shut."

"Who had a key to unlock it to start with?"

THE HIDDEN CONGREGATION

"It sounds like you're blaming me. I'm the one who held this congregation together when Petersen became obsessed with Angel."

"Oh," cried Angel. "How could you!"

"Hush," said Elmer.

"Oh, I forgot," said Nehmi. "It was you who were obsessed. You got the minister."

"Mr. Nehmi," said Ox, "you are sounding less and less like a friend of the congregation."

"I don't believe what I'm hearing," said Elmer. "All these years you pointed a finger at Ammahn, and now it's beginning to look like it was you all along. Tell me I'm wrong."

Ammahn faced Nehmi. "Easy to accuse someone not around to defend himself, right Nehmi? I always knew there was something not right about you. It was one of the reasons I wanted to come back here."

"This is beginning to sound more serious than locking someone in the basement," said Tom Fitzgerald.

"It is," said Ox. "And you and Amanda and Sarah and Chris deserve an explanation. I'll give you a quick summary in a few minutes. Mr. Nehmi, I don't like making accusations, but the circumstances point to you. We are all waiting for you to give us a full explanation. Someone locked Sarah and Chris into that horrible place. We heard you say you didn't have the key. We heard Ammahn trying to get Sarah and Chris out. You were doing just the opposite. And you know what happens in such circumstances. Now just tell us why."

"I don't need to explain anything to you people. The fact is, your own built-in lust is the problem, and if they rolled around in there, good for them. I'm sure they enjoyed it."

Ox turned to the Frankles and Fitzgeralds. "Okay, time I clued you in. Those candles have some kind of aphrodisiac effect.

Somehow that dust in there contributes to it. Someone with a mind so evil it's sick, has trapped others in there, including me and Cynthia. The object is to destroy relationships, families, the congregation, and the church. Cynthia and I got out, but it was a close call, just as with you two. The effect dies after you have been out for a while. Don't feel guilty or think you are immoral. It's far from it. I want to meet with all four of you in my study right now. I also want Cynthia to be there."

Elmer, Joe, and Ammahn backed Nehmi against the wall next to Petersen's portrait. "Nehmi," said Elmer. "I want all of your keys." Nehmi folded his arms and just looked at them.

Tom Fitzgerald walked over to them. "Empty all your pockets now or I'll flatten your face. That was my wife you locked in there. You made her a victim, including me and my children. Now empty every pocket or you will know what a victim feels like."

Nehmi didn't move or change expression. Elmer, Joe, and Ammahn moved aside to let Tom in. Tom stepped forward with obvious intent. Nehmi quickly began emptying his pockets. Ammahn held out his hands and Nehmi dropped keys, coins, wallet, some notes, a ballpoint pen, and some loose change.

Ox looked back at Nehmi while herding the group up to his study. "Mr. Nehmi, after this meeting, I will see you. I think under the circumstances you will want to find another job. Elmer, Ammahn, would you accompany him to his locker in the men's room so he can empty it out. Please examine everything in his locker. If you can wait to meet with me and Nehmi after the meeting, and with the Fitzgeralds and Frankles, I would appreciate it."

CHAPTER FORTY-THREE

Ox closed the door. "Sarah and Chris, you've just been put through an ordeal you won't soon forget. I know. Cynthia and I were tricked into that dirt basement as well. We have recovered, but it took a lot of strength and determination. That's why I asked Cynthia to be here, and of course, Barbara has a vested interest, as do Tom and Amanda. For your information, there were others in the congregation who were caught up in that plot. So you are not alone. We know what you experienced and you will feel it to a lesser and lesser degree as the days pass."

Tom Fitzgerald shook his head as though to cast off some clinging question. "Aphrodisiac candles? Aphrodisiac dust? This kind of thing is new to me. And in a church? How can that be? I just don't know what to make of it. Is this Nehmi going to be arrested?"

"Believe me. We will take care of Mr. Nehmi. The important thing now is for the Frankles and the Fitzgeralds to understand what was attempted and to realize their own partnerships are sound. Sarah and Chris are not immoral or loose. They are victims."

Sarah was still holding her hands to her face. "Thank God you all got there in time."

Tom put his arm around her shoulder. "And thank God for the explanation, because otherwise it would have been a blow to our marriage."

Sarah let out a wail.

"It's okay. I believe all this, as unbelievable as it is." Tom pulled her close.

"Okay," said Ox. "I want to leave a standing invitation to you four individually, in couples, or as a group, to come discuss your feelings and any problems coming from this experience. And Tom, on the way out, if you see Nehmi, resist clobbering him. We are going to handle it." Ox stood up and that was a signal for the others to leave.

Ammahn and Elmer came in escorting Nehmi as though it were the last mile. Not a dead man walking. Nehmi was angry. He looked ready to spit nails.

"You won't believe what we found in his locker," said Elmer, holding a bundle of candles. "These were in a panel behind his locker. Wouldn't have seen it if we hadn't removed his work trousers. And that's not all." He placed a wax bottle on the desk. "This is the famous elixir he claimed Ammahn provided Petersen. And this is the stuff for painting on bodies to make them flammable."

Ox stared at the evidence, then Nehmi. "I guess this pretty much wraps it up."

"If you weren't all evil to start with, it would never have worked. I just let the evil out that was embedded in your souls. And you all enjoyed it. You call yourselves good people. You aren't. You should admit who you are instead of pretending to be good with never an evil thought in your heads. Hypocrites."

Elmer's face had turned a deep red. "Hypocrites? You call us hypocrites? You're the champion hypocrite of all times. Pretending to be our friend. Your whole life is a lie. And you're a murderer."

THE HIDDEN CONGREGATION

Ox hoped Elmer didn't have high blood pressure or he would have a heart attack.

Elmer turned away and leaned against the wall.

"You're the murderer, Elmer. You are all murderers. And you killed your spouses just for sexual pleasure. You murdered your wife. Burned her alive. Why don't you call the police?"

Ammahn jerked Nehmi by the arm, turning him so they were face to face. "You nematode. Everybody in this room knows who the murderer is. We could dispose of you right now and nobody would ever miss you. In fact, we have the materials to do it with." He pointed at the evidence sitting on Ox's desk. "It would be a justifiable execution. Only we could do it without the elixir. Let you feel the pain just as you did Petersen's wife."

"You wouldn't dare. You don't have the guts."

"And afterward, I could split your skull."

CHAPTER FORTY-FOUR

Ox was at a loss as to what to do with Nehmi.

Ammahn put his big hands on Nehmi's shoulders and pushed him down into a chair. He kept his grip so tight his knuckles were white. If it hurt Nehmi, he didn't show it.

"We can't let him go," said Ammahn. "He's pure evil."

"I know," said Ox. "He could implicate the congregation—making them all victims again."

"Let him," said Elmer. "He can't hurt me any more than he already has."

"You're all weasels. There's nothing you can do to me. You're gutless," Nehmi declared. Ammahn slapped him on the side of the head. "Maybe we should stake him out in the dirt basement and do the same thing he did to Petersen's wife."

"Then we sink to his level," said Ox. "But I admit there's a certain appeal. An eye for an eye."

"Let's take him down and stake him, then we can talk about it." Ammahn winked at Ox. Apparently, Elmer caught the wink.

"Maybe we can douse him with the incendiary liquid and leave him to think about it while we decide what to do with him. I'll be glad to drive some stakes in. Joe will help me."

"You gutless weaklings. I'll just take a nap," Nehmi said.

THE HIDDEN CONGREGATION

Ox was reluctant. "I don't think so. That's what he would do."

Ammahn whispered to Ox, "It's a place to keep him until we can figure out what to do with him."

Ox still had misgivings. "I just feel uncomfortable with this."

Elmer nodded. "I understand your feeling, but there's no choice."

"Well, okay, but we have to come up with a solution by tomorrow."

"You wimps don't have the guts to do anything. I can come and go as I please."

Ox gave Elmer the key. "You know I can't go with you."

Nehmi laughed. "Hypocrites. All of you."

Several hours later the congregation had a meeting in the dining room. The Fitzgeralds and the Frankles had not been called. The pit would have required more explanation than anyone wanted to give. Ammahn, Elmer and Joe were still covered with dust.

"He's down there, staked out," said Elmer. "We doused him and he just laughed."

"If he's the devil, burning wouldn't hurt him," said Hilda.

Ammahn shook his head. "He's just an evil human being. Got warped somewhere along the way."

Elmer turned to Ammahn. "We all owe you an apology. We were certain you were at the back of the whole thing."

"As Ox said before, you were all victims, including being victims of his lies. Evil can dissemble automatically. It goes with the character. Besides, you were all too desperate to see beyond what was thrown at you."

Hilda slumped and bit her lip. "But I'm ashamed for being so blind. How could he fool us all? And for so long? All these years. We trusted the devil."

WILLIAM T. DELAMAR

"You didn't know," said Ox. "You grasped at straws, the first straw you could reach. Ammahn is right."

"Forget apologies," said Ammahn. "We have to decide what we are going to do with him. He's staked out down there and completely unafraid. I've seen a lot of evil in my life, but nothing like this. Ox is right. We can't turn him over to the police because he can implicate all of you and destroy the church, which was apparently what he had in mind from the beginning."

"How long do we keep him down there before we let him loose?" asked Joe.

"Maybe we could just leave him down there to starve," said Hilda.

"No," said Ox. "That would just create more bad images."

"Why don't we just leave him there overnight," said Hilda. "Maybe he'll worry some."

"Yes," said Joe, "and tomorrow, let's all meet down there. Get in dirty clothes so we can join him around the pit and tell him we are going to sing to him as part of the program before we burn him."

"You can't burn him," said Ox.

"Ox is right," said Elmer. "But we can scare the bejesus out of him."

"That might make us all feel better," said Ox, "but you've got to face up to the fact that we will have to let him go."

"I know," said Elmer. "And we will have to face the fact he might come back and burn down the church. Maybe we'll keep him there for a month. Hand feed him each day. We men can take on that job. Maybe we'll get an inspiration."

"Elmer, we just can't do this," said Ox. "I'll go along with keeping him there overnight, but we'll just have to come up with a better solution. Tomorrow, we'll have to bring him back upstairs."

THE HIDDEN CONGREGATION

"What if he gets loose?" asked Hilda.

"Not the way I tied those knots," said Joe. "In addition we used tape. No way. Also, the door is locked. He can't get out."

"Tomorrow is decision day," said Ox.

CHAPTER FORTY-FIVE

At ten o'clock in the morning, they were all there—the remnants of the congregation, covered with dust. Ammahn stood at the back out of deference. He looked at Nehmi's evil grin and couldn't remember having ever seen so much evil packed into one person.

"Here we are," said Elmer. "Just like old times," he added sarcastically.

Nehmi looked up at him and laughed. "Don't you wish? All of you had a good time. Humping in the dirt."

"We are here again, but this time it's different," said Hilda. "This time we aren't trapped by an evil monster. Maybe we should fill in this space with the dirt we just crawled through then seal the door."

"Maybe we should do all that with him still in here," said Joe.

"We don't want that image under the floor and in our minds either," said Elmer. "It's time to start the program." He handed out the sheet music. "Too bad Cynthia can't be here to provide music. What we don't have in quality, we'll make up in quantity."

And they began to sing. They sang some of the old favorites like: "Just As I Am," "Rock of Ages," and "Amazing Grace." They sang until noon, then joined in for a chant.

THE HIDDEN CONGREGATION

"We forgive you and receive forgiveness in return.

"We forgive you for there's one thing we can learn.

"Love for each other is powerful and right.

"Love for each other will give us all sight.

"We forgive you.

"We forgive you.

"We forgive you."

Then they started over, only this time, after each line, they gave a clap. Ammahn just stood there and observed.

Halfway through, Nehmi looked at Angel. "I notice you've been looking at my naked body. Does it make you hungry? Why don't you strip and lie down on top of me and let me bring back memories."

Angel took out a match, struck it, and dropped in on him. "Burn in hell."

Everyone jumped back as he burst into flame. They stood like statues, listening to his screams.

Ox stood looking out of the window at the Schuylkill River and the traffic on the roadways on both sides. From his study, he could hear nothing from the dirt basement. He doubted the singing and imprisonment would have any effect on Nehmi. What were they going to do with the man? Nehmi was definitely going to cause problems, but they were going to have to let him go and simply face the consequences. Trouble, nothing but trouble. He had never had to face anything like this. And at this point, he himself was probably guilty of aiding and abetting. But they were all going to have to face it. Tying Nehmi and holding him in the basement was a bad decision. If anything, it would make it worse. Unfortunately, there just didn't seem be a solution.

He thought he heard sounds from the dining room. They were being awfully quiet. He hurried down the steps, through the kitchen, and there they were, standing around Petersen's portrait as though paying homage to him. They were covered with dirt. The floor was a mess. He hated the dirt basement smell. And there was something else, the smell of something cooking, and it struck him. No! They wouldn't.

Elmer and Hilda had their arms around Angel who was hunched over with her hands covering her face. The group was silent. Ammahn was the first to see him as he approached. Even he seemed shaken.

"Well . . . the best laid plans . . ."

"What happened?"

Elmer shook his head. "Angel took care of the problem."

Ox waited.

"Dropped a match on him."

Hilda looked at Ox, but turned away.

"They burned him?"

"Actually, it was Angel."

Ox didn't know what to say.

Ammahn said, "The idiot taunted her. Big mistake."

"And she just happened to have matches with her?"

Elmer was still shaking his head. "My take on it is she wanted to, but didn't have the nerve until he propositioned her. She told him to burn in hell."

Ox watched the group huddled together.

Ammahn said, "I think they may all be in a state of shock. No doubt, it brought back bad memories."

"We can't call the police," said Ox.

"The only thing left is his skeleton. I'll bury his bones out on the farm. I can put them where no one will find them."

CHAPTER FORTY-SIX

Two weeks later, Ox still wasn't over his shock. He felt guilty of murder. He had never really liked Nehmi, but he could never kill anyone, not even a murderer. The congregation seemed on a high. They had become an even more cohesive group and a candle burning ceremony seemed the right way to celebrate their newfound freedom.

Billy and Martha ran along ahead of Ox and Barbara on the way to the church.

"I think you should give Angel a raise."

"The way she's been behaving in the last two weeks, I think she gave herself a raise. I've never seen so much energy."

They turned up the walkway into the courtyard.

"Looks like your entire congregation is already here, the whole thirty members. But they look like they're alive. Look at them. I've never seen so much laughing with this group. You know what? A weight has been lifted."

"There's been an amazing transformation." But Ox was still concerned over the killing.

Angel met them halfway up the driveway. "We all want candles. We think everyone should burn a candle."

"Wait here." Ox went up to his study, unlocked his desk and opened the double drawer. There they were . . . the bundle of black candles from Nehmi's locker. He gathered them up and went down to the courtyard.

"Here they are," he said, handing out the candles. "I stored away half a dozen at Ammahn's suggestion for lab analysis."

Elmer was concerned. "Are you sure the odor won't cause you a problem?"

"Not a chance, and anyhow, Barbara is here to protect me."

"Cynthia says not to worry about her, but I remember how strong it all was at one time."

"Not to worry. We are outdoors where there's no dust to contribute."

The Frankles and Fitzgeralds each had two candles and were standing at the dining room entrance, all smiles. Joe started dancing around the courtyard and soon so were the rest. They were laughing and crying. With their free hands, they held each other. Hilda kissed Angel. The newest couple, Emmett and Jessie May, each held a candle, but they seemed to only watch the others.

"Mommy, can I burn a candle?" asked Martha.

"Me, too," said Billy.

Barbara knelt and gave each of them a candle. "Now be very careful not to let the flame get near anything, including yourselves. You don't want to get burned."

Billy stood by Martha and jumped up and down, holding the candle straight out in front of him.

Ox watched the congregation. It occurred to him this was the first time they had done anything together since the things they shouldn't have done. "I think they've become a family again, this time in a positive sense." But at what price?

"Makes you feel good, doesn't it. You may have a chance to get this church on its feet again after all," Barbara said.

THE HIDDEN CONGREGATION

Elmer joined Ox and Barbara. He was clearly amused at the two children holding candles. "Ox, we all met last night and we're ready to help you rebuild our church."

Hilda had followed him. "Yes, and we want to have a candle burning ceremony every year on this same date. We are celebrating each other and the future. Not only that, we discussed something else. We need to have a memorial garden in the cemetery. We need to celebrate and recognize those who have gone. Nothing ostentatious, just little plots of flowers tucked away somewhere in the cemetery. We'll all work on them, and we might put a little brass plaque in each of them so their names won't be forgotten."

"We'll talk later," said Elmer, and they went back to the celebration.

"Hidden away," Ox mumbled to Barbara. "The hidden congregation. Hidden no more."

CHAPTER FORTY-SEVEN

The bishop leaned forward and peered over his clasped hands at Reverend Darner. "This contribution by Hosannah Lewis is a godsend. This will provide that church an endowment that will last for many years. Christie must have done something right. He feels everything should be sold rather than keeping the house. He's probably right. What I don't understand is, why we haven't heard from Nehmi."

"I've tried to contact him several times, but I get no answer," said Reverend Darner.

"Well, he had expressed genuine concern about so many members running off to join some kind of cult. He even implied they had been burning other churches in the area. Keep trying to get him. Maybe somebody in the cult got him. Crazy stuff going on there. Why would this lady commit suicide? Will we ever know what has really happened there?"

"I don't know, Bishop. Maybe eventually, Christie can tell us."

"Maybe. But in a way, I'd prefer he kept it to himself. Might be best to keep it hidden."

CHAPTER FORTY-EIGHT

Ox and Barbara were relaxing on their front porch. Martha was telling Billy how to hold a teacup with two fingers.

"You hold the handle with your thumb and the main finger, with your little finger sticking out."

"Why can't I just hold the stinking cup with all my fingers?"

Ox and Barbara grinned at each other. "Sounds like a declaration of independence," murmured Barbara.

"A few other people have gained their independence," said Ox. He gazed up at the sky. Dusk was just beginning. "I almost feel like there should be a rainbow up there. Almost."

"The burning still worries you, doesn't it? It's probably best to just forget it, rainbow or no rainbow. In a little bit, we'll see lightning bugs. Guess that'll have to do."

"This has been the strangest experience of my life."

"This has been the strangest experience in anybody's life."

"Guess I'll have to start looking for a sexton to take Nehmi's place."

"Talk about poetic justice."

"The mills of the Gods grind slow, but sure."

"Is anybody going to miss Nehmi?"

"I don't even know if he had a family."

"Well, at least you don't have to explain it to the congregation."

"Except maybe that strange new couple, Emmett and Jessie May Dobson."

"Strange?"

"Well, it's just that during my sermons, they keep giving each other uh-huh looks and seem to be studying the congregation."

"Uh-huh looks?"

"It looks like they're passing judgment on everything. And after the sermon, they never come over to say anything. Sometimes, I get the impression they don't want to be there, but they keep coming."

"I've not had any contact with them. Maybe if they had children. They did pop into the nursery once, looked around, then left. Didn't say anything."

"They probably never even noticed Nehmi. Probably wouldn't know him from Adam's house cat."

"Well, the whole thing is probably a closed chapter now."

CHAPTER FORTY-NINE

At the police roundhouse, Sergeant Oster looked at Emmett and Jessie May as though they were stray dogs needing a hard kick.

"You're telling me you never even talked to that Nehmi character, and now he's gone? What's with you guys? Jessie May, you got brains. Emmett here's 'bout as smart as a hoagie, but I expected more out of you. Have I got to go out there myself?"

"Sarge," said Emmett, "I think Nehmi had something to do with that fake suicide of Hosannah Lewis. I think he did it and flew the coop."

"That's a stretch, hoagie brain. What would he get out of it? He wasn't in the will. What do you think, Jessie May?"

"I can't see any connection. But it's strange he disappeared after the new minister arrived. Nehmi has been there for so many years."

"I think you're pointed in the right direction. Maybe it's time for us to add some pressure. Why don't the three of us go to church this Sunday in full uniform?"

"That would blow our cover," said Jessie May.

"Forget cover. It's time to unwrap."

"Damn right." said Emmett.

"My money's on the minister, but the jury's still out on that Nehmi character. We've got to find him. And the minister has to know where he is. After all, he's an employee."

"Right," said Emmett.

"And if he turns up, you two nab him and talk turkey with him."

"You want we should bring him in?"

"No, hoagie. Just talk to him like you are about to can him. I'll talk to the minister."

"What about Mr. Weiss?" asked Jessie May.

"If you can't find Nehmi, talk to Weiss."

"And that Ammahn character?"

"Him, too. We've got to spread the net. We start this Sunday."

Jessie May and Emmett headed up the stairs to their desks.

"I don't think that minister is involved. Do you?" asked Jessie May.

"I think they're all involved. What makes you think he's not?"

"He just sounds like a real minister."

"A week ago, you thought otherwise. What's changed?"

"I've been thinking about some of the things he said in his sermons . . . especially about good and evil. I think he's good."

"Crap."

CHAPTER FIFTY

Ox was aware that Elmer and Joe were busy cutting grass and pulling weeds in the graveyard. Now he could hear them talking as they came up the stairway. They were either finished or taking a break.

"Hot day," said Elmer as he and Joe walked into Ox's study.

"You guys ought to take it easy. We'll wind up planting you out there."

"Half done," said Joe. "The rest is downhill."

"Well, since you're here, I wonder if you would help me move Petersen's picture up here where it used to be."

"That's a good idea," said Elmer.

"I thought you said we should take it easy."

"You should, but you don't want to stop too suddenly. Besides, the sun's not burning in here."

"I think we ought to remove that word 'burn' from our dictionary." Elmer stood up.

"Show us the way, Preacher."

Ox smiled to himself. They were now able to joke about the problem. The new chapter had really begun. The congregation was being reborn.

In twenty minutes, the picture was back in its place. Angel peeped in. "That's where it belongs." Then she was gone.

Ox studied the portrait. "Yes. He belongs here. He was a good man."

"And the world must never think otherwise," said Elmer. "Come on, Joe. Let's get a cold drink of water then move slow."

"I'm with you."

Ox sat behind his desk and studied the portrait. The eyes seemed to study him. *I'm watching out for your congregation, old man. But they may not need watching out for anymore. You never knew it was Nehmi—or did you? My God, you did know. He was the one passing the materials on to you. He had control of you. Through that horrible basement, the dungeon. You couldn't call the police because of what you had all done.*

Ox ran down the stairs and caught Elmer and Joe just as they were about to head out the door.

"We've got to get rid of that basement."

"How?" asked Elmer.

"We'll expand the nursery by ripping out the wall and push all the dirt up to fill in the pit area. The only thing left will be a crawl space. Hosannah's contribution will pay for it and we will eventually need a larger nursery anyhow."

"I buy it," said Joe.

"Me, too," said Elmer, "and I know a contractor who could do a good job."

"Can you call him today?"

"Consider it done."

CHAPTER FIFTY-ONE

Sunday Morning. The old group was there early. Ox watched them talking to each other. It reminded him of a weekly club. Maybe they could start a book club. He felt good about the congregation. There were a few new faces again. He had made the right choice at coming here. Then he saw Jessie May and Emmett. They were in police uniforms and they were with another policeman. They were police? The three sat in the back pew. Jessie May looked apologetic. Emmett looked full of himself.

The congregation hadn't noticed the three uniforms. Ox remembered the conversation with Barbara. Emmett and Jessie May hadn't really participated in activities with the other members. Now he knew why. They were there as part of a police investigation into the disappearances. He had planned to make some comment about the memorial garden, but not now. The other policeman looked older, more mature. He was probably their boss. There was a kind of swagger about him even sitting.

Ammahn came in and sat across the aisle from them. Emmett whispered something to the older policeman, who then glared at Ammahn. Ammahn ignored them.

WILLIAM T. DELAMAR

Ox realized a new chapter hadn't started for the congregation after all. He considered changing the subject of his sermon, but realized it had been posted. He proceeded with the "Formula for Happiness: Looking Forward to the Good Things, Forgetting Any Unhappy Past Things." He saw Emmett whispering to the older policeman with each reference to the past. The old chapter had been ripped back open.

When the service was over, most of the congregation wandered to the dining room for coffee and socializing. The police continued to sit.

Ammahn walked over to Elmer and Joe. "You may not have noticed we had a visitation from the police. They sat at the back pew and we know two of them."

"The police?" said Elmer. "What two do we know?"

"Emmett and Jessie May Dobson. That may not be their real names. They are in uniform."

"Damn. You can't trust anyone," said Joe.

"What it means is the church is under investigation," said Elmer. "Maybe for Nehmi's disappearance, maybe for more."

Joe and Elmer were quietly letting the others know, when the three officers came into the dining room. Jessie May looked clearly embarrassed. They quickly moved over to Ox.

"Mr. Christie, I'm Sergeant Oster. We need to talk to you in private. Now."

"Is there a problem, Sergeant?"

"If you don't know there's a problem, you were born yesterday."

"I beg your pardon?"

"Do you want to talk to us in private here, or would you rather come with us to headquarters?"

"We can go upstairs to my study."

Elmer came over quickly. "Is everything okay, Ox?"

"As far as I know, but Officer Oster seems to think otherwise."

THE HIDDEN CONGREGATION

"Officer Oster, I'm Elmer Weiss, a longtime member of this congregation. Can I or any other members of the congregation be of assistance?"

"Do you know what happened to all those people who disappeared from this church?"

"Officer Oster, I wish I had an answer for you, but we don't know where they are. And that's ancient history. Happened long before Dr. Christie came here."

"Maybe you ought to join us in Mr. Christie's study. And ancient history or not, this case is not closed, and we plan to find those people."

Elmer answered, "I can't tell you how much all of us wish you could bring them back."

"I can't tell you how much we want to nail anybody responsible."

"I'd be glad to join you in Dr. Christie's study." He placed emphasis on "Dr."

In Ox's study, Oster sat in Ox's desk chair. He put his feet up on Ox's desk. "Did your bishop send you here to attempt a cover-up?"

Ox looked at Oster's boots and wondered what kind of human being operated like that. "No, of course not."

Oster removed his boots from the desk and sat up slowly. "Do you want to come down to the station house with me?"

"Am I under arrest for something?"

"You are about to be."

"For what?"

"I'll think of something."

Ox said nothing.

"Where is Emil Nehmi?"

"I don't know. He didn't appear for work and we haven't heard from him."

"We want to talk to him about all the disappearances from here in the past."

"Well, if he can tell you anything, there are people here who would be grateful, but I'm sure you talked to him before. I wasn't here at the time, but I have heard about it."

"Who told you?"

"I did," said Elmer. "My wife was one of the people who left."

"Where did she go?"

"I wish I could tell you."

"You people aren't any damn help at all. Where does Nehmi live?"

"The personnel file is in the church office. I'll go over and get it."

Ox stepped across the hall to Angel's office. He could hear Oster's rasping voice. "So your wife left you. You two have an argument?"

"No," said Elmer.

"So she just up and left? Just like that?"

"That's right," said Elmer. "I can't explain it."

"Can't or won't?"

Ox stepped back in with the file. "His address is 1147 Hoosac Street. The index card says that's in the northeast section of Philadelphia."

"Phone number?"

"Nothing listed here. I think he rented. Might not have had a phone, or if he did, it isn't listed here."

"Well, how did you get in touch with him?"

"Didn't need to. He was always here. From early in the morning to late at night."

"Didn't you think that was strange? How did you contact him?"

"I never needed to call him. He was always here."

Emmett finally had a comment. "Shit."

THE HIDDEN CONGREGATION

Oster stood up. "We'll be talking to you later. Don't either of you leave town for any reason."

Ox called Angel. "Ring Hilda and call the group. We need an emergency meeting right now." He told her of the meeting with Oster, and Jessie May and Emmett. He could hear the trembling in Angel's voice.

No sooner had he put the phone down, but it rang. It was Hilda. "We saw you go up to the study with the police. Should we have a meeting?"

"Yes. You're about to get a call from Angel asking if we can meet there."

"Yes, and I will help her make the calls."

"Elmer's here, so you don't need to call him."

Barbara came in as Elmer rushed out. "What did the gendarmes want? Are we in trouble?"

Martha looked a little worried. "What's a gendarme?"

"Nothing to worry about, sweetie," and Barbara swept her up in her arms and kissed her.

"Hard to say. I'll tell you all about it later—at Hilda's. We're having a meeting."

Barbara frowned. "I'll get something for the kids to play with."

Everyone was there except the newer members. Ox let Elmer relay the conversation with Oster. When Elmer sat down, everyone in the group looked angry. Ox was relieved they didn't look defeated.

"We've all got to be on the same sheet of music," said Ox. "They don't know anything and they can't prove anything."

Rebecca Crum, who had never said anything in any of the meetings, now spoke up. "Maybe we should just tell them what happened and get it over with."

"No," shouted Joe.

245

"No, Rebecca," said Elmer. "I know you've always had deep feelings of guilt. We all have. But keep in mind we are all in this together. If you tell them, they have us all. I for one want to do something worthwhile for this church at least to try to make amends. I want to give what's left of my life to that. We can't do that in prison."

Rebecca nodded, but didn't look too sure.

"Keep in mind too. If any of us break, it also hurts Ox. And Barbara and the kids downstairs playing."

"Okay. I'll keep my mouth shut."

"Okay," said Ox. "Elmer told them just the right thing. When Oster asked where the people were, Elmer said, 'I wish I could tell you.' You don't know anything. You don't know what happened. It's history. There's nothing to be gained by confessing to anything. They may or may not question you. For some reason, they think Elmer had something to do with it, and me, and I think maybe they suspect Nehmi. And that brings up another thing. I told them I didn't know where Nehmi was. I told them he just stopped coming. They have his address and no doubt will follow up on that. Maybe they will think he skipped out."

Joe stood up. "I just want to say I'm disappointed with Emmett and Jessie May. Obviously, they were just plants. I bet they aren't even married."

Hilda looked pensive. "I never did like that Emmett. He seemed strange, but Jessie May looked okay."

"I have to say," said Ox, "she looked almost apologetic the whole time. I think she's a nice person, and I don't think she thinks any of us are guilty of anything. Or if she does, she doesn't want to."

On the way home, Barbara whispered. "We'll put the kids down for a nap and talk."

"Yeah. We need to. This is not going away."

CHAPTER FIFTY-TWO

Ox didn't want Barbara to know how worried he was. Oster's rasping voice kept ringing in his ears. *"We'll be talking to you later. Don't either of you leave town for any reason."*

Was he under suspicion for something? Could he be arrested? What would happen to Barbara and the kids? And a third one on the way. He kept reassuring himself. The police knew nothing. There was no evidence. He was sure the congregation would keep silent. But Oster didn't appear to be a man who would give up easily. It occurred to him that Oster was the kind of police officer law-abiding people would want.

All of a sudden, he felt like a criminal.

The kids were napping. Ox and Barbara sat in the living room and sipped coffee.

"Ox, this doesn't look good."

"I don't think any of the congregation is going to tell them anything."

"That group has really suffered, but if only one of them makes a slip, they all go, and I'd be lying if I didn't say I'm worried about you."

"What could they ever charge me with?" But he knew full well he could be charged with aiding and abetting and probably obstruction of justice and a long list of other charges. Oster was out to get him and everybody else he could invent a charge for. Ox didn't want Barbara to worry.

"I don't know, but that Emmett and Jessie May must have been nosing around. Could you be charged for aiding and abetting, or whatever they call it?"

"No, I never aided them in what they did."

"What about hiding what they did?"

"The only person who would expose anybody was Nehmi."

"Well, what about him? Could they charge you for his disappearance?"

"Barbara, they have nothing to go on."

"Well, I'm worried. This case is old as the hills, and yet here they are spying around and making threats. Something's going on."

"Don't worry about us. Worry about the group. They're the ones who are vulnerable."

"I'm not so sure. With that crazy Emmett and that crazy Oster, anything can happen. You know they are going to watch everything going on. They might pick up on the most innocent thing."

"That gives me a thought; the graveyard plaques. They've got to be careful what they say on them. I'll get Elmer to talk to them all. They can't mention death, just missing."

CHAPTER FIFTY-THREE

Jessie May and Emmett found Hoosac Street in the northeastern section of Philadelphia. "Crazy name," said Emmett.

"Lot of crazy street names."

"Lot of crazy people in this case."

"Some of them may be as crazy as you."

They drove until they came to the 1100 block and slowed down.

"1147. There it is," said Emmett.

Jessie May pulled over in front of the small frame house. "Why would anyone paint a house orange?"

"To make it even uglier?"

Jessie May went up to the front door while Emmett scooted around to the back. She knocked and peered in through the door glass. Not a sound. She rapped hard on the door. Nothing. She walked to the attached garage and peered in through the windows. No car. Looked like some kind of workshop. No room for a car. There was no car in the driveway. No car in front of the house.

Emmett joined her. "I don't think anybody's in there."

"There's no car here. He may have vamoosed."

"I'll call downtown to see what's registered in his name." He headed for the squad car. "Put out an all-points."

Emmett came back. "Can you believe that guy drives a blue Edsel? That's a dinosaur."

"Should be easy to spot."

"You know what? My gut tells me this guy's a killer. I'm busting in."

"No, wait. We'll get a court order."

"Court order, court schmorder. I'm going in now." He marched over to their car and yanked open the trunk. He came back with a crowbar. Jessie May watched as he jammed the bar through the lock plate of the front door, and with one jerk forced it open. He walked in still carrying the crowbar.

Jessie May stayed in front of the garage. She knew any evidence found would be useless with an illegal entry.

"Why did I get linked up with this idiot?" She figured he would have to come out sooner or later. Nothing to do but wait. Then the garage door opened.

"Look at all this crap he's got stored in here. He could burn down the city. Looks like he's been making fireworks. He got boxes of dynamite, gunpowder, cans of kerosene, a whole, damn arsenal. And look at this, an old-fashioned candle mold. He's even got a computer hooked up in here."

"Too bad none of it can be used as evidence. You couldn't wait for the court order."

"No time for that. We've got to catch this bird. He's the one we're looking for. Let's get out of here."

"Might as well, now."

"We find this guy and the case is solved."

"Come to think of it," said Jessie May, "there were a bunch of churches burned a few months back. You don't suppose . . ."

CHAPTER FIFTY-FOUR

They were all at the graveyard, planting flowers, pulling up a few stray weeds that had been overlooked, and placing the plaques for those missing. Each time a plaque was placed, everyone gathered around. It was a quiet time.

Ox noticed that some of the members who had come only occasionally to church were now acting as though they were part of the family. It was a good sign. It was a sign of healing.

The plaques were all quite simple. There was the name of the person, hidden in memory, with the words "missed deeply." Nothing else. No secrets exposed.

When they were all finished, they walked back into the church, sat quietly in the dining room and drank coffee. Ox left them to themselves and went up to his study.

He looked out the window and saw Emmett and Jessie May walking toward the graveyard.

"Good Lord." He headed down the steps and out the side door. "Damn." Ox entered the graveyard just as Emmett was talking.

"Missed deeply. Does that mean buried deeply? Load of crap. Planting flowers ain't gonna make it go away. Who do they think they're fooling?"

Jessie May made no comment. Emmett saw Ox. "Okay, preacher. You'll be interested in knowing we found Mr. Nehmi's car parked a block down the street. How do you suppose he left here without it? Or is he hiding somewhere in your church? Do we need to get a search warrant?"

"The church is open. You can go anywhere you want to. Try not to make a nuisance of yourselves." Ox was surprised at his own aggressive feelings.

Jessie May had been kneeling by one of the plaques. "Dr. Christie, are these people dead?"

"I don't think anyone can answer that question, but my congregation is suffering and you aren't making things better for them."

"Dr. Christie, you must understand, it's not our job to make things better for them. It's our job to find out what happened."

"Let me know if I can help you."

"It would help us if you could tell us where Mr. Nehmi is."

"I have no idea where he is, but I'm sure he isn't in the church."

"He may have been involved in a number of church burnings."

Ox didn't hide his surprise. He remembered reading about the church arsons in Philadelphia.

"Knowing him as you do, would it surprise you if he burned churches?"

"It would surprise me if anyone did such a thing. And you must remember, I haven't been here all that long. I didn't get to know him all that well."

"Shit," said Emmett.

CHAPTER FIFTY-FIVE

Ox felt exhausted. The three months he had been with the church seemed more like three years. He walked down toward the dining room. *Don't police have to pass an IQ test?* Jessie May seemed intelligent, but Emmett was dumb as a post. Either that, or he was trying to fill the role of what he thought was a hardnosed cop. The old congregation was still there. They were sitting in a circle facing each other. As he entered, Elmer was talking.

"Think of as many ideas as you can for us to help get this church back on its feet. What's been done in the past can't be undone, but we must do everything we can to at least make up for it in some degree."

"Elmer," said Ox. "Jessie May and Emmett are outside. You might want to watch what you say in case they come within earshot."

"I think it's time for us to go over to Hilda's house," said Elmer. "Ox, why don't you join us?"

"I'd kind of like to stick around."

Angel came hurrying into the dining room. "Ox, the bishop is on the line."

Ox trudged back up the steps. Somehow, he didn't feel any desire to talk to the bishop. "Hello, Bishop Markham. What can I do for you?"

"Oxford, we were just wondering how things are going for you and thought a short visit might be in order. Reverend Darner and I thought we would drop in on you some time the week after next. Maybe Tuesday week. How would that be on your schedule?"

"Bishop, any time would be all right. I would fit my schedule around your visit. Is there anything in particular I can do for you?"

"No, but I would like to chat with some of the church leaders: Mr. Weiss, and maybe Mr. Nehmi, and others you might suggest."

"I can certainly arrange that, Bishop, but Nehmi has left. Mr. Weiss and Miss Danziger and any others will certainly be honored to talk to you."

"I'm surprised to hear Mr. Nehmi has left. He always seemed so concerned for the well being of the congregation. Maybe you could talk him into coming around for a chat?"

"Unfortunately, Bishop, he seems to have just disappeared. We don't know where he is."

"I'm surprised. Did something happen to upset him?"

"We can't put our finger on anything ... except ... the police are looking for him. They think he may be connected to some arsons at local churches."

"That sounds outlandish. But the police have just about blamed everybody for the disappearances of some of the congregation. There was a member of the choir who seemed involved. But that's old news. We can discuss that more next Tuesday. We'll let you know the time of arrival."

Ox stood and gazed out the window. It seemed the bishop

THE HIDDEN CONGREGATION

had been fed misinformation by Nehmi. What did the bishop believe? Why hadn't the bishop told him of the problems if he knew of them? That didn't seem honest.

At that moment, Jessie May and Emmett passed under the window on the way from the graveyard. Jessie May looked up and signaled they were coming in.

Great. Now they were going to want to look in every corner of the building.

Ox called Angel. "When Jessie May and Emmett come up here, give them a tour of the building like you did for me when I first came here."

He could hear them coming up the steps.

"Do I have to?"

Ox stepped out into the hall. "What do you want now?"

"Dr. Christie, we need to know where Mr. Nehmi is."

"Jessie May, I have no idea where he is."

"We don't have a search warrant, but we can get one if it's necessary. Can we search the premises?"

"Go right ahead. Ms. Rush can show you around if you like."

"That would be helpful and would you also accompany us?"

"I have other things to do."

"I know, but it would help clear the air if you came with us."

"As far as I'm concerned, there's no air to clear. I'll be in my study."

In his study, Ox could hear Angel's voice describing the large meeting room as she took them on the tour. He heard Emmett's voice, "We've seen this. Show us the rooms behind closed doors." Their sounds faded away.

Ox realized he had become more assertive. It must have been the basement experience. That was enough to make anybody testy. No doubt about it, it had been a growing experience. And now the bishop was coming. What for? It had to

255

be in relation to all the past trauma. How much did he know? Ox had a very strong feeling the bishop hadn't leveled with him. He felt a bit used—not the right kind of feeling regarding one's bishop.

He thought of his own path in religion. He had been a Baptist as a boy. He could hear the song he had sung when he was a little sunbeam. Tiny voices singing, "Jesus loves me, this I know, 'cause the Bible tells me so . . ." And each Sunday, the minister would cry real tears because Jesus died to cleanse us of our sins. No one could explain to him how Jesus dying had saved him from sin. Especially after he had stolen a toy soldier from the dollar store. Ox joined the Episcopal church, sang in the choir, carried the cross and led the processional each Sunday morning. He had tried to be inspired. He thought of the old Episcopal priest. He sensed the man had seen something in him, but it didn't take. Then came a stint in the army. Pure hell. Sherman was right: war really was hell.

He came back an atheist. No god could allow such unmerciful killing. There was no God. We were all an accident. Particles of matter chancing together. A curious dance like dust particles in the air.

But as he got older, he kept seeing signs. Little things that alone meant nothing, but cumulative—something. One day, he realized he had slipped from atheism to agnosticism. He could no longer say there was no God. He could only question. Signs. Then, he saw his grandfather—his grandfather who had died before Ox was born. He was standing in the next yard just looking at Ox. More like studying him. Ox had gone on into the house. When he looked back, he was gone. He had an old photograph of him, standing in what must have been his back yard, feeding chickens, and wearing a black suit and a black string tie; the same suit and string tie he was still wearing.

THE HIDDEN CONGREGATION

Ox wondered. Was his grandfather an angel? Had he come back to guide him? Had he been there all along? Had he kept him out of harm's way? When he went into the service, he had been selected for weather school and as a result, was somewhat removed from direct danger. He had watched the other young men. Most of them drank. Some were away from home for the first time and the drinking symbolized their escape from home—freedom. Later it was an escape from where they were. He had never needed an escape. He had never rebelled. He had just followed whatever path opened up for him.

A belief came to him. A God created everything and set up a system of angels to move everything in the right direction. God had gone on to other things. It was up to the angels to set things right. That explained all the ungood in the world. God wasn't letting horrible things happen. The angels weren't able to control everything. Then he realized it was a collective effort. Everyone was a part of it, himself included. A kind of collective energy focusing through a system of angels. Maybe that was where the term "host of angels" came from. We all formed a single soul. It was up to everyone to work it out. We could advance or deteriorate.

Where did the bishop fit into all this? A hierarchy on earth. Was it needed? Well, maybe to help people come to terms.

Emmett walked in without knocking. "We need to get into the room off the nursery. It has a padlock on it and Ms. Rush says she doesn't have the key."

Ox was startled by the thought of Emmett and Jessie May going into the dirt basement. There would be no candles, but . . . "That's an unfinished basement, nothing but dirt. There's nothing in there."

"All the same, Dr. Christie, we need access to complete our search." Jessie May sounded apologetic.

"Hey! We'll get a warrant and search your damn house, too. You want to give us a rough time?" Emmett leaned forward and squinted at Ox.

"Have it your way." Ox got the key to the padlock from his desk drawer. "Let's go."

Ox unlocked the door. What was going to happen when Jessie May and Emmett walked into that area? No candles had been lit in there for a while, but the dust . . . He opened the door and stepped back to let them in.

Emmett rushed in ready to spring into action. He stood in the dust and Jessie May walked in behind him. "We have a flashlight out in the car. I'll go get it."

"I have one upstairs. I'll get it for you. I hope this will be the end of your suspicions that we are hiding Nehmi." Ox stepped in and looked around. There was a faint smell of something, but diluted. He left.

He took his time walking up to the fuse box by the entrance to the sanctuary. Maybe if the odor got to them and something happened, it would end the investigation. He got the flashlight and slowly walked back to the dirt basement, feeling a little guilty.

The two of them were standing side by side in the same place. They seemed to be looking deeper into the dirt basement, but they were really just standing there. They weren't talking. Ox stood in the doorway for a few minutes then said, "Here's the flashlight."

"Thank you," said Emmett. "That was very thoughtful of you. I hope we didn't put you to too much trouble."

Ox stepped back. Was Emmett being sarcastic? He almost sounded genuine. He handed over the flashlight.

Emmett played the beam of light around in the basement, to the far end, to the corners, on the ceiling, and clicked it off.

THE HIDDEN CONGREGATION

"Nothing in here. Guess we bothered you for nothing. Sorry." He handed the flashlight back to Ox.

"Um . . . no problem."

"Emmett's right. We've been imposing."

"It's all right, Jessie May." Ox wondered what kind of change had just taken place.

"No, it's not all right," said Emmett. "We've imposed—me in particular."

"You were just doing your job, Emmett," said Jessie May.

Ox led the way out. "Are . . . are you two all right?"

"We're fine," said Emmett. "Never better."

Jessie May stepped back in. "There's something peaceful about this place. It might make a good meditation room."

Emmett, who was already standing by the nursery door, said, "Crap. It's just a dirt basement. Look at all the dirt clinging to my trousers."

"Oh, Emmett," said Jessie May. "You can be a pain. Just brush it off. A little dust never hurt anyone."

"Well," said Ox, "is there anything else I can do for you two?"

"No, thanks," said Jessie May. "We feel better about everything now."

"Shit," said Emmett.

CHAPTER FIFTY-SIX

Ox entered his study and sat in one of the easy chairs reserved for guests. He sat looking out the window at the sky. What had happened in there? A change in personalities? Emmett seemed almost human for a few minutes. And Jessie May, while always more courteous, seemed even more so and polite even to Emmett.

"Dr. Christie?"

It was Jessie May. "Yes?"

"I would like to join the church."

"Well, I think you have already done that."

"No, I mean in my own name and for real. Emmett and I were only here on assignment."

She blushed slightly. "Sorry about that. But in another way, I'm not sorry. I feel a real attachment to this church. I want to be a real member. My real name is Jessie May Fremont, not Dobson."

"What about Emmett?"

"He said he would wait in the car."

"Are you two partners?"

"Only on this case, and as far as I'm concerned the case is closed. Nehmi's gone and whatever he did will stay with him until he's caught."

THE HIDDEN CONGREGATION

"Jessie May, did you feel anything unusual in that basement?"

"Now that you mention it. It just felt so peaceful in there. I could have stayed there for hours. I can only say, I felt more at peace than I have for years. It's kind of a unique place. Maybe it should be kept unlocked for people to go in and just sit. Maybe you could call it the Peace Room."

"The Peace Room." Ox tried to swallow his surprise. "That really is something to think about."

"Anyway, can I sign the book with my real name?"

"You bet. We're lucky to have you."

Ox sat thinking about it. Peace Room? All the dust. What about At Peace Room? Were Jessie May and Emmett unique? Would anyone else be affected the way they were? Should he leave the door unlocked? Open, with a few chairs? At Peace, it had a double meaning.

At the dinner table, Ox mentioned the effect the room had on Jessie May and Emmett. "Let's walk in there together tomorrow. See how we feel. Might be good to test it out cautiously on a few new people. We could always be around to monitor."

"What does 'at peace' mean?" asked Billy.

Ox expected Martha to have a comment, but she didn't. She looked the question, too. "It's a place where you forget your worries. You're too young to worry."

"I worry," said Billy.

"What do you worry about?" asked Barbara.

"I worry you're going to make me wash."

"Good idea. Time to go and get washed. Then come back down for a story."

Going up the steps, Billy said to Martha, "See?"

"Our little boy is growing fast," said Barbara.

"Thank God the place he's growing up in has improved."

"Babe, do you have any idea what that room could do for the church if the effect is real?"

"Yeah, but that's a big if. It's hard to imagine the dust without the candles having such a different effect."

"Is there any such thing as dust analysis?"

Ox thought about it. "Ammahn knows someone at Penn. He mentioned he could get the candles analyzed."

CHAPTER FIFTY-SEVEN

Ox told Angel to let everyone know the bishop would be visiting.

Ammahn asked, "What's the old buzzard coming down here for?"

Ox laughed. "I don't know for sure, but I think he wants to see how I'm holding up, given past problems."

"That means he knows more than he's saying."

"I guess that means everyone will have to be told to clam up, like with the police. We'll have a meeting at Hilda's, but I suspect by now a briefing's not necessary."

Ox decided it would be appropriate to mention the bishop's visit during the Sunday service. He was surprised to see Emmett come in with Jessie May. That could only mean Oster had not closed the case. They weren't home free yet.

After the sermon, there was a lot of talk about the bishop and why he was coming. "I guess it's an honor," said Elmer. "He's never been here before."

"Why now?" said Hilda.

"Where was he when we needed him?" said Angel.

"That's what I say," said Joe. "Who needs him?"

"We need to welcome him in honor of the office he holds," said Ox. "I think we should have a state dinner in Hosannah's dining room. That'll be on the agenda at the meeting at Hilda's."

"You mentioned an 'At Peace' room downstairs," said Elmer. "Will that be on the agenda?"

"I have some concern about that," said Hilda.

Barbara came over and tugged at Ox's arm. "Cynthia and I need to talk to you—up in your study."

In his study, Cynthia said, "You and I are the logical people to test the At Peace Room."

"Are you crazy?"

"No. Barbara and I have worked it out. We go in. We sit in chairs a few feet apart facing away from the door, which will be open. Barbara will monitor. We can judge the effect."

"I'm not at all sure of the effect on Jessie May and Emmett. Maybe they were ready for a change in their relationship."

"Babe, you said yourself Emmett was civil for the first time. It might have worn off, but it was real for the moment. It's worth a try."

"Yes," said Cynthia. "What's the worst that can happen with Barbara keeping watch? I want to try it."

Ox watched as Barbara set two wooden chairs about ten feet into the dirt basement and a little over a foot apart. Ox sat with Cynthia to his left. Ox was worried this could just start the cycle over again. He looked straight ahead. The basement was quiet. He could almost hear the dust settling. He could see nothing but darkness in front of him. There was a faint odor, but new, different. Nothing to worry about. He relaxed. The visit by the bishop would be uneventful. It would probably be a good thing—put things behind everybody. Nehmi and the threat were gone. The ministry was going well. He had noticed a few more visitors today. And the kids were growing in all the right ways. Barbara was wonderful, and expecting another baby.

THE HIDDEN CONGREGATION

Life was good. Better than good. The congregation had come back to life. The memorial garden was evidence of that. And Ammahn was a good human being. Philadelphia was an interesting city. He was happy he had come. The room was so quiet he could almost hear the absence of sound.

Like a vacuum, no sound allowed, wonderful. He closed his eyes. But he didn't sleep. There were too many happy thoughts.

"Okay. Time to evaluate." Barbara put a hand on his shoulder.

"Wow," said Cynthia. "I was just hearing the most wonderful music. It sounded like a thousand violins."

"That was really restful," said Ox. "I just replayed the last month."

"You two realize you were only in here for five minutes?"

Ox shook his head. "It seemed like a lot longer. Maybe we ought to call it the therapy room. I think I could have been with a hundred people in here and I wouldn't have been aware of anybody else. And in my mind, Cynthia wasn't anywhere near the place."

"Cynthia, did you sense Ox nearby?"

"No, I think I was floating on a cloud somewhere."

"Well, we've just had a good test of the room. Now we need to try it out with a group."

"Your psychotherapy background is showing," said Ox.

"Speaking of that," said Barbara, "maybe we could add some additional odors to really put people at peace. We change from the candles with the negative effects to something that will increase the positive."

"Maybe we ought to test it out on Oster," said Ox.

"Yeah, sure," said Barbara. "While you're thinking about neutralizing the police force, let's think of ways to improve on this room."

WILLIAM T. DELAMAR

"Right. For one thing, we need flooring. The dirt should be pushed back and maybe we should build a brick wall to keep the dirt back and give the place the appearance of a room."

"What about some faint lighting?" asked Cynthia.

"I'll tell you what," said Ox. "You two decide and we'll pay for it with Hosannah's money." Ox had started to head back to his study, then stopped. "But we need to really test this first. We need to bring the whole group back in."

CHAPTER FIFTY-EIGHT

Ox was surprised to see Ammahn come through the doorway. On Tuesday afternoons, he was scheduled to be at Penn.

"What brings you here at this hour?"

Ammahn plopped his briefcase on a chair and pulled out a folder. "Give a gander at this." He tossed the folder on Ox's desk.

"What is it?"

"Candle analysis."

Ox grabbed the folder and opened it.

Ammahn leaned over the desk. "The candles were made of animal fat infused with everything on that list."

Ox read out loud, "Essence of banana, cherry, fig, peach, cardamom, coriander, ginger, saffron, and yohimbe."

"They're still analyzing. Those are the elements they have definitely identified."

"These don't sound threatening. Sounds like a gourmet special except for the yohimbe. I never heard of it."

"The chemist thinks it's the combination with the animal fat. They haven't identified which animals other than goat at this point."

"Better tell them not to burn those candles."

"Not a chance. They've ground them up for easier analysis. They think there may be some kind of bird included. First they thought a mouse, then a bat. He said it might be a few more weeks."

"How would Nehmi get something like this?"

"You can get all kinds of information from the Internet. There are all types of people selling stuff and giving away harmful information to the social misfits of the world."

"Interesting." Ox shook his head. "I don't know what good it does for us to know this now."

"Maybe this one will give some possible guidance." Ammahn pulled another folder from his brief case and slid it across the table to Ox. "This is the analysis of the dust."

Ox picked it up and read it out loud. "Lavender, rosemary, spearmint, cinnamon, chamomile, flax seed, lemongrass, peppermint, valerian root, white willow, yarrow. I don't know. Sounds like a chef's spice rack."

"I have heard of some of those being included in aromatherapy and for relaxation."

"I sure didn't feel relaxed when I was in there with Cynthia."

"Maybe the dust removes tension and inhibitions so the candle mixture can take control."

"Maybe. It certainly made me feel relaxed."

CHAPTER FIFTY-NINE

Bishop Markham and Reverend Darner arrived in a stretch limousine. They wore business suits—no trappings of office. The bishop was a large, portly man, and Reverend Darner just the opposite.

"Dr. Christie, I'm sorry I was unable to get here at an earlier date. I hope everything here is to your satisfaction." Bishop Markham grasped Ox's hand with a warm, friendly grip.

"I think I made the right move in coming here, Bishop."

Ox walked the two visitors through the church, giving them a tour. Actually, Reverend Darner had been there before. He had preached on Sundays after Petersen's death. Ox wondered why the bishop had never been there before.

As if in answer to his thought, the bishop said, "I must apologize. I really should have been here long ago, but there's been a problem. It's my own problem—a health problem. I'm seriously considering stepping down because of it. I felt I should come down here to do anything I could to help you. I knew there had been unexplained happenings here, and I didn't mention them to you for fear you would decide against coming to Philadelphia. And the fact is, I was just too exhausted to extend the search for a minister here any farther if you had said no." The bishop shrugged his heavy shoulders. "I hope you will see your way clear to forgive me."

"Bishop, I'm happy to be here."

The tour of the building had started upstairs, and as they came down into the dining room, the bishop headed for a chair.

"I exhaust easily. Do you mind if we rest a moment?"

Reverend Darner placed his hand on the bishop's shoulder. "I'm not sure you should have made the trip."

"Reverend Darner is my physician. Actually, he's my psychiatrist. I'm suffering from depression. Have been for years. Ethan and Betty Petersen were my two best friends. They were the perfect couple. I sensed trouble when they stopped communicating with me, but I thought it was something I did. But when all those people disappeared, I knew something strange had happened. I did nothing to help. I let them down."

"Whatever happened was not your fault," said Reverend Darner.

"I just know I could have helped. I feel it in my soul. Dr. Christie, how is the congregation? Anything about the missing members?"

Ox was beginning to feel as though he was hearing a confession. "Actually, they're doing well and the congregation is slowly growing, but the missing members are still missing. I think the congregation is ready to move on."

"Obviously, you've been a great help. I only wish there was something I could have done."

"Bishop," said Reverend Darner, "let's cut the tour short. A building is just a building. Let's go up to Dr. Christie's study and chat. You need to rest." He turned to Ox. "I tried to talk him out of coming, but he feels guilty."

The three men made their way back to the study, Ox in the lead. "Whatever happened seems to have been beyond the

THE HIDDEN CONGREGATION

power of some very intelligent people to control. But now they are dealing with it in a constructive fashion. They have started a memorial garden in honor of those who are missing. The entire congregation seems to have come back to life."

"Obviously your doing."

"I don't think I can take the credit for that. I think they came to the realization on their own. I think it was a group effort. What's past is past."

"Thank you for whatever you did," said the bishop.

He settled into a cushioned chair. It was obvious the little bit of effort to walk though part of the building had worn him out. "My problem is mental, not physical. I'm a nutcase."

Reverend Darner shook his head. "I keep telling him he's not a nutcase. Depression is a recognized malady. It can be cured."

"If I could be cured, why am I still such a nutcase?"

"Give it time. Take a vacation. Get your mind off things that bother you."

Ox couldn't help but think of the dirt basement, the Peace Room. If he took him down there and it did nothing for him, they would think he was crazy. Best to test it with the congregation first. If he could think of a reason to get him down to the nursery, maybe it would just happen.

"Bishop, why don't we walk down to the nave and chancel. You should see the beautiful artwork, the chandeliers, the wooden paneling. It's truly a beautiful place of worship. You should see it."

"Yes, you are right." The bishop pushed himself up from the chair.

They made their way slowly downstairs. Ox flipped on the lights as they entered the huge place of worship. "I know it's a little farther, but let's go to the back. It's that much more impressive."

They sat in the back pew.

"It is marvelous," said the bishop. "And peaceful."

"The first time I saw it, I thought of the great cathedrals of Europe."

"There was a lot of money in the original congregation here," said the bishop. "They made large donations, built up a large reserve."

"Maybe in time, we will be able to recapture that."

"I think the donation from Hosannah Lewis might be seed money for that. Oxford, I want to talk to you about that. It's what I really came down here for." The bishop leaned forward and placed his hands on the back of the pew in front of him. "I don't know what happened here, and if you ever find out, it's your duty to protect the congregation. They come first. I knew some of them. I knew Hosannah and Stuart. There were good people involved in whatever happened. Not bad people. Your duty is to protect them. That's what I wanted to say."

CHAPTER SIXTY

A block away in a squad car, Jessie May sat behind the wheel. Beside her sat Oster. And in the back seat sat Emmett.

"One of them was the bishop. Bet it was the big one. Got fat off everybody else." Emmett leaned back with his hands laced behind his neck.

"Oh, Emmett, when did you become an expert on bishops?"

"Okay, you two. Shut up. They've been in there long enough to get comfortable. Let's go."

Jessie May inched the car on toward the church. She turned up into the courtyard. "The side door is usually unlocked."

"I want to question that bishop," said Oster.

"Would that really be proper? After all, he is a bishop."

"He ain't God," said Emmett. "He's just a damn bishop."

Oster grunted, "If we keep pumping, somebody's going to crack."

"But it reaches a point where it's excessive."

Oster glared at her. "There's no such thing as excessive when you are trying to solve a case."

They entered through the side door and heard voices coming from the sanctuary. They turned that direction and caught sight of Ox and the bishop exiting toward the down stairway. "I wonder if they are going to the dirt basement," said Jessie May.

Emmett remained silent.

"Why would they be going to a dirt basement?" Oster asked.

"I don't know," said Jessie May. "Just something interesting about it."

"Like what?"

"I don't know. I guess you just had to be there."

Oster gave her a dubious look.

They headed down the steps.

Ox was standing in the doorway to the dirt basement.

"Okay, Preacher, I want to talk to that bishop," Oster declared.

"I'll get a chair for you to join him." Ox moved over to a row of chairs along the wall and grabbed one.

"I'd like to go in, also," said Jessie May. She walked over and grabbed a chair.

"So would I," said Emmett.

The three officers stood behind their chairs just behind the bishop and Reverend Darner.

No one spoke. They were all faced toward the dark end of the area. Finally, the three officers sat. Ox still stood in the doorway. The only light came from the nursery.

After ten minutes, Ox said, "It might be more comfortable if we all sat out here in the nursery."

All five stood up at the same time. The bishop and Reverend Darner seemed a little surprised to see the other three.

In the nursery, Oster addressed the bishop. "Sir, are you Bishop Markham?"

"Yes. What can I do for you Officer?"

"Sir, I'm Officer Oster and I'm sorry to bother you, but I need to talk to you about the disappearances of a number of people from this congregation."

THE HIDDEN CONGREGATION

"Officer Oster, I wish I knew what happened to those people. Their disappearances have depressed me for years. Ethan and Betty Petersen were among my closest friends. I would give anything to know what happened here."

"I'm sorry for your loss," said Oster. "It must have been hard on everyone, but it's still an open case and I would like to be able to pick up the loose ends."

Emmett and Jessie May remained silent. The bishop sat in one of the chairs along the wall.

"Officer Oster, I could never thank you enough if you were able to solve the mystery. What I understand from Dr. Christie here, Mr. Nehmi might have had a hand in what happened. He seems to have disappeared."

"He's one person on the suspect list."

"There's a list of suspects?"

"Yes. Mr. Nehmi, this Ammahn character, Dr. Christie, and Mr. Weiss."

"Dr. Christie was nowhere near here when all that took place."

"We were concerned he might have been sent here to cover up what happened. We thought he might have something to do with Nehmi's disappearance."

Emmett seemed to regain his natural aggressiveness again. "My money's on Nehmi."

"We've searched every inch of the church for him. He's not here," said Jessie May.

"Maybe he's in cahoots with Ammahn," said Emmett.

"Where does Ammahn live?" asked Oster, who also began to show signs of his natural aggressiveness. "Maybe we ought to go there right now with you gentlemen to see if Nehmi is there."

"I'll have to get his address from the office," said Ox.

"We'll all go to the office. No phone calls."

WILLIAM T. DELAMAR

They all walked up the stairs. The bishop seemed to have regained his energy. "We could all fit in my stretch limo. We might as well get full use of it."

"We'll take the squad car. Emmett, you ride with them and follow us."

CHAPTER SIXTY-ONE

Angel called Elmer to let him know what had happened. Elmer said he would let everyone else know.

"We should still prepare for the dinner at Hosannah's tonight," said Elmer. "The bishop wasn't feeling well. I hope he'll be all right."

"We'll just have to hope for the best."

"If Oster finds out what happened, could we all go to jail?"

"There's no way he's going to find out."

"Even Ox could be charged for covering it up."

"Angel, quit worrying."

"The whole church could be destroyed."

"Angel, none of that is going to happen. Now, stop the worrying. Everything is going to be all right. Quit being so damn timid. Where's your spirit? You weren't timid when you told Nehmi to burn in hell."

"Oh," she said. "Could I be charged with murder?"

"Not unless all of us are. Your secret is safe."

"That Oster scares me, Elmer."

She could see him in his heavy boots. He could stare a hole into a person. She trembled thinking of him.

CHAPTER SIXTY-TWO

The two cars traveled north on the Skuylkill Parkway. The lead car was driven by Jessie May. Oster sat by her side. The second car, the stretch limousine, was driven by a chauffeur. In the back face-to-face seats, sat Ox, the bishop, Reverend Darner, and Emmett.

Oster watched Jessie May. "Do you know where the house is?"

"Yes, I got a map from the Internet when I thought we might need to question Dr. Laval."

"But you don't think that's needed anymore."

"No, I don't. I don't have any idea what happened to those people, but I think Nehmi might have had something to do with it."

"What if we find Nehmi with Laval? Would you still think they were acting alone? Could it be possible Elmer Weiss was working with them? And Christie was brought in by the bishop to help hide it?"

"I just don't believe any of that. There's nothing to support it."

"I'm not sure police work is for you."

* * *

THE HIDDEN CONGREGATION

In the stretch limousine, Emmett sat next to Reverend Darner and faced the bishop and Ox. "I see you've decided to admit all those people were killed."

"Admit what? What are you talking about?" said Ox.

"Those plaques in the graveyard. Didn't even want to give them gravestones?"

"The plaques don't mean they're dead. The plaques mean they are missed."

"Why did it take so long for them to say 'Heck, I miss you'?" Emmett grinned like he had caught him.

Ox wondered how Emmett ever got to be a policeman. "I think it's taken a long time for these people to finally come to grips with the fact they are gone. The plaques simply express their hope they will all return. Hope is all they have. They have all suffered. Don't take their hope away from them."

"So you don't want us to find out if they were murdered?"

"It would be really strange for that number of people to be murdered and nobody know about it."

The bishop interrupted. "Young man, Dr. Christie has done a remarkable job in helping these people deal with a traumatic loss. Imagine if someone close to you just disappeared. Put yourself in their shoes. I realize the police have a duty to perform, but consider the quality of mercy. Be kind. Think of what they have all gone through. You are a better person than you act."

Ox was surprised to see Emmett lean back in the seat and look out the window. They continued on in silence.

After three wrong turns the cars turned into a small dirt road leading down to a wooden house with a porch. There was a car with a University of Pennsylvania emblem on it parked beside it.

Oster leaned forward. "There's a cross above the door. I don't trust people who wear crosses to show how good they are. I want to question this Ammahn Laval. Let's see how willing he is for us to search the house."

Oster and Jessie May stepped onto the porch while Emmett ran round back in case Ammahn or Nehmi tried to escape. Oster pounded on the door. "Police! Open up."

No sound from inside. Emmett came running round the corner. "There's no back door."

"Guess this is the only way in and out. What a crappy little house. Guess they don't pay eggheads much, about what they deserve. Crappy little place sitting in the middle of nothing."

"Well, it's kinda like a little summer place," said Emmett. "Maybe he doesn't need a larger place. Can't really judge a man by his house."

Emmett looked surprised by his own comment. It was as though his conscience spoke before he did. Jessie May and Oster stared at him. Neither said anything.

Ammahn came from behind them and stepped on the porch. "Something I can do for you?" He was carrying a small plastic bucket with some brownish objects in it.

"What's in the bucket?" asked Oster.

"Amber."

"What for?"

"Just samples."

"Samples for what?"

"If you must know, amber from certain levels down in the earth are indicative of the great pine forest that use to spread from the northeast to the southwest in this country. Roughly two-thirds of it is now gone. Do you care?"

"Frankly, I don't give a rat's ass," said Oster.

Jessie May spoke up. "Dr. Laval, we are looking for Emil Nehmi. We'd like to search your house to rule out the number of places he could be."

THE HIDDEN CONGREGATION

"What makes you think he could be in my house? I don't harbor criminals."

"Look buddy," said Oster. "Doctor or whatever, we have a short list of suspects for some possible murders and you can help us to shorten the list. We want in."

"So I'm a suspect?"

"Everybody's a suspect."

"That's a short list?"

"We can get a warrant if we need it. You can make it easier on yourself if you just open the door and let us search. If he's not in there, we're on our way. What's it gonna be?" Ammahn stepped to the unlocked door and opened it. "Come in. Have a ball. Just don't mess with anything."

Jessie May and Emmett climbed the stairs to the second floor.

"While they're searching, I have a few questions for you," Oster said.

"Make it quick. I have a lecture to prepare."

"You just recently joined the Church of the One Soul. What lead you to that church?"

"What's the problem with my picking that church? Can't I pick my own church?"

"I'm asking the questions. Why did you join it?"

"Because I wanted to. It was my choice."

"Listen, you smartass college professor . . ." Oster seemed to catch himself. "Dr. Laval, we're just trying to solve a possible crime."

"If you are referring to the disappearance of a number of members of the church, say so. I wasn't even in Pennsylvania when all that happened. I was in California, and I object to your line of questioning. If you have more questions, I'll be upstairs in my study."

"I could take you downtown."

"What are you going to charge me with, freedom of religion?"

Ammahn went up the steps.

Oster stood in the middle of the small front room. "Damn college professor." He kicked the small rug and discovered the trap door. "Emmett! Jessie May! Get down here."

He bent down and opened the trap door just as Jessie May came down the steps.

"Go out to the car and get the flashlight."

Emmett straggled into the room and peered down into the basement. "What the hell's down there?"

"That's what you are going to find out."

Emmett felt his way down the steps cautiously. He couldn't see what was below. Oster trained the light down on him. "Dark down here."

"What do you see?"

"Nothing. Too dark."

Emmett switched on his flashlight.

"Now what do you see?" Oster demanded.

Emmett played the light around. "Just a little room with a dirt floor." He stepped off the ladder. He could feel a faint breeze. "Must be an opening somewhere. I can feel air moving." Then he saw the cave opening. "There's a tunnel down here."

"See where it goes."

"Not a very big opening, but this might be where Nehmi is hiding."

"I'm coming down."

Emmett knelt down to peer into the tunnel. He trained the light into it. About twenty feet in, the cave bent off to the right. He could hear Oster coming down the steps. On his hands and knees, he crawled into the cave.

"Okay, Nehmi. Here I come."

Soon, he was crawling on his belly, pulling himself along

THE HIDDEN CONGREGATION

with his elbows. Flashlight in the left hand and gun in the right. Maybe Nehmi was farther down hiding in the dark with the bodies of all those people from the church.

The tunnel curved off to the right. *Got to move slowly. Nehmi might be waiting.* Emmett extended his left arm and shined the flashlight around the curve. He inched forward. Nothing. Just more tunnel. It was getting smaller. He pulled himself forward. He still felt a little breeze. Another small tunnel forked off to the left. Which way to go? Went right before, go left this time.

He couldn't see behind himself. There was not enough room to turn his head. The tunnel was getting smaller—he might have to back up and go the other way. *Damn. Must be what it's like to be buried.* He backed up and heard a faint noise. Was it breeze along the dirt? What if Nehmi's waiting back there? He couldn't see going backward. His left leg caught in a hole off to the left. Had he come that way? Could he have passed a hole and not seen it? *Okay. Go that way.* It was getting tighter. He had to squeeze through—can't be right. He moved forward again. There was a tunnel to the left and a tunnel to the right. Which one? Go right—just a guess.

Every tunnel seemed to go down more. But he couldn't be sure. He couldn't tell up from down, right from left. Where was he? Another sound. Were those eyes ahead? Yellow. Or was it imagination. What was the sliding sound. A snake? He began to back up, but didn't know where he was going—the tunnel was tiny. He wouldn't be able to defend against a snake or a rat. What has yellow eyes in the dark? He stopped and tried to relax. He took a deep breath. He closed his eyes for a moment. He opened his eyes. Nothing there. Nothing anywhere. He didn't know where he was. Buried. Dust in the air. The flashlight was getting dim. He didn't want to be in the dark. He backed up more, but he seemed to be going down, not up. Where was he?

He didn't know if anyone could hear him. Where was he? He called out, "Can anyone hear me?" No response. It sounded like he was shouting down a well.

The light went out.

Ammahn got curious. It was too quiet downstairs. He peered down the steps. Jessie May was standing by the trap door. He came down.

"Where's Emmett and Officer Oster?"

"Down there."

"What are they doing?"

"Emmett's checking out the tunnel."

"He went into the cave?"

Ammahn scooted down the steps. He could see Oster from the light above, but no sign of Emmett. "When did he go in?"

"Twenty, thirty minutes ago," Oster said. "You worried about what he might find in your tunnel?"

"No. Worried about him." Ammahn pulled a candle out of the small cabinet on the wall and lit it. He grabbed a flashlight and walked over to the cave and listened. Nothing. "You haven't heard anything since?"

"He's a good officer. If Nehmi's down there, he'll bring him out."

"You've no idea what he's gotten himself into."

Ammahn knelt in front of the cave and shouted, "Emmett, can you hear me?"

Not a sound. Ammahn shook his head.

"You trying to warn Nehmi he's coming? I ought to pull you in right now."

"That's a complex cave system down there. I don't doubt for a minute that he's lost and can't find his way back. He's probably in one of the small offshoots. It's the same as being buried alive. There's a little air down there, but in the offshoots, you breathe

THE HIDDEN CONGREGATION

as much dust as air. He won't last much longer. You have an officer in danger. There are two reasons why I wouldn't suggest you go in after him. One: you're too fat to fit into the offshoots, and two: you're too stupid. There'd just be two officers in danger."

"I ought to run you in right now."

"For what, making an accurate description of you? I'm going in after him."

"No, you're not going to warn or help your friend Nehmi."

"Nehmi isn't down there. Your officer is in danger. I can go in and I will. It's my house and you're here without a warrant."

"I'm a radio call away from a warrant."

"Well then, you better go get one." Ammahn squatted and planted the candle in the dirt near the entrance to the cave. Oster turned his back to Ammahn.

"Jessie May," called Oster. "Get on the car radio and get us a warrant to search the house."

"We've already searched," said Jessie May.

"Don't argue with me. Go do it."

Ammahn slid headfirst into the cave.

"And furthermore, don't ever argue with me when I tell you to do something," Ammahn heard Oster say.

"It might help if I knew why we needed a warrant," Jessie May said.

"Because if this jackass goes into his tunnel, I'm going to arrest him."

Ammahn was around the curve in the cave and he could still hear Oster bellowing at Jessie May.

"Hey!" Oster shouted after him.

Ammahn trained his flashlight ahead. He called out, "Emmett!" He heard a faint yell that sounded like "Come back here." He could hear the familiar sound of air moving over the dust. He was soon pulling himself along by his elbows. He came

WILLIAM T. DELAMAR

to the first division and decide to go to the left, assuming that's what Emmett would have done—left, right, left, right. How easy it would be for someone unfamiliar to get lost. Still plenty of time to get him out, unless he panicked. He had heard of one cave explorer who had a heart attack and died, thinking he was buried alive. Or maybe he had thought he was about to be attacked by some hidden creature, a prehistoric leftover. Anyhow, when they found him, his fingernails were torn off—apparently from digging frantically at the cave wall.

Ammahn took another right and another left. He couldn't go much farther in this offshoot. It would get too small, but he needed to check it out anyhow. Nothing there. He backed out. He decided to back up and try alternate offshoots. If that didn't work out, he would have to go back near the entrance and take the first right instead of the first left. He called out for Emmett again. He heard nothing.

He crawled back to the primary artery and shined his light in both directions. Then he took the next alternate. And there, he saw two feet. He crawled up to Emmett and touched his ankle. Emmett screamed.

"It's me, Emmett. Ammahn. Back up toward me. We'll get out of here."

But Emmett didn't move. Well, he was alive, or he couldn't have screamed. Ammahn took his belt off and wrapped it around Emmett's ankles. He began to back up, pulling Emmett after him. In a little while they were back in the primary artery. Ammahn crawled up next to Emmett. "You okay, Emmett? You able to crawl out of here?"

Emmett opened his eyes. "My God. I'm alive."

Ammahn unwrapped the belt around Emmett's ankles. "Take my flashlight and crawl straight ahead. I'll correct you if you make a wrong turn."

THE HIDDEN CONGREGATION

Emmett crawled out of the cave, with Ammahn right behind him. Oster was standing at the foot of the steps.

Emmett remained on his knees. He was caked with dirt and taking deep breaths. "Thank God. Thank God. I was dead. I know I was dead."

Ammahn stood over him. "A common reaction. This is no place for amateurs. I'm glad I found you. There are stretches of that cave system I've never been in."

"I would have never gotten out of there."

Jessie May called down, "The warrant's on the way."

Oster called back, "We don't need a warrant, dumbass. Stupid tunnel."

Ox, Bishop Markham, and Reverend Darner waited in the stretch limousine outside Ammahn's cabin.

"I don't know what's going on in there, but Ammahn is a member of our congregation and I'm going in. It's been over a half hour."

"That lady officer smiled at you when she came out," said the bishop. "If that's any sign, everything should be all right."

"I don't think they're beating him or anything, but I'm his minister. I should be there."

Ox got out of the car just as Oster stepped out onto the porch. He was followed by Emmett, who looked like he had been dumped in a compost heap. Ammahn stood in the doorway. He waved to Ox and began to brush dust off his clothing.

"Time to head back," said Oster. He and Jessie May got into the squad car. Emmett came over to the limousine. He stumbled almost as though he were drunk. He stood by the car, waiting.

Ox walked over to Ammahn. "Everything okay?"

"It is now." Ammahn told Ox what had happened.

Oster reached over and blew the car horn.

The bishop's chauffeur got out and opened the car door. Emmett seemed to suddenly realize he should get in.

Ox got into the limousine beside Emmett. "Are you going to be okay?"

Emmett leaned his head back. "Yessir."

"Ammahn told me you got trapped in that cave. That must have been a harrowing experience."

"I thought I had died. I think I went to sleep."

The car started moving and Emmett closed his eyes.

Ox left him to his own thoughts.

At the church, Jessie May came over and helped Emmett out of the limousine. She put her arm around him and they walked over to the squad car. Oster shouted, "We'll be back!"

CHAPTER SIXTY-THREE

Oster propped his heavy feet up on his desk. "I don't know what you two have been doing on this case. Don't you have anything other than a few straws to grab?"

Jessie May said, "For my money, it was Nehmi. I know it's all circumstantial, but everything we really know points that way."

"Malarkey," said Oster. "He might have been part of it, but they're all in it together. Christie was sent here to hide their guilt. I think Weiss and Christie are both concealing evidence."

"Sarge," said Jessie May. "There's nothing to substantiate that."

"It's your job to find something to substantiate that. That's what you're being paid to do."

"I thought we were being paid to discover the truth, not to pin a rap on somebody."

"You pin the rap on that crowd and you'll be finding the truth. Don't tell me what you are supposed to be doing. You're supposed to prove that crowd is all guilty of murder. Period. Damn them all. They're just another cult and we treat them like a cult. Period."

Jessie May persisted. "Sarge, they believe in God, just like the rest of the churches."

"God, my foot. What's this nonsense about a single soul? We all joined at the hip or something? They even think they have a bishop. Only Catholics have bishops."

"Episcopalians and others have bishops. There's no law against having bishops."

"Listen, Jessie May. I'm getting tired of you protecting them."

"I'm just trying to be objective."

"Objective my ear. I want convictions."

Emmett had been sitting as though he were somewhere else. "Did Nehmi kill Hosannah Lewis and make it look like a suicide?"

"Possible," said Jessie May.

"That's wishful thinking," said Oster. "Maybe Christie put him up to it. She left a lot of money to their damn cult. She didn't leave any money to Nehmi."

"I don't know," said Emmett. "Why did Nehmi disappear after the suicide? It makes him look guilty."

"Emmett, we can't pin this on one person. In fact, what about Weiss? He was the one who found her. Was he even in church that day?"

"He was, Sarge," said Jessie May. "We saw him get up and leave in the middle of the service."

"Well, there you have it. He left to kill her."

"He left to go see why she wasn't there."

"There you go. Defending everybody but Nehmi. That damn Christie has put a lid on everything. They're all guilty."

"Sarge, it all points to Nehmi, and even that's guesswork. We may never know where those people are or even if they are alive. They could be in a Turkish brothel for all we know."

"Jessie May, I'm beginning to wonder if you belong in police work."

"From what I learned at the police academy, I do."

THE HIDDEN CONGREGATION

"We'll see." After a while, Oster said, "If we can't prove Christie's in on it, I'll find a way to frame him. Maybe we should bug his office or his phone."

"Waste of time," said Jessie May. "Time to bury the past."

"Like they buried all those people? It's time we got them together for interrogation. We'll start with the group and I'll have the bastard. You two don't have the guts. Then you two can be your own sweet selves and get to each of them individually. We're going to crack this case. I want to see them all fry."

CHAPTER SIXTY-FOUR

Angel leaned over her typewriter. She wouldn't look at Ox. "I'm afraid."

"He knows nothing. He can't hurt you."

"He scares me."

Elmer stood to one side. "Ox is right. He can't hurt you. We all need to stick together."

"Can't you tell him I'm just the secretary and know nothing?"

"He wants us all there, Angel," said Ox. "If you don't come, he'll think you're hiding something. You have to be there."

They were all assembled in the dining room, seated in a large circle—all except Angel who was still in the church office. The bishop and Reverend Darner had not arrived. Cynthia and Barbara came in and sat in chairs along the side of the room.

Ox began. "I asked you to be here an hour before Oster is scheduled so we can be sure we are all more or less on the same sheet of music."

Elmer said, "I'll go up and get Angel."

"Keep in mind the importance of giving him nothing. You are not just protecting yourself. You are protecting the church."

THE HIDDEN CONGREGATION

At that moment, Oster burst through the door. "So. I thought you might be meeting ahead of time. Need to get your stories straight?"

He was followed by Jessie May and Emmett in their full uniforms. Both looked uncomfortable.

Oster strode to the center of the circle. "I know every one of you is guilty of murder and I'm going to prove it, and you're all going to rot in jail."

"Officer Oster," said Ox. "These people have been through enough trauma without being accused of murder. It's absurd."

"And you are covering up. That makes you guilty of obstruction of justice, and I'm sure I can come up with some other charges. You all belong in jail."

Elmer came in with Angel.

Oster leveled his finger at Elmer. "I know you are guilty of murder and obstruction of justice. You can bet charges will be brought. Who's the murderer with you?"

"Miss Rush is the church secretary."

Oster walked toward Elmer and Angel. "You're going to jail for murder, lady."

Angel slumped to the floor. Elmer grabbed her as she fell. He knelt beside her and looked up at Oster. "This is insane."

"She knows she's guilty. She's faking." He stalked back into the center. "You're all guilty. Every one of you, and you're going to pay for it. Are you all going to fake passing out?"

Hilda ran over to Angel. Then she ran to the kitchen.

"Sergeant," said Jessie May, "you've really stepped over the line."

"Get the hell out of here! You think they're all innocent. I know better. They're all going to fry. Out. Out!" He pointed to the door. "You're off the case. Be in my office in the morning." Jessie May and Emmett backed out the door and left.

293

Elmer was cradling Angel and Hilda was holding a cold cloth to her forehead. Everybody stood, talking at the same time.

"This meeting is over," said Ox.

"What do you mean this meeting's over? This meeting's just starting."

"This meeting is over. If you want to charge us, do it. Charge us or get out. Harassment is not legal. That's not policing, that's Gestapo. And that's all you are. Charge us or get out." Ox pointed at the door.

To Ox's surprise, Oster headed for the door.

"You haven't heard the last of me." And he was gone.

Everyone crowded around Angel. She was sitting up, leaning against Elmer "Give her room," said Elmer. He helped her to her feet and led her to a chair.

"Everyone sit for a minute," said Ox.

Jessie May and Emmett came back in.

"Everyone," said Jessie May. "We want to apologize for what just happened. Officer Oster has been under a lot of pressure."

"That's no excuse," said Joe. "The man's a sorry excuse for a human being."

Others were nodding and agreeing.

"We've had enough of police," said Mary Jane.

"Please," said Jessie May. "Let Emmett and me get an official police meeting on record and help us get past this."

"Jessie May," said Elmer. "Enough is enough."

"I know. And you people have been through hell. What can we do to help?"

The outer door opened and the bishop came in, followed by Reverend Darner. "I hope I'm not too early."

"You're right on time," said Ox. "Everybody settle down. Let's allow Jessie May and Emmett to do their job so we can all relax.

THE HIDDEN CONGREGATION

We need to get all of this behind us. You've all suffered loss. It's time to recapture your lives."

The bishop and Reverend Darner stood off to the side next to Barbara and Cynthia.

Jessie May began, "The police wondered why, after all this time, you decided to place those plaques in the graveyard."

Elmer answered, "We miss them. It's that simple."

Emmett finally joined in. "But why now? Why not five years ago? Or ten years ago? They've been gone now—what, fifteen years?"

"I can tell you why," said Hilda. "It's because we finally realize they aren't coming back."

"That's right," said Joe. "Dr. Christie has brought us to our senses. He's the new broom. He woke us up."

"That's why Hosannah killed herself," said Hilda. "She finally admitted to herself that Stuart wasn't coming back. She's been good as dead all these years anyhow. She's no longer suffering."

"Speaking of Hosannah," said Jessie May, "is it possible Nehmi killed her to make it look like a suicide before he took off?"

"Why would he?" asked Elmer.

"Well, she left a lot of money to the church," said Emmett.

"That wouldn't help him," said Elmer.

"No," said Mary Jane. "Hosannah missed Stuart something awful. She cried a lot."

"Was Stuart the kind of person who would just run away?" asked Jessie May.

"He didn't seem like it," said Mary.

"He was wealthy, stable, loving," said Elmer.

"We have wondered if Nehmi had something to do with it," said Hilda.

"What about the others?" asked Emmett. "Were they the kind who would just up and go?"

They all joined in. There was a wave of no's throughout the room.

"To the police, it looks strange," said Jessie May.

"It was strange," said Elmer. "Strange hardly describes it."

Ox was surprised to see Ammahn come in. Ammahn stood along the wall near the bishop.

Jessie May continued. "Elmer, did you and your wife have children?"

"Yes. They had already left the nest." Elmer had a faraway look.

The room grew quiet.

"And the minister's wife. Was she the kind who would just up and leave?"

"It was horrible," Angel moaned almost to herself.

Neither Jessie May nor Emmett seemed to hear her. Elmer wrapped his arm around her again.

Oster came in and slammed the door. He looked around the room and focused on Angel. Ox realized Oster was looking for the weakest link.

Oster didn't come into the circle. Instead, he walked around the backs of the group. He stopped behind Angel. He leaned forward near her ear and shouted, "What do you know about Nehmi's disappearance?"

Angel, surprised, jumped up. "Burn in hell." She ran from the room and up the stairs, crying.

Oster watched her go.

Elmer quietly got up and went up after her. Jessie May and Emmett remained silent. Oster pushed into the middle of the circle. "Doesn't that cemetery out there worry any of you people?"

Ammahn stood up. "Of course we worry about cemeteries. Everybody worries about cemeteries. Don't you worry about

THE HIDDEN CONGREGATION

cemeteries? One day you will be in one and people can walk on your grave. There are more people under foot than above. There are layers of dead—dust— debris—carbon. The air we breathe is filled with gasses from under the earth. We breathe old life. We're just part of the cycle. But we worry about cemeteries. What's your next question?"

"Would you like me to place you under arrest?"

"For what? Answering your question? You ought to be arrested for asking stupid questions. Or maybe you can arrest me for expressing my opinion. You are a flea-bitten excuse for a policeman."

Oster was getting red in the face.

"Furthermore, you don't have a shred of evidence to support your ridiculous accusations. There's a difference between good police work and badgering. Maybe you ought to go back to police school. You've proven one thing. Policemen don't have to take an IQ test."

"That does it. Jessie May, Emmett, cuff him." Oster charged across the room. Jessie May and Emmett both restrained him.

"Sarge, let's go outside and let Emmett and me summarize our findings. This guy's baiting you."

Emmett and Jessie May pushed Oster toward the door.

"I'll be back, smartass."

The door closed behind the three of them.

Ox walked over to Ammahn while everybody stood and clapped.

"You just out-badgered the big badger."

"He had it coming."

"You met him head on and it was effective. Maybe he'll leave us all alone now."

"I'm part of this congregation now and I'm involved. These people need protection."

Bishop Markham said, "I don't know what happened here, and I don't really want to know. Whatever happens next, you must protect the church. And by the church, I mean the people in it."

"Yes," said Ox. He remembered wondering if he wasn't obligated to turn them all in. He looked at Elmer and Angel and Hilda, and realized how right he was to hide the terrible truth. They were all guilty of being trapped, himself included.

"Oxford," said Bishop Markham, "Reverend Darner and I must be getting back to New York. We'll have to miss your big dinner. Please pass our apologies to your congregation. I must say, you have handled the situation admirably."

"Bishop, I had no choice but to do what I did. Anyone would have done the same." It was just as well they couldn't be at the dinner. With all the interference, it wasn't ready anyhow. "I'll pass on your apologies. I'm sorry you can't be there."

In his study, Ox replayed the events. He was amazed by Ammahn's challenge to Oster. Oster was nobody to fool with. Then he remembered Ammahn went into the cave to find Emmett. The man was fearless, and Emmett had not seemed the same since. Was it because of the cave or was it his exposure in the dirt basement room? Or was it both? Thinking of the room, he decided to herd the congregation there after the dinner. He would force the issue if necessary. It would represent a celebration. They could now face their demons.

Then it hit him. Nehmi had taken pictures. From where? There was no place to hide down there. How did he take pictures? Did he watch the orgies? How twisted was he?

Or did someone else take them?

Ox kept pondering. What was the answer? How could Nehmi have taken pictures if he wasn't in the dirt basement? He had searched the area and there just wasn't any place he could have

THE HIDDEN CONGREGATION

hidden. And if someone else took the picture of Petersen's wife, then who? Elmer after all?

He realized Nehmi was some kind of genius. He had to be to have done the things he did so effectively, but such a twisted genius. He had become much more than a caretaker. He had held the congregation together after the destruction, but why? Did it please him to see the remnants of what had been?

He had been in the youth group when he was a boy. Maybe he felt out of place because the others came from money. Maybe he felt rejected because of it. Maybe he really was rejected. There would be no way to ever know. What is it that allows people to become twisted? Did he have some way of watching the orgies? He remembered the first time he saw Nehmi and the impression he gave—the eyes of a watcher.

The pictures had to be taken from up above. Was there a hole somewhere upstairs in the flooring? Was there a hole under a pew?

He went down to the sanctuary and judged about where the pit would be beneath him. He crawled around under the pews looking for an opening. Nehmi would have been clever in concealing it. He looked for anything that could be a small hole or a peephole. He ran his fingers over the rug looking for any irregularity. The rug fit snug against the pew supports.

He sat on a pew near the front and stared at the flooring, then he saw something. The rug seemed worn a little more near one of the supports. He gripped the support and it swiveled off to the left, leaving an opening in the floor. It was dark below and he could see nothing, but he inserted a ballpoint pen and it cleared through. And no one in the dirt basement would have seen the hole. The lighting was too poor.

Nehmi had hidden under the pew. No one else would have been around upstairs, and he could watch. He could watch it all. A twisted genius.

Ox had a curious feeling. He had made a discovery, but at the same time, he had been willing to suspect Elmer. He had actually judged and misjudged. Judging and misjudging, they went hand in hand.

Then another thought flashed into his mind. Were there more pictures somewhere?

CHAPTER SIXTY-FIVE

Ox and Barbara stopped midway on the steps to Hosannah's front porch. The door was open and the lights in the front hall gave the impression of a palace. Three chandeliers in a row gave the appearance of a thousand candles. Ox had been impressed by the house in daytime, especially the marble floors, but something about it now made it seem gigantic. Ox had been in the library with Hosannah, but had not seen the rest of the mansion. The walls in the front hall reflected gold. A mahogany staircase curved upward to the stained-glass windows on a landing and beyond.

Hilda and Mary Jane scurried across the hall carrying dishes into what had to be the dining room. Ox and Barbara were early. They had found a reliable babysitter for the kids.

They stood in the dining room doorway—more chandeliers. The table was longer than an average house. Hilda and Mary were giving directions to four of the other women who had been present for the church services, but had generally kept to themselves. He knew them: Elizabeth Weimann, Carolyn Carver, Marjorie Bannister, and Patricia Stallings, but they had never really participated much. He was glad to see they had been drawn in. Hilda and Mary Jane were responsible for that—two good souls.

Elmer came up behind them. "Nice touch, involving those four. Pulls them back into the group. They need that."

Cynthia came in. "I can't believe this was a home. It looks like something you would see in a cloud formation."

"Stuart was a financial genius. He made a lot of money and lived well. He also gave millions to charity. He was a wonderful individual. We all miss him."

Hilda had stopped for a moment behind him. "We miss all of them. Maybe we can talk about them now." She hurried off to the kitchen.

"Yes," said Elmer, more to himself. "Maybe we can talk about them. All of them."

Most of the congregation was there, thirty-five people. Even so, they only filled half the huge table.

Hilda, Mary Jane, and their helpers had produced a seven-course dinner. There were bowls of fruit every five feet. It would be impossible to eat everything. The main course was beef stroganoff from Hilda's parent's recipe.

Ox gave the opening words, not a prayer—more like a testimonial. He concluded with, "I don't think I really knew what ministry was until I came here. I feel I have been welcomed into the family of souls, and I thank you all."

Elmer said, "Ox, in a real sense, you have helped to restore our souls. Each event in our lives changes us—every good thing and every bad thing. It's up to us to make the best of it. Sometimes it takes a jolt for growth to take place. You have been that facilitator. We are all indebted to you." He raised a glass of wine and said, "To Ox."

Joe stood and said, "We all are who we are regardless of chance. To us."

The dinner became a celebration. There were more testimonials.

THE HIDDEN CONGREGATION

Hilda said, "God is treating me better than I deserve. I feel hope for the first time in more years than I can count."

One after another, Mary, Rebecca, Cynthia, all stood, and one by one gave testimonials of hope and thanks.

Ox stood up. "This has been a celebration of the spirit. Now there's one last thing that needs to be done. This afternoon, I set up chairs from the dining room in the space off the nursery. We need to go there and have a short meditation then go home."

Elmer objected. "You know we can't do that. It's insane." He looked uncomfortable saying it in the presence of new members, but it was for their benefit.

"I want you all to trust me. I have spent time in there and it is peaceful. There's something special in there. Something new. Something that wasn't there before. Trust me. It will be the final closure."

Everybody stood up, the older members more slowly. Some of the newer members looked a little puzzled.

"Let's all walk together," said Hilda. "We can come back here for cars."

They all filed into the nursery. Ox had left the lights on. The door to the dirt basement was open. Chairs were arranged in a large semicircle facing the darkness. Quietly, they all filed in and sat down.

CHAPTER SIXTY-SIX

Jessie May and Emmett sat in Oster's office. They were early for a meeting and stared at the empty chair, anticipating his arrival.

"I'm thinking of quitting the force," said Jessie May.

"That would be a mistake," said Emmett. "You're a good cop. Better than me. The police need you. You keep a calm head. Not many of us do, at least, not me."

"Don't underestimate yourself Emmett. All you need is a little patience. In fact, you're showing more patience. I've noticed a real change in the last few weeks. I think you're a born-again cop."

"Born-again cop? What the hell does that mean?"

Jessie May laughed. "Damned if I know. Maybe it means you've seen the light."

"Seen the light. What the hell does that mean?"

They both laughed as Oster came in.

"I'm glad you two find something funny. What can we do to hang that damned Ammahn?"

"How about if we charge him with having a smart mouth?" said Emmett.

"Maybe I should fire you for having a smart mouth."

Emmett laughed. "Well, the fact is, he *has* a smart mouth."

THE HIDDEN CONGREGATION

"Nobody ever accused you of being smart."

"Sarge," said Jessie May. "There's really nothing we can charge him with. I think he was just concerned about those people in the congregation. They each lost someone close and have no idea where they are. Maybe they really have suffered enough."

"Yeah, I'm beginning to think so. But that man has a really smart mouth. I'd like to bury him."

Jessie May smiled at Emmett. "I think if we could find Nehmi, we could put an end to this whole case."

Oster snarled. "Well, I just want to be done with this case. Maybe it all falls on Nehmi."

"Everything points to him," said Emmett. "Those people really don't know anything. I'm sure they wish they did."

"When did you become so damned considerate of anyone?"

Jessie May said, "I agree with Emmett. Nehmi could be in South America or India by now. For all we know, he jumped in a river and drowned. So it's good night Irene."

"Shit," said Oster.

"What to you want us to do, Sarge?" said Emmett.

"Okay. The church is off the hook. It was Nehmi who got rid of all those people. And if it wasn't him, who cares? Crazy bunch of people anyhow. I'll keep the case open just to keep Nehmi high on the wanted list."

CHAPTER SIXTY-SEVEN

"Our flagship church seems to be growing again," said Bishop Markham. "I guess we'll leave Oxford Christie there."

"Seems like the best thing to do," said Reverend Darner. "That Ammahn what's-his-name really told off the police."

"Many years ago they had been a very vocal congregation. Maybe they'll make a comeback," said the bishop.

"The Sundays I filled in, they were like the living dead," said Reverend Darner. "When the sermon was over, they all left. They acted like zombies. I never really got to know any of them. None of them welcomed new people. Those that came in didn't return."

"Looking back on it, maybe we should have retired Ethan Petersen. He was getting old, and after his wife disappeared, he just seemed to lose all will. It was all so strange."

"I still can't figure out what brought all that on. Maybe if I could have gotten to know some of them it might have come out. Neither the church secretary nor the caretaker, Nehmi, took time to talk to me. They were just in and out."

"I wish I knew what brought it all about. But I guess it's all over now."

"One would hope so."

CHAPTER SIXTY-EIGHT

Everyone was seated. There was total silence. Ox had never experienced such silence. He felt completely at peace. It was as though the silence was a solid thing. He thought of the song, "The Sound of Silence," Did silence have a sound? Maybe it sounded like a light sprinkle. He closed his eyes. How many people had died here? Ox imagined the presence of those gone. He relaxed. It was as though his mind emptied out. With the soft sound, he imagined soft light from somewhere, angelic. His mind floated with sounds and lights—pale gold lights, flowing into the corners of the entire area—soothing, seeping into the corners of the mind. Was this real? Was he dreaming? Soft music mesmerized. Soft light soothed. Nothing mattered but the music and the light.

Ox opened his eyes. He looked at his watch. They had been in there for almost an hour. Had he fallen asleep? The congregation was sitting quietly. All of them had their eyes closed. He touched Barbara's shoulder. She opened her eyes, looked at him, and slowly smiled.

She shook her head. "I was asleep and dreaming."

When she spoke, the others began to open their eyes. Ox watched as they readjusted to where they were.

"Let's go out to the nursery. Bring your chairs with you."

They followed him, becoming fully alert as they left the room.

"That was amazing," said Elmer. "I feel like I just had a catharsis."

"I feel like I just had my soul cleansed," said Hilda.

"Ox, thank you," said Joe. "I would never have gone back in there if you hadn't insisted."

Angel sat and took a deep breath. "I feel all right for the first time I can remember."

Mary Jane sat down and said, "I feel like I just came back to the real world."

The rest just sat as though too stunned to talk.

Finally, Larry Pregle said, "I think I could have stayed in there all day."

Elizabeth said, "I'm not going to have any more bad dreams. I feel like I'm free."

"Okay," said Ox. "In case it hasn't struck you, we have something special in this room. Is there anyone here who did not feel at peace in there?"

"It was wonderful," said Sarah. "I don't want to ever leave here."

There were a lot of yeses and head nodding.

"I think we ought to call it the angel room," said Joe. "That room is so different, angels must have had something to do with it."

"Why don't we just call it the Peace Room," said Elmer. "No one can deny we all felt at peace for the first time in years."

"We should redesign it, put a floor down," said Mary.

"Hosannah left us a fortune," said Joe. "The least we can do is fix it up and dedicate it to her and Stuart."

"If you will all leave it up to me," said Ox, "I'll take care of it and we will have a dedication ceremony."

THE HIDDEN CONGREGATION

"Will it always be left open like it is now?" asked Mary.

"That's why I removed the door," said Ox. "If it has the same effect on everybody else, I may never need to offer counseling."

"Maybe it's just us," said Mary Jane.

"I don't think so," said Ox looking at Cynthia.

"Yes, you're right," said Elmer. "We may have something special. Let's not do too much fixing."

As the group left, Cynthia came over to Ox. "I feel purged. And that room now has its own music—violins and oboes."

Ox explained to Barbara, "Cynthia hears music to fit each place she goes. The elements that somehow got into the dust have a calming effect. They remove problems from the mind, making a clean slate. Add the black candle mix and there's nothing to stand in the way. I think now we need to add more of the calming aromas to make the room even more effective. Let each mind draw its own pictures on the slate."

Elmer came over. "How did you manage all that harp music? And the clarion trumpets—nice touch."

CHAPTER SIXTY-NINE

Church was over. The congregation was having coffee in the dining room. The noise level was evidence of the change that had come over the group. Only a few months before the after-service dining room had been more like a morgue. Now, there was laughter and shouting across the room. Everyone stayed after church. There were greetings and hugging and endless conversation.

Emmett came in through the side door. He walked through the sanctuary and down the steps to the nursery. Sarah Fitzgerald and Amanda Frankle were still there with some of the children. Emmett walked past them all and into the dirt basement. There were several chairs positioned facing forward in the semi-darkness. He sat on one.

When Emmett came out, Sarah, Amanda, and the children had left. Emmett went back upstairs. He found Ox still in his study.

"Reverend Christie, I want to join the church."

CHAPTER SEVENTY

The kids were in bed. Barbara and Ox sat on their front porch watching the daylight fade.

"Your congregation has doubled. Prior to you being here, there had been no new members for fifteen years. If I weren't already married to you, I'd marry you."

"What are you, a minister groupie?"

"I could do a lot worse."

"Well, that's quite a compliment."

"I thought so."

"I think circumstances have played in my favor as far as church growth is concerned. The Peace Room is bringing new people in. Word has gotten around. People sit in there and want to stay."

"Parents come to the nursery for their children then they all go in there for a while. Everyone comes out relaxed."

"How could something so good come out of something so horrible?"

Barbara yawned and stared out at the leaves falling like rain. "Makes you think, doesn't it?"

"Have you noticed anything unusual about the lighting in there?"

"The overhead lights and a little bit of lighting from the nursery. Nothing unusual about it. Why?"

"I guess there could be some reflection from something," said Ox.

"Seems to be enough. Most people close their eyes when they are in there."

"Yes," said Ox. "I guess they can dream their own lights. Maybe a few angels can help out."

"Well, the world can always use angels. The congregation has been in need of one for a long time."

"I'm glad the weight has been lifted from their shoulders, but every now and then, I worry about the criminal implications."

"Yeah, me too, Babe."

"I also recognize the church is obligated to protect the congregation."

"That can be a real conflict."

"What if one of them, in a fit of consciousness, confesses?" Ox put the thought out of his mind. "I wonder what any of my classmates would have done here. I wonder what any of my professors would have done?"

"I think what you have experienced isn't taught in school."

"You're right," said Ox. "This has been a crazy experience. It's a crazy city. I guess I can have an impact here."

"Or vice versa."

"I worry sometimes that more pictures might turn up. Did Nehmi take more and hide them somewhere? If someone found them, would they know what they were?"

"I doubt it, Babe. And even Oster, by now, has gone on to other things."

"Well, like Ammahn says, the past is always with us."

ACKNOWLEDGMENTS

I owe thanks to my wife, Gloria Delamar, for her insights. She is a writer, editor, and teacher. She caught any errors I missed in this novel.

ABOUT THE AUTHOR

William T. Delamar was born in Durham, North Carolina, in a home full of books, which ignited a love for reading. In high school, he worked part-time at Duke University Press, further increasing his insatiable desire for literature.

He served in the navy as a weatherman, received his bachelor's degree from the University of Pittsburgh, and a master's degree from Antioch University. After thirty-five years' experience in hospital organization and development, ranging from methods and procedures examiner to CEO, Delamar became a founding member of the Hospital Management and Information Society. Under his guidance, it grew from twenty-eight members to thousands internationally.

Delamar was on the board of the Philadelphia Writers' Conference, having served five times as president. His works include: *The Hidden Congregation*, *The Caretakers*, *Patients in Purgatory*, and *The Brother Voice*. He crossed over to join his wife Gloria in 2022.

THE REVEREND CHRISTIE MYSTERIES

FROM OPEN ROAD MEDIA

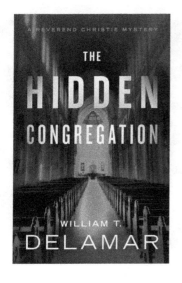
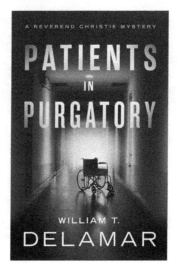

Find a full list of our authors and titles at www.openroadmedia.com

FOLLOW US
@OpenRoadMedia

CPSIA information can be obtained
at www.ICGtesting.com
Printed in the USA
JSHW021258190723
44980JS00006B/4